THIS SIDE OF BABYLON

THIS SIDE OF BABYLON

James Stoia

atmosphere press

Published by Atmosphere Press
Cover art by Rachelle Rioux

Cover design by Nick Courtright

This Side of Babylon
2020, James Stoia

atmospherepress.com

CHICAGO

1

Lennox Adler started selling himself to the commercial machine sometime in 2014, the same year Obama signed a $1 trillion spending bill which allocated funds to Science, Space, and Technology. While that administration was rocketing U.S. dollars into a program that was initially a dick-measuring contest with other superpowers, Lennox was walking the garbage mound wastelands of Astoria, Queens, in search of some means of supporting his New York addiction. The white-bagged refuse piles camouflaged beneath a few inches of powder East Coast snow made it look as though the sidewalks were barricaded by two-feet high snow drifts which reeked of Taverna Kyclades' leftover seafood.

"I didn't give a shit about New York. I was an opera singer, for heaven's sake, and I never contracted that illness of the soul that beckons its followers with a siren-like call to death. I emigrated to its murky shores in search of love, and not the kind of sadistic ball slapping the city is renowned for. She was a gorgeous, curly-haired fire-sprite who I intended to marry, not some metal skyline of protruding erections. We met during undergrad, went our separate ways for grad schools, and then I moved back home while she went down that dizzying New York rabbit hole. Alice was once again allured to the land of screaming queens and cheesy cats. Personally, I don't think New York is a lover at all. It has no love to give."

"I've had three-and-a-half blowjobs in my illustrious life."

"And a half? Did she lose interest halfway through?" Lennox asked jokingly, not expecting a retort other than a sheepish chuckle. That bold of a statement with its farcical implications had to be a joke, or at the least a distorted exaggeration.

"Yeah, kind of..."

"What the fuck?!"

The response wiped away any planned comedic comeback. "There's no way that's real," he thought.

"We were in the car and things started to get heated. I think we were talking about galaxies and planets, or something like that. I'm not sure if it turned her on or what, but she immediately went for my belt. I just laid back and let the whole thing happen. It was awesome. Then she stopped, looked up at me, and said, 'I want to go home now.' That's how I got a halfsie."

"Did she ever explain what happened?"

"Nope. Never saw her again after that night."

"By choice or did she just not care to see you again?"

"I think I might've tried to text her a few times after that night, but she never responded."

"Wow..."

"Actually, I think she might've called me a few weeks later. I didn't pick up, just let it go to voicemail."

"Did she leave a voicemail?"

"Nope."

"Maybe she remembered the big bang between your legs and needed a refresher."

"Classy, real classy Lennox."

"I mean, let's be honest. A grade school boy has probably had more blowjobs than you. Consider the halfsie your mulligan, a learning moment. You don't woo a girl with conversations about stars, cold dark matter, or our inevitable demise as a species. Exploding stars have never gotten anyone laid, ever, except maybe Einstein. I bet he smashed everything in sight, or out of sight. You are not Einstein. Lay off the meta-philosophical-intellectual humdrum and focus on fulfilling the other part of your *halfsie-conundrum*. The universe wants you to be whole, so does America, so do I. Don't be a dumbass."

"You're a real motivator, an inspiration to us all, Lennox." Alastor could not have imbued his comment with more sarcasm.

"You're the Harold Hill of our generation, convincing all the inhabitants of the world that a River City Boy's Band will solve all our problems. Nuclear warfare? No worries, give everyone a tin drum. Ethnic Cleansing? Just let your worries disappear with an oboe reed. Clandestine destabilization of third-world countries for the sake of monetary gain? It can all disappear with the movement of a trombone slide."

"I mean, you know Harold Hill got laid at the end of it all. He was an altogether different music man after Marian the Librarian got him singing."

"I immediately regret telling you."

"Al, if you can't discuss such profound things with your brother, then there's more wrong with this world than any one of us has realized. It's a dark moment in the history of humanity when the wise counsel of a caring brother goes ignored, nay, when the edifying wisdom of a world-traveled sage remains abandoned by the wayside of life's travels."

"What the hell are you talking about? Seriously, sometimes I wonder if you even notice when no one is listening."

"You're listening, Al. You'll always be here to listen." Lennox batted his eyelashes and mimicked what he imagined to be the culminating moment between Alastor and his galaxy lover. Lennox was well aware of Alastor's disdain for hugs, but he could never pass up the opportunity to put his brother into an intensely uncomfortable situation. Seizing the feigned heightened emotional quotient of the moment, Lennox lunged across the faded blue-grey sofa and aggressively threw his arms around Lennox. "My poor, misfortunate, *halfsie* brother."

"You're an idiot."

"And you're squishy. I thought you started working out. Clearly not."

Alastor hated to be reminded about his recent lack of self-care. He typically enjoyed being physically active, but the past few years had not been kind to him. His days were a continual cycle of work, home, couch, repeat. Any strength and vigor he'd once had gradually decayed with the hours spent allowing his emotional dam to burst and flood his entire mind. So, when Alastor shoved Lennox completely off the sofa, it wasn't an acquired physical strength, honed through hours of gym time, that aided his endeavor. It was the burbling of angst and frustration which began to seep into every muscle fiber of his body.

Alastor was becoming a Samson who was divined by the supernatural force of hate and misery; the driving whip of resentment would eventually lead him to the colossal pillars of Dagon.

"Jeez, maybe you have been working out. Give me a warning next time, Hercules."

"I don't know how many times I have to tell you I don't like hugs. You do it just to annoy the crap out of me. You deserved every bit of that."

"Fair enough. Dishing out your own brand of raging justice, I can get behind that."

"I'm thinking of getting two cats."

"Where the fuck did that come from?" 'Oh hey, my name is Alastor and I like books, and coffee, and walks on the beach, and, oh look, squirrel!'

"Was that supposed to be me?"

"No, it's a critical interpretation of the inner dialogue of the dog from UP; of course that's you. Why the hell do you want to get cats?"

"I think it would be good for me to have something to look forward to when I get home every day."

It took Alastor a long time to admit out loud that he was lonely, three years to be exact. In the scarce amount of conversation between the two brothers during the past year, it was a subject never openly mentioned but always looming. Lennox had not expected everything to come to the forefront that night, especially with a coffee table full of empty shot glasses, chewed up limes, and thousands of salt grains. Tequila and truth were a noxious combination.

Lennox didn't move from the floor. He continued to sit where he'd landed after his brother flung him off the sofa. Alastor looked across the room, passively observing the two windows on the opposite wall, and Lennox stared at the blank white wall to the left of the sofa. Lennox's Chicago apartment was a two-bedroom palace compared to the New York City shithole he'd lived in for two years with his wife. The Chicago apartment had a balcony with a distant view of the downtown skyline. Lennox occasionally woke up early in the morning, before his wife even noticed, and watched the fog and dew dissipate with the announcement of the sun, giving way to a sparkling metallic vista. It was the only reason Lennox insisted they stay in the city for another year. There was no amazing job, or a once-in-a-lifetime opportunity that kept them living in a city that cared little for the well-being of its citizens. Lennox knew what cold indifference was. Queens, New York, introduced him to it and Chicago relentlessly reinforced it. But the vista from the balcony was enough to feed his self-hate for staying in the city while also resurrecting his hope that there was something more beautiful. He stayed in the city for a longing he couldn't explain.

"You know, I envy you and what you have here. I love the city. There's so much to see, so many loud sounds, great places to eat, hidden gems to explore. You don't have much of that in Wheeling. Living there leaves a dull taste in your mouth, kind of like licking a battery and then having a strange tingling always remind you that you have a tongue. Without the battery, you forget you even have a tongue. But once you know it's there, you'll constantly be thinking about the awkward boneless lump in your mouth."

"We're talking about a tongue, right?"

Lennox did not try to conceal that he wasn't prepared

to discuss more serious subject matter than had already been introduced. Blowjobs and movies, fine. Anything more and the three-quarter empty bottle on the table would have been for nothing. He purposefully avoided asking intrusive questions in search of some liberating truth that would shed some light on what Alastor was going through. Their parents wanted to know, their siblings wanted to know, probably even the homeless Puerto Rican drunk on the corner of Division and Rockwell wanted to know. They all needed to know what the hell happened to Alastor. To them, Alastor's life was a celebrity-type addiction that no amount of disclosure or 24/7 coverage could assuage.

"I actually already got the cats."

Lennox gathered it was futile putting it off any longer. The levies had been breached and the floodgates were open. After two years, it was time to go down into the heart of darkness.

"When? What? You have cats now? When the hell did that happen?"

"I got them a while ago. That's why I haven't been able to come down as often. I've been trying to get them on a feeding schedule that won't have them throwing up on the carpet. I swear they throw up just to keep me from going to work in the mornings. It's also taken me some time to get adjusted to them, and then to being able to leave them alone for trips like this."

"You do you, Brosephim."

"You do realize that you're adding the Hebrew suffix on that word which refers to the masculine plural form?"

"Who the fuck are you, the syntax police? Tequila makes you too literal. What are their names?"

"Arthur and Edna."

"Like the Mouws?"

"Who the hell are the Mouws?"

"You know, the missionary couple that spent time with some small primitive people on a deserted island."

"Where did you possibly read about that?"

"I think it was on a Bazooka bubble gum tattoo."

"Ah, the literary backbone of this great country. I once had a tattoo with a Buddha on a turtle."

"You mean a dragon turtle?"

"Nope, just a regular oversized turtle. It might still be somewhere buried at Mom's house. I kept it because it reminded me that, regardless if it's a huge turtle or a dragon turtle, Buddha still gets to wherever the hell he wants to be. We only expect it to be a dragon turtle because that's what we've been conditioned to anticipate. Buddha doesn't give a shit either way."

"We are some privileged-intellectual-expounding bullshitters. They should make a tattoo about that."

"Why are you still on the floor? It can't be comfortable at all."

"Shut up. My place, my rules. I don't tell you to put on pants when you're at your place, do I? I probably should since I'm sure you've answered your door while you were in your underwear."

"I was tired and I needed my food. Also, I didn't realize I didn't have pants on until the delivery guy gave it away by trying way too hard not to look down."

Lennox put his left hand on the sofa, his right hand on the coffee table, and lifted himself up. He sat down by the right corner of the sofa, elbows on his knees, hands supporting his face, watching the same two windows on the opposite wall which overlooked the balcony.

"Shit, I got salt all over my beard." He hadn't felt his hand accumulate a good amount of the salt that had been spewed across the table and floor while they'd demonstrated their lack of skill in taking tequila shots. "Now it's going to seep into my pores and spike my blood pressure. Goddamn salt!"

"I don't think that's how it works."

"No shit that's not how it works, but let a man explore every facet of the imaginative process, will you? We are staring at two windows with the blinds drawn. I have to imagine what's beyond those windows."

"Len, you know what's behind those windows, you live here."

"You never know, *Al*. It's Chicago. It could've burned down without anyone noticing. Or the municipal overseers could've come by and taken it as compensation for owed back taxes. The city doesn't like to see its inhabitants succeed. One foot on their necks, one hand up their asses."

"What? Why are they getting fisted?"

"Who said anything about getting fisted? What the hell is wrong with you? Seriously though, stop calling me Len. You know it pisses me off."

"Then stop calling me Al."

"Deal. Do you want another shot?"

Before Alastor could answer, Lennox had already picked up the two shot glasses that were knocked over in his heave from the sofa. He filled the two glasses to the brim, almost completely draining the bottle. The brown tinted liquid swooshed back and forth from an unsteady pour but somehow managed not to spill all over the hardwood floors. The brothers still had not made eye contact.

"You know one, or both, of us is going to be sick."

"And that's okay. It's Friday. Now take your shot."

"No more limes?"

"Nope."

"Where's the salt shaker?"

"Buddha probably took it with him."

"Here's to taking a tequila shot without lime or salt."

The two brothers had once made it a prerogative to meet monthly, regardless of personal travesty or habitual indifference. Alastor didn't mind driving forty-five minutes to Lennox's Chicago abode because the city enticed him and exacerbated his Romantic allure of the artist's urban life. Alastor was not an artist, neither by inclination nor by training. He worked in Research and Development for a large, heartless corporation that had a fetish for seeing its employees dressed in all white from head to toe. There was probably even a bylaw that regulated what type of underwear they wore, including the color. Alastor dropped blood bags from a ladder for a living. Of course, there wasn't blood in the bags when they were dropped, but envisioning the possibility of red color splattered across the pristine white canvas of their uniforms was most likely the idea of some corporate big shot needing a desk to hide his pronounced excitement. The company's headquarters building was located in a cornfield that may have doubled as a set location for one of the horror movie trilogies. It was an idyllic location for corporations to avoid larger taxes and their employees to fantasize about being in a horror flick. Alastor hated horror movies. He didn't see the point in tricking your body's stress response to a stimulus that was, for the most part, utterly ridiculous and unrealistic on every level.

"Bleh. That never gets easier to take, no matter how many you've already had. Seriously though, you have two cats now?"

"Yup."

"Two of them?"

"No more, no less."

"Hmm."

"What time is Miriam coming home?"

"I thought you were sleeping over tonight? You shouldn't drive in your thoroughly impaired condition. You might piss off some trigger-happy police officers."

"I am sleeping over."

"Oh, you are? Awfully presumptuous of you to think you can just auto-invite yourself over to my bumble abode."

"That's a crappy joke."

"I thought it was quite clever. The bumble was in reference to my growing fascination with bees."

"Yeah, I got that part. It's the pretending you're a good host that goes over my head. It's only 10 pm and we're already out of tequila. Are you keeping the better liquor for the queen?"

"No. I stopped paying tribute to that foreign land ages ago, although I do like Beefeater. I will happily offer my currency up for a dry gin."

"We're drinking tequila."

"It's also imperialistic, in its own unique way."

"Mexican Tequila is imperialistic?"

"Yup. Let's rid ourselves of such imperialistic propaganda. Away with you, thwarting bottle! Let your influence ne'er more be seen."

Lennox knocked the bottle off the coffee table and onto the area rug in the spirit of anti-imperialism. The emptied bottle bounced several times before coming to a halt on the hardwood, creating the impression to the tenants on the first-floor that a cannon ball had been dropped.

"That was uncalled for."

"Yeah, I realize that now."

"This means we haven't reached the goal yet."

"Why did I just get the feeling we were waiting for Godot or someone?"

"Because we're both drunk and you knocked a tequila bottle on the floor."

"I mean, should we go get more alcohol? Is that wrong? Should we bring Mr. Morality into the conversation? Is there enough room for him on this couch?"

"Let's just wait a little bit. Let's just allow it all to settle. Maybe we call Godot and Morality over a little later."

Both brothers leaned into the back cushions of the sofa as though simultaneously pulled back by a Marionette string. Their gazes drifted to the two windows across the room. So many of their formative years were spent on a similar couch at their parent's house. That couch was forest green and was entirely inviting and cozy. Alastor and Lennox spent most of their summer and winter vacations playing video games or watching telenovelas. It was on that green couch, in the Adler childhood home, that Alastor was sitting when Lennox came home from New York and announced to the family he was getting engaged. It was on the same couch that Alastor informed Lennox he was ready to propose to his fiancée.

"Shit. I still have salt in my beard. I can taste it."

"Lennox, I never told you this, but she disappeared for two weeks and I had no idea where she was. She wouldn't answer her phone. Her friends had no idea where she was staying. Her family were none the wiser about who she had become. I freaked out. I don't think I slept for those two weeks."

"Damn."

"That was during the worst of it. I was sleeping on the floor every night. Never asked her where she went, what she did, or why she did it. I tried to give it time, hoping maybe it would correct itself."

"I'm really sorry."

"Yeah, me too. I like my cats, though."

"You have to realize how it sounded coming from your mouth at that exact moment. You sound like a cat lady. Catwoman had all those cats and she still got thrown out of a window. Just saying."

"Are you comparing my life to Halle Berry as Catwoman?"

"You know we're brothers when we both think of Halle Berry as Catwoman, and not Anne Hathaway."

"I mean, it's Halle Berry."

"Truer words have ne'er been spoken."

"Sorry it took me so long to reach out to you. I know I called you the night I was on my way to tell Mom and Dad, but I didn't mean for it to go that long without at least seeing you. I got stuck in the torpor of it all. Things slowed down so much that sitting on my couch felt like the only way to watch everything safely transpire. I meant to call, you know that, right?"

"Yeah, I know. Don't worry. You never have to

apologize to me. If you have a dead corpse to bury, let me know the time and place and I'll help you dig."

"I think I'm ready for bed."

"Let's go brush your teeth. Trust me, you'll thank me tomorrow."

"You're clearly a seasoned pro at getting shit-faced. Onward! You can lead a horse to water..."

"Just get up."

"You know, in the amount of time it will take us to get from the sofa to the bathroom, we could just as easily get to the balcony. I mean, it'll be one blind man leading another but we shall prevail, should you choose to accept this mission."

The decision wasn't very difficult for Lennox to make. He could not stand having the *spins* and going to bed. The Adlers would take a summer trip to Portland, Oregon every summer during the 90's to visit their relatives. There was one enormous hill on the way to their Aunt Lena's house the boys looked forward to. Their mom would usually be the one driving, so she didn't understand the full impact of the sensation the boys felt when they drove over and down the hill. She would maintain a healthy speed throughout, and when the car dropped over the apex of the hill, the boys had the feeling their stomachs were dropping out through their urethras. To Lennox, having the *spins* and going to bed felt like going over the hill over and over again, eyes closed, wishing throughout the night it would stop.

"I'll get the lighter."

"*You get a line and I'll get a pole, honey...*"

"Your process of association is getting a bit watered down."

"Nah, it's getting tequila'd up. Do you remember when we all used to go to McHenry Dam? I remember one year there was a torrential downpour, and we were caught unprepared in the middle of it. I mean, we were in shorts and tanks planning for it to be a fantastic summer day. Dad went off fishing somewhere and Mom let us run around wherever we wanted. It didn't matter they didn't see where we were, it was our time to let loose. Then it started to rain like crazy. You know when you have a full bladder, and when you finally let go it splashes all over the toilet bowl? That's how the top of that lake looked. I've never seen water jump up that high. Every splash seemed to clear a two-foot vertical. Mom didn't have to say a word or send the National Guard to find us. We just instinctively knew to go back to where she was going to be. That was so comforting to me, and still is. We packed up all our stuff in record time and sprinted to the minivan. Dad, with a black garbage bag draped over his body, was last to arrive at the van. Now that I think about it, I don't think Dad ever fished after that day. At least I don't remember him ever picking up a fishing pole after that. I wonder what happened to him out there? I imagine he was kind of like Peter; he went fishing one day, caught a shit ton of fish for the masses, the ingrates didn't appreciate what miracle they were a part of, so every time Peter had some time away from his day job, he would fish for himself. Remember when the big guy came back and found him snacking on some fish on the shore? Peter sure as hell wasn't spending his time fishing for the ungrateful riffraff. He had a small fire going with enough fish to feed himself and a few compatriots. I think Dad exhausted his fishing skills that day. We were a bunch of ingrates, probably still are."

"You still have stellar exegetical skills, Alastor."

"Do you know that Mom and Dad are still there?"

"I'm fairly certain they've moved on from McHenry Dam. The housing situation there is terrible. Also, too many mosquitoes."

"Mom is still there, at the rickety picnic table, setting up a place for each of her kids to come back and feel like they are still loved and expected. Dad is out there, fishing for his kids in the direst of circumstances to make sure they have everything they need to continue through this shithole existence. Mom and Dad never left that spot for me. It's so every time I get caught in a rainstorm, I know where to go."

"I know what you mean. Do you need anything?"

"The night I called you from the road, I was heading to Mom and Dad's. I was scared out of my mind. My brain kept telling me to take every exit off the highway, screaming I was headed for a world of hurt. I don't remember how I got there, but I waited in the car for a while. I didn't tell them I was coming, I just showed up. You know how Mom and Dad are always home."

"I'm glad they always are."

"They were so quiet. Even after I was done talking, they sat for some time without saying a word. Mom was looking down at the table, Dad was rolling up a napkin like he always does when he's thinking. Even though I couldn't see her face, I knew Mom was crying. I didn't hate her for crying like I usually do. I mean, I don't hate her, per se, but it usually forces me to deal with issues on an emotional level. You see your mother crying, you're most likely going to be crying along with her. I think Dad eventually said, 'okay' or something curt like that. I didn't hold it against him. I just wanted to tell them."

The outside furniture on the balcony was nestled in a corner. The alley across the way had so many tagged garage doors it might as well have been an art exhibit. The door leading back into the apartment had clearly been made to fit a different door frame. Behind the huddled furniture was a wooden stairway which led to the dark abyss of the trash area, and in front of it all was the view of the skyline. The brothers stumbled onto the balcony landing and pulled out two chairs and the table. Alastor sat facing the brightly lit Chicago mirage, while Lennox ignored the art gallery behind him and plopped down in front of the malformed door to the apartment. Miriam and Lennox had attempted to create an urban garden on the balcony, but two months into the project and all they had to show were several pots full of soil and two withering tomato plants. There was a chattering of European Starlings that had pecked their way into the brick of the apartment building, waiting for the absence of humans to pick away at the sprouting blossoms. No one utilized the balcony during the day, partly because of the blazing Chicago heat and partly because of the squatting family of birds. At night, however, the understanding was clear: for human-use only.

Lennox twirled the red Bic lighter in his hand, occasionally dropping it on the floor, and Alastor rested his head on his folded hands atop the speckled table.

"I see the birds have increased the frequency of gifting you their excrement. I count twelve more white specks than I did last time."

"Alastor, you're full of shit. I know you've never

counted the poop stains. I highly doubt you're even capable of counting to ten right now, let alone the increase of bird shit on this table from the last time you were here."

"You're always so critical of *my* imaginative process. I imagine I've kept track of all the stains and have recalled with exciting precision the increase in the bird's metabolic rates given the evidence of fecal matter."

"There's almost as much shit coming out of your mouth as there is on this table."

"Remind me again why you brought a lighter out here?"

"Force of habit."

"Dare I ask what this habit is?"

"Nothing noteworthy."

"Just as well. *Sittin' on the bank 'til my feet get cold, honey...*"

"I dated this girl who used to live in Washington: the state, not the crime center of America. I was finishing up my Master's in Oklahoma and I flew all the way to Portland to see her."

"I thought you said she lived in Washington?"

"She lived in Washington, but it was on the border with Oregon. I consider pretty much anything on the West Coast as Portland. Anyway, I flew into Portland airport to see her. Now before you make a smart-ass comment about "flying *into* an airport", may I remind you it's the English language, so lay off me. I landed in Portland and she picked me up in a silver Lexus SUV. Mind you, I was a broke grad student, spending money I didn't have on a ticket to see her, and I see this luxury SUV coming to pick me up. I was torn. I was beyond excited to finally see this gorgeous girl, but felt so inferior compared to where she was in life. I think she was a pharmacist, or anesthesiologist, or bone doctor, I can't remember, but she was unforgettable. I was standing on the curb, at PDX, with a duffle bag of clothes to last me the weekend, wondering what the hell I was doing there. Well, I knew what I was doing there, but maybe she didn't?"

"Is that a question I'm supposed to answer?"

"One of the days I was there, it might've been a Saturday because she wasn't working. Anyway, we went to Canon Beach at almost the exact spot where they filmed the Goonies sequence. Great iconic place, pivotal to our childhood, and I should've been so excited to be there, right? Instead, I was holding my shoes and socks in my right hand, khakis rolled up past my ankles, and shivering because it was so damn cold. It was only March or April, not the right time to be going to the beach. She wanted to walk close to the water so the waves could reach us. Well, the water did reach us and it was, I am not exaggerating, -273 degrees Celsius. I can't remember anything else from that entire trip. The water was so damn cold!"

"Why were you wearing khakis?"

"I think I was trying to impress her? This was a girl unlike any other. She had you confused whether you were coming or going."

"You're telling…"

"Nope. Let that joke just pass on by."

"Did you at least make an effort to find One-Eyed Willy a treasure?"

"I immediately regret telling you the story."

"Is this the lavish, heart-felt story about you and Miriam?"

"No. Just the divinity of a green blur across the room

that stole me away like no god could ever do."

"Is that your convoluted way of saying this was before Miriam?"

"Yeah, way before."

"I had no idea you met the Green Lantern at a party. Is this your way of coming out to me? Was there stellar roleplay involved, maybe some light intergalactic travel? Did you lock eyes across the room, and boom, you saw stars?"

"I've peed off this balcony before."

"I'd be disappointed if you hadn't."

Lennox misplaced the lighter almost immediately after they'd sat down outside. He assumed it had fallen through the oversized spaces between the five-inch wooden planks, kind of like a baby throwing a toy over a high-chair and believing it to have fallen into an abyss. He constantly needed something to fidget with, but since he misplaced his item of comfort, Lennox was relegated to focusing all of his excess energy into moving his leg up and down; a tic that, when noticed, agitated Alastor to no end. Alastor frequently admonished him by saying, "It's like signaling you have something to say without actually saying it. I know you're thinking about something cause your leg is moving like the horny version of Thumper. Out with it, man!" Lennox would never retort. He would calmly stare into Alastor's eyes and start moving both legs, offset in rhythm and synchronization.

The movements of Lennox's nervous twitch were especially pronounced outside in the stillness of the evening. There was never any worthwhile breeze on the balcony. The buildings were all so close together that the only moving air was from the neighbor's box fan, or exhaust from the window ac units. Even though there was a vacant parking lot next to the apartment building, the movement of the wind dissipated in the alleyways and gang breezes. The night air was stale, but it had an edge to it. It wasn't crisp or refreshing, but it was nevertheless felt. The Chicago air gave off the impression of an invigorating quality while it slowly suffocated its victims.

"Lennox, would you, for the love of god, stop shaking your leg."

"I've lost the lighter."

"Will wagging your leg up and down help you find it?"

"You never know. The energy created by the motion could send vibrations throughout the unseen, causing a rattling noise upon impact with the lighter. Or maybe if I shake my leg hard enough, you'll get annoyed and look for it instead. Either works."

"It's so hot outside. At least I think it's hot. I'm either sweating from the heat, or the tequila is seeping out of my pores."

"I give more credence to the tequila-pore hypothesis."

"Was she hot?"

"She was something."

"Do you ever wonder?"

"In moments of insanity, I do. I lose focus and grasp of what's really here, of what I have, or at least what I think I have. I more just reminisce. When I was in grad school, I created a symbol that was also a puzzle. I sent her a letter with the symbol and asked her to decipher it. She wrote me back and said she had spent an entire day staring at it, so much so that when she closed her eyes, it's the only thing she saw. She also included we shouldn't communicate anymore. It read something like, 'P.S. I deciphered your symbol. I can't talk to you anymore. Goodbye.' If memory serves correctly, she may have included a 'god bless' in there."

"That was very patriotic of her."

"Fulfilling her duty to god and country."

"Gobble, Gobble, America."

"Was that an ad hoc performance by the patriotic turkey? Wow, we haven't been graced by that miraculous fowl since the Bush era."

"I swear, Bush Jr. said the exact line. There is no possible way I came up with the slogan all on my own. I've come up with some zingers in my time, but to have created such an inspirational tagline to such an inspirational figure..."

"It's possible as well as probable."

"You still drunk?"

"A little bit. You?"

"A little more than a bit. Have you ever mentioned her to Miriam?"

"Yeah. We discussed what happened during the year we were apart. Not that she owes me information or I her, but it's better to know and not feel like there was intent to deceive. She had her loves and I had mine."

"You have a great one, Lennox. She is hilarious, beautiful, intelligent, really what every sullen sap looks for in a life partner. I wish I could find that."

"A rose by any other name would still be a rose, only it would be mislabeled."

There were no awkward moments of silence between the two Adler brothers. The time Lennox and Alastor spent without saying anything was used to recharge their brains and reinvigorate their stamina for keeping up with each other's digressions and interjections. They were two years apart in age, Lennox was older and Alastor never allowed him to forget his advanced years compared with the beaming youngster. As children, they did not exhibit any of the closeness they shared later in life. They fought extensively into young adulthood; the last fight either of them could recall was when Alastor turned the radio on during their morning commute to high school. Lennox needed half the day to ready himself for greeting existence and half the day to wind down. There was about twenty minutes of prime time in the middle to safely interact. That morning kerfuffle was the last remnant of two bickering brothers.

After the interregnum of discord, Lennox went off to college and the following year Alastor decided to commute as an undergrad. When the two brothers reunited after grad school, both lived at home under the principled roof of two loving parents who could not fully comprehend the redefining of identity required of immigrants within a cultural behemoth. Their parents mostly kept to the ways and ideas of, at least according to their children, a foreign land devoid of a refined understanding of, what is essentially, a cultural hodgepodge. Their parents had resented Lennox for having gone away to school, being the first and only child to do so, and there was perhaps some credibility to the allegations they took it out on Alastor, the only remaining child not married or gallivanting about.

"Lennox?"

"I haven't gone anywhere."

"Do you ever explore the cavernous places of your mind, cataloguing the situations we're forced into that, somewhere down the road of eventuality, become shaping influences in our lives? As vigorously as we try to convince ourselves afterward, the fact remains we would never have willingly chosen to participate in those times. We wish we were all-knowing or that our life's vision was keener, but it turns out to be completely and utterly apart from us."

"Sometimes I wonder which places have the best fish and chips. It's hard to find a place that makes it right, you know, with the batter/fish ratio not being completely in favor of the batter. Beer batter, pssh, who the fuck actually cares. I just want my cod to be the focus of the meal."

"If Mom hadn't forced you to join me and Chris Darnell on the Wisconsin hiking trip, you would most likely have remained a crotchety piece of shit."

"You make a fair point. I was so pissed you pressured me into going. All I wanted to do was stay in bed and text my girlfriend. Then you come whining about how you wouldn't be able to go unless I chaperoned your whimsical adventures."

"Hardly whimsical. We planned that trip months in advance."

"Well, Mom knew how to ensure you left on her terms."

"Never seemed to work with you though."

"I was a miserable runt. When someone becomes as inured as I was, at times still am, no amount of tactical maneuvering or emotional manipulation would find success in the endgame."

"You should get that checked out."

"Yeah, probably. Here's the damn lighter. Did you see me put it in my pocket?"

"No, but it would've come in handy on that hike. Three

suburban high schoolers trying to light a fire with flint when neither of us even knew how to spell the word. I don't think I had a bowel movement the entire trip. The efficacy of the beans was blocked by an intestinal dam of crackers and macaroni and cheese."

"I recall our dining experience entailed some oatmeal."

"Just added to the blockage. We ran out of water by the end of the three days."

"So much for a month of advanced planning. Look at you two now, a lab technician and a nurse. Thankfully, society has placed its future in your more than capable hands. We should all hope we won't run out of water."

"You know both set of parents adamantly wanted us to get married."

"You and Chris? That's news to me!"

"They kept touting it wasn't 'decent' for two young people to be dating for so long without establishing credibility to the eventuality of life-long fidelity. My favorite bundle of edification was, 'holding hands implies sexual activity.' They didn't want people getting the wrong idea."

"Makes sense. Holding hands is the epitome of intimacy, the paragon of desire, a stepping stone to the crimson A, and I don't mean the Alabama kind."

"She didn't want to get married. I'm not sure if it was the echoes from all directions that wore her down or a decline in her mental prowess, but there we both were. I've blamed both her parents and ours, but I'm left with the clarity that all I can do is choose to never do the same to anyone. Knowing how much hurt and catastrophe came from a process that, in its essence implies celebration, heralding of trumpets, streamers of good-wishes, gives me little aspiration to perpetuate a fairy-tale. The day had a lot of make-up and patchwork, divertissements to detract from the putrid odor emanating from a hope that, like milk in the sun, turned rancid. No one knows this, but after I had to have my gallbladder emergently removed, the doctors pulled me to the side and informed me that, according to my tox screen, I had traces of poison in my system. It's what triggered my body to essentially shut down, piece by piece."

Lennox struck the lighter. A small flame blazed against a muted and deeply darkened backdrop. The red hue of the flame clashed with the bright blue of the skyline, as though a star were bursting in the midst of its twinkling, dwarfed kin.

"I tried to get her to take her meds, but I couldn't watch her every second of the day. I panicked whenever I closed the apartment door behind me. I couldn't make her stop taking what she was taking when I didn't know what was happening. I started throwing up at work, forcing myself to be sick in order to leave with a legitimate reason. The first time I did, I arrived to find her sprawled across our kitchen floor, a powdery film dusting the top of her head. She had slipped and knocked it all over herself. I tried not to inhale as much as possible. It all spiraled out of control without any repose after that. She seared with hatred because I knew."

Alastor buried his head in the crater formed by his folded hands. His sobs were inaudible, but his upper back moved in broken meter as he inhaled, then exhaled. Lennox released the igniting mechanism of the lighter as the two were stranded within the cacophony of stale city air, gleaming office lights in the distance, and the tapping of falling, disintegrated brick.

"I have the air mattress already set up in the second room. Let's get you to bed."

"Can I just sleep out here?"

"Yes, but let's sleep inside first and then come sleep outside."

Alastor leaned against Lennox as the two brothers made their way back into the apartment via the misshapen door. Alastor depended completely on Lennox to stabilize and direct the movements of the conjoined duo. Alastor spent more than he expected, and had little left to get him to where he needed to go.

"Let's get some water and Aspirin. You'll thank me tomorrow."

"Again with the seasoned advice from the seasoned pro."

"That's me."

The bathroom in the apartment was small, able to fit one regular sized person but only half an Adler boy. Lennox had to wait outside the bathroom door as Alastor splashed some water onto his face in the vain hope that sobriety was hidden in its molecules. It hadn't taken more than two splashes before the greenery of Alastor's diet was splattered all over the sink basin. Water mixed with what was most likely the remnants of a spinach salad, and clogged the sink drain. Alastor attempted to unclog the sink with his hands, but instead knocked over Lennox's and Miriam's toothbrushes into the puddle of spinach, water, and stomach acid.

"Eww, that's gross. Your toothbrushes are floating. Never mind, they sunk. Seriously, that's gross."

"I can see that, Alastor. Don't worry, just get to bed. I'll take care of it."

The two brothers swapped positions. Alastor stomped his way from in front of the sink into the second room, and Lennox squeezed into the hobbit-sized bathroom. Lennox removed the two toothbrushes from the basin and immediately threw them away. He didn't even attempt to unclog the drain. That was an issue better tackled, and hopefully resolved, the next day. In the meantime, Alastor had plopped onto the queen-sized air mattress, on top of the neatly spread linens, while still wearing his jeans.

"Alastor, take off your pants. You're going to be too uncomfortable wearing them at night."

"Don't touch my pants. They need to stay on. You peeping Tom, stay away."

"Okay. Goodnight, Alastor."

"Goodnight, Lennox. Love you."

"Love you too."

2

"Good morning, lovely."

"Ugh...it's a morning. Still too early to know how good it actually is."

"If you can form that cohesive a thought, you're awake enough to be nice."

"Good morning, my love."

The sunlight was particularly boisterous and intrusive in Lennox and Miriam's apartment. The ceilings were vaulted and measured a non-standard ten feet in height, allowing free reign to the sunlight to bounce around. There was no corner in the two-bedroom apartment not brightly lit mere seconds after sunrise.

Miriam was an early riser so an apartment with at least two windows in every room appealed to her more than to Lennox, who abhorred waking up to the blinding light.

"Why again didn't we get light-cancelling curtains?"

"Because after my husband has his first cup of coffee, he doesn't see the point in spending the money."

"Smart man that husband of yours."

"Did you guys have fun last night?"

"We did. When did you get in? I didn't feel you come into bed."

"It was around one. You were already knocked out and mumbling 'she's not here.' Were you dreaming about me? Did you miss me? Were you so very lonely without me? Aw, poor Lennox is devastated without his wife."

"You know me, utterly dependent."

On the weekends, Lennox looked forward to sleeping in but Miriam could not alter her tendency of waking up at six. She would try to show some compassion for Lennox and wait until at least eight for his wake-up call, but she was impatient to connect with him. She would sit up cross-legged on the bed, face him, and gently introduce external stimuli to wake him without agitating him. She would start by blowing air on the back of his neck, then moved to pulling the covers off of him with her toes. As a last resort, she would whisper 'good morning' over and over again, never exceeding the volume of a light whisper. Lennox was an extraordinarily light sleeper and was accustomed to her tactics. He never mentioned he was aware of her attempts to condition him. He knew she loved the playfulness of those mornings, so he let those moments calm his excessively rough and agitated nature.

Miriam and Lennox had met while both were pursuing their undergraduate degrees. Miriam, being the keener entity in the relationship, fell in love with Lennox long before he himself realized they were destined. He was cast as Don Ottavio in a performance of Mozart's *Don Giovanni* and from eight rows back, she decided to love him. They met again the following year, Lennox as Nemorino and Miriam as Adina in Donizetti's *L'elisir d'amore;* this time Lennox mustered up the stones and offered his number.

They would have to wait several months after that fortuitous meeting to connect. Miriam accidentally inputed Lennox's number into her phone under someone else's contact info, and every time Lennox texted her, she supposed it was some other creep trying to seduce her.

"Did you get a chance to tell him?"

Lennox turned over to face his sitting wife. She hadn't washed off her eye makeup from the night before, making her blue eyes even more pronounced. He knew she'd been waiting all morning to find out the answer to that question. She most likely woke up before seven and showed superhuman restraint in not waking him up earlier.

"No, I didn't have a chance to." Miriam's face subtly showed signs of sadness, unnoticeable to the average observer but blatant to Lennox. "He finally opened up last night about what happened, though. I didn't think he would be able to handle it if I sprung it on him. I'm sorry."

"It's okay. I'm glad he's finally talking to you about it. Is he okay?"

"It feels like he's at least moving now. It's more than I thought would happen."

"Do you need me to give you some more time to talk with him?"

Lennox understood Alastor required time. Alastor needed to navigate through his subconscious before he could express himself to others. Lennox ideally would have liked to give Alastor a little more time; he wanted to know his brother had at least made it three-quarters of the way through the parted sea.

"Time to talk about his divorce or about us?"

"Either or, hopefully both, but whichever he's ready

for."

"Do you want to invite him to breakfast, get him talking some more?"

"You've paved the way to my heart. Do you want to go to Hash?"

"Sounds great. Let me see if he's awake. He wasn't feeling too well last night, so extraordinary measures might be needed to get him up."

"Hey, what happened to our toothbrushes? I came home last night, went to brush my teeth, and they weren't there."

"I just thought it was time to change them out. We've had them for a few months, you know, oral hygiene and all. I'll get some new ones out for us?"

"Before you go out there, could you please put some water to boil for the French press, just in case you guys decide to hash it out now? Better safe than sorry; Mama needs her coffee."

"You and me both. Do you want me to bring you a cup in here when it's done?"

"No, I'll come out there in a little bit."

It was the beginning of a very humid summer in Chicago. All the wooden doors expanded and had to be forced open with the brunt force of a lowered shoulder and a wide stance. The apartment had a small window ac unit, but neither the main bedroom nor the other room received any of the cooled air. The hundreds of cracks, spaces between windows, and gaps underneath the doors offset the cooling efforts and instead heated the Adler's apartment. Lennox and Miriam usually slept with a box fan propped up on their wooden dresser, but Lennox placed it in the other room to make sure the fully clothed, passed out Alastor would not drown in his own sweat. The Adler boys tended to sweat considerably more than the average human being.

Lennox turned on the electric kettle, ground some Dark Matter coffee beans, set up the French Press, and loudly clanked down three mugs onto the countertop. The noise and smell wafted throughout the apartment, bringing a comforted smile to Miriam's face. When Lennox finally shoved open the second bedroom door and heard a startled Alastor scream out, "No, not the cats," he knew there was no need to check if his brother was still asleep.

"I might as well be in the hostel in Budapest with all this racket."

"If that were the case, I would've kicked your ass to the curb at first light without giving you a chance to grab your stuff."

"How did we get our stuff back?"

"We gave that tourist group of bicyclists ten Euro."

"That's right. Damn Tour de France wannabees never gave me back my pocket watch. Ass hats said it wasn't where I said it would be. They took it. Ass hats."

"I'm making some coffee; do you want some?"

"No shit you're making coffee. It's either that or you're clearing up your slaughter room where you just ground up the bones of two backpackers and then started playing a drum solo on your drum set that sits in the corner."

"Wait, the drum set is in the slaughter room?"

"Could be."

"That's dark. Even for you."

"Yeah, I regretted it as soon as I said it."

"So, yes or no to the coffee?"

"Did you try to take off my pants last night?"

"Of all the things, that's what you remember?"

"Bleh. I can still picture your floating toothbrushes. Again, sorry about that."

"Let's keep the toothbrush incident between us. For all anyone else knows, I threw them out on a whim, okay? Let that memory, the green pukey, drain-clogging memory funnel all the way down."

"The drain clogged in real life. I definitely remember that."

"I changed the circumstance to fit the metaphor."

"So then, you did try to take my pants off..."

"I thought you would be more comfortable."

"That's weird. Pants always stay on, regardless."

"You're an idiot. I'm making you a cup of coffee. Try not to puke it up."

The electric kettle finished boiling the water and the ground coffee beans were in the press. Alastor rolled around from one side of the inflatable bed to the other to see whether or not his body was ready to get up without vomiting.

"What's the verdict, yay or nay?"

"I think I'm good. That aspirin you gave me before bed must've been the key to success."

"Miriam and I were planning on going to get some breakfast at Hash, you up for it?"

"I would love to, but I'd better get back home. I haven't left the cats alone overnight very often, and I want to make sure they're okay."

"You're leaving now?"

"Yeah. I'll probably get home and sleep the rest of the day. I don't want to infringe upon your time with Miriam."

"You're not infringing upon anything. At least stay for

some coffee."

"No, really, I'm going to head out. I promise, I won't wait as long before we meet up again. Thanks for everything, I had a lot of fun."

"My pleasure, anytime."

"You're the only person to have ever seen me drunk."

"You're the only person to have ever knocked over my toothbrush into a basin of spinachy vomit."

"Ah, the joys of brotherhood."

The two brothers hugged; all apprehension of physical contact dissipated the night before. Alastor knew Lennox understood his need to slowly introduce himself back into society, and Lennox believed Alastor would keep his promise to visit more often. Lennox yanked the front door open, nearly unhinging it from the wall, and said goodbye to his brother.

As he watched Alastor walk down the yellow plastered hallway to the stairwell, Lennox remembered bits and pieces of the conversations they'd shared. As his brother moved further away, Lennox acknowledged the role reversal the last time the two were together. It was at Alastor's apartment, and Lennox was saying goodbye and giving his brother a hug. He recalled turning to go down the hallway, and seeing all the pictures on the walls. There were frames covering the entirety of the two walls with not even an inch of white between adjacent pictures. It was as though he was walking down that hallway again, except now all the pictures morphed. They weren't romantic, they weren't sweet, they weren't innocent. They were all pictures of Dorian Gray. Dorian had fractured his soul into innumerable pieces and placed himself within those frames. They displayed his beauty and elegance with a contoured sense of sophistication that delineated fragile softness. Dorian projected himself as a glorious being, a transcendent beauty among the savages, an ethereal representation of a regal visage, yet, the true Dorian was unabashedly hideous. The hallway was meant as a rouse, a deception, the most sophisticated reveal of any known magic trick. It was meant to leave a twisted impression, a false sense of having observed sincerity.

Lennox saw his brother leave and watched him walk away in every single one of those frames. It wasn't only one Alastor leaving, it was hundreds of Alastors reflected in those frames, slumped shoulders, bleeding wounds, gashes, sobbing. Lennox couldn't breathe. He couldn't leave like that again, he couldn't let Alastor leave like that again.

"Hey, dingus, you want to meet up again next weekend?"

"Uh, sure. I mean, I don't have anything going on, I don't think. I'll text you and let you know."

Lennox felt a little more at ease considering Alastor's initial, instinctual reaction to the invite wasn't an outright rejection. He unclenched his fists and lowered his shoulders. His breathing returned to normal and the hallway returned to its piss yellow color. There weren't any more picture frames on the wall and his brother seemed taller to him. He walked back into the apartment and rammed the door shut. The smell of the coffee had already made its way to the main bedroom. The aroma of the fresh brew seemed brighter, crisper and more awakening.

"Did Alastor just leave?"

"He said he had to get back to his cats. We're planning

to get together again next weekend though."

"Alastor has cats?"

"I'll be in the room in a minute. I'll bring your coffee in there and we can talk about my brother's fecund fanciness for felines."

"That sounds pretentious."

"Don't I know it."

Miriam liked her coffee black and Lennox preferred it sweetened and with milk. He took after his father who, every morning before work, would have what was more accurately described as a glass of hot milk with a little coffee flavoring. Miriam slowly weened Lennox off of dairy, convincing him that almond milk was the superior tasting coffee accompaniment. "There's a reason why I'm 6' 3, Miriam. It's because I drank whole milk as a child. Why don't you want me to be happy?" Whenever Lennox noticed himself slowly changing due to his love for Miriam, he would teasingly and jokingly ask her that question.

Miriam and Lennox were happy. They had been together for eight years, dating for five, apart for one, and married for three. Miriam attended grad school in Iowa and Lennox in Oklahoma, both deciding to end their relationship in the second year. It was not a breakup that looked towards future reconciliation, with no anticipation of a storybook ending, let alone a storybook wedding. They did not speak for an entire year. It was after graduation from grad school that both of them happened to share the same emotional parameters; they missed each other. On his way to his parent's home from Oklahoma, Lennox stopped in Iowa and they met at a small breakfast spot called Bluebird in Iowa City. They didn't reconcile nor did they keep in touch immediately after breakfast. They did, however, both purchase a coffee mug from Bluebird as a reminder of the day. Lennox poured the steaming, aromatic coffee into the mugs, looked at the symbol of a bluebird next to the handle, and remembered their intermission.

"Here you are, black and strong, just like you like your men."

"Then I clearly married the wrong man."

"I am, after all, your starter husband. Now's the time to figure out what you really want."

"Smart ass."

They didn't shy away from the subject of their one-year separation, their intermission, bestowing it with such importance and solemnity that occasional reflection of the time was typical. It was in that year Lennox realized he wanted to spend the rest of his life with Miriam, and she learned how strong she became through trials of great sorrow and moments of intense study. Miriam didn't think about those difficult things when she saw the mug every morning. She felt like she was home. She had waited so long for Lennox to decide what he wanted and the intermission gave her *carte blanche*. She allowed herself to hate him, to miss him, and at times regret him.

Miriam's mother died during the intermission. In her most profound moment of despair, Miriam reached out to Lennox, hoping to at least have an ounce of something she recognized. She sought out something familiar, something that was there before her mother died, but Miriam faced the sorrow alone. Over the course of healing, she discovered she was more than able to figure out her life by herself. In that year, Miriam recognized who she was, what she wanted and where she wanted to be, regardless of external life-related circumstance. She always loved Lennox, and in that time, she learned to love herself even more.

Miriam had a sister, Rachel, whom she commiserated with during the intermission. While Miriam was in grad school, her sister had moved to New York to try her hand at becoming a waitress. Unlike Miriam, Rachel had no ambition to better herself in terms of a career. Rachel craved the glitz and the glam of New York with no aspiration to be seen or appreciated within the millions of passing faces. When Hurricane Sandy hit the East Coast, Miriam couldn't reach Rachel, inducing Miriam to call Lennox for comfort and reassurance. He didn't answer. His unavailability solidified Miriam's renewed relationship with Rachel. With the passing of their mother, the two sisters strengthened their bond and commiserated over the stupidity of men in their lives and, often, the veneration of their mother.

"So Alastor has cats now? When did that happen?"

"I think he actually got them a while ago, Arthur and Edna."

"Like the Mouws?"

"Exactly like the Mouws."

"Are they saving him like the human Arthur and Edna saved the Dayaks?"

"The language barrier might be more formidable in Alastor's case. He knows limited feline. It might take longer for them to purr into his heart of hearts."

"Terrible play on words. I expect more from you. Good coffee though, starter husband."

Just like the first morning after having moved to

Humboldt Park, the Adlers serenely laid on their queen-sized pillow top mattress with the same Bluebird coffee mugs. Miriam and Lennox made it a ritual to lay in bed with coffee and connect with each other every Saturday morning.

"Why did your parents give you and your siblings such non-Romanian names? I mean their names are Mădălina and Florin. Where did they get Graham, Katelyn, Lennox and Alastor? You sound like an aristocratic family awaiting a resurgent march to arrive at the front steps of your white palace."

"That's Russian. We are *not* Russian."

"Same thing, isn't it? You're all Communists."

Miriam was well acquainted with all the right buttons to press to get Lennox riled up.

"Is this where I'm supposed to make a commentary on your Jewishness, or lack thereof?"

"There is no lack; it's really nonexistent. I'm an inheritance Jew."

"In that case, I'm an inheritance Romanian."

"I know your last name was shortened, but seriously, what's with the pompous sounding names?"

"When my parents moved here, they tried to leave Romania behind. That meant fitting into this country. First names like Ionel, Mirella, Mihai and last names like Dehelean, Handra, and Ardelean would've been met with suspicion. My parents wanted to make their children's lives easier, even within the minutia of everyday American life. Having to correct the teachers on how to pronounce difficult names would draw too much attention to a people who lived in constant fear: a parting gift from their home country. Remaining in the background, innocuous and unobtrusive, in my parent's minds, would lead to an easier and more favorable life in this country."

"Lennox and Alastor aren't exactly the easiest names to pronounce."

"My parents stopped giving a shit after the first two kids. Graham was exceptionally successful at assimilating into everyday life and Katelyn was pretty enough that no one cared. My parents probably took note, observed carefully, and eventually decided to do whatever the hell they wanted. It took them long enough, though."

"What do you think of the name Findlay Rose?"

"For a girl?"

"Yeah. I like names for girls that sound like boy's names when shortened. Findlay Rose, Fin for short."

"Let me think about it."

"You don't like it?"

"I just think it's weird to call a girl by a boy's name."

"But it's only a nickname. She could decide what she goes by, Findlay or Fin. Well, I like it even if you don't."

"I need some time with the idea. I didn't say I don't like it. I just need to get familiarized with it."

"Growing up with names like Gherasim and Ioana are perfectly normal, but Findlay, Fin for short, throws your head for a loop, huh?"

"You really get me. What about a boy's name?"

"What about Michael Lazar? The first name sounds normal and then the Romanian middle name. What do you think?"

"I can get down with that name."

"Are you sure you don't need some time with that one, too?"

"You really get me."

"I get you're purposefully being difficult, a tad dickish even. So yeah, I think I get you. Are you for sure meeting with Alastor again next weekend?

"Nothing is for sure with him nowadays. We simply make plans and hope for the best."

"Do you still want to go to Hash for breakfast? I'm getting kind of hungry."

"I can definitely eat. You want to go right now or wait until after you video call Rachel?"

"She cancelled, so we can go right now. I don't feel like waiting around for a few hours for her to possibly change her mind and decide whether she is in the mood to talk. Let her sulk, I'd rather eat."

The walk from the Adler apartment to the breakfast spot in Wicker Park could have been either economical and quick, or scenic and prolonged. Lennox consistently chose the quick route, however ugly or uneventful, and Miriam chose the scenic route. When they first moved to Chicago, the prerogative was to learn the lay of the land as quickly and efficiently as possible. They calculated the quickest way to get to the Blue Line, which was the gateway transportation for their usual destination spots. The Division Bus stopped right outside their apartment.

After the first year in Chicago, Miriam started researching nicer routes to all the places they liked to go, including Hash. Lennox wanted the straight shot down Division, then down Western Ave, whereas Miriam would take him through a labyrinth of side streets which she purported was shorter. There were community gardens and public art installations, an array of art graffiti, painted murals, and gang-related tags that decorated the streets which Miriam decided to take.

Lennox seldom ordered the same meal twice, except when it came to Hash. He habitually ordered the Lox Benedict, and Miriam the Truffle Hash. When they felt impulsive and momentarily took a break from saving money to eventually buy a house, they would both get a cup of the fresh squeezed orange juice, and Miriam would add two iced coffees with almond milk to their order.

"I love this place so much. I wish we could've convinced Alastor to join us, but maybe I can talk him into to it next weekend. You never mentioned why Rachel cancelled your video call today. Why was she sulking?"

"She's still pissed about the money thing."

"Still?"

"I don't expect you to understand. We're all we have of family. She helped me through some really dark times, and saying no to my sister was difficult. I know you and I are trying to start our own family and working toward that goal, but it sucked to have to say no. I realize it was an impossible situation; we don't know what they're going through or what they needed it for, and I recognize we sacrificed a lot to get where we are. I don't regret telling her no, but I just want to convey to you that it sucks. I feel very off not being able to talk to my sister, not having the same closeness we had, and having something drive an ocean-sized gulf between us. How would you feel if it were Alastor and not Rachel in this situation?"

"Well, Alastor loves you. Rachel..."

"My sister does not hate you; I've told you that before. You two are just figuring things out. I've said this before; I need my sister and my husband to at least endure one another. I don't expect you two to swear oaths or create pledges of harmony. I just need you two..."

"Lox Benedict and Truffle Hash?"

"Yes, that's us, thank you."

Food on the table was an implied ceasefire to any form of disagreement between Miriam and Lennox, especially at Hash. Regardless of how hungry they allowed themselves to get, or level of anger which arose, the placing down of food saved the Adlers from many torturously drawn out arguments.

"Do you think your parents ever regretted leaving Romania, or at least miss it? Is it still home for them?"

"They had to leave out of necessity. My dad was in the army and my mom had already left for the States. The government didn't look favorably on spouses espousing Western propaganda by fleeing the home land. By association, they were also suspicious of spouses of espousing spouses. If my dad would've stayed, none of us kids would be here; they would've eventually executed him. The States became their home, and I don't think that place would be the same for them, even if Romania has made strides in the right direction. They've changed, it's undeniable, regardless of value-added judgments whether or not for the better. If my parents went back, even to visit, it would be a foreign land. It would be a place that existed without them for all these years. Romania kept going regardless of them. To go back to a place like that would not be home. If, for the past thirty years, Romania remained desolate, forsaken, and uninhabited, leaving a snapshot of a place which has retained most of its characteristics of what used to be, then yes, it would still be home for them. It wouldn't have outgrown its people, or progress without them, or forgotten them. It would be a land that waited, broken and alone, for its people to return. It would be a place that retained hope in a people who would resuscitate and revive its broken limbs, reestablish its altars, and build up its former glory. It would be a symbiotic hope exchange."

"A place like that doesn't exist anymore. If that's what you consider home, then no place is home. Home is nowhere, it can't subsist. If we left our apartment tomorrow, I mean stop paying rent and leave, our landlord would move our things out, keep what is valuable to him, and find another tenant. It would change the instant we leave. We can have a connection we feel with a given place, like your parents and the States or Romania, but even that connection has to adjust. Places change, time changes, we change. I guess by 'home' I meant a place where they can see themselves again and again; somewhere they choose to be day after day. My mom used to tell me stories about Babylon. I didn't realize until college, but she didn't prescribe to a traditional interpretation of Jewish stories. She was a beautifully simple woman. She used to tell me Babylon was everywhere and nowhere. You can live within Babylon, outside of Babylon, or away from Babylon.

"Those who live within Babylon gather a great matter of wisdom, luxury, pleasure, and happiness. They live with a sense of security, comfort, and pay tribute to others. They depend on the wealth from the shared land, the wealth of the city's inhabitants, and the wealth of the leadership. They're all rich and comfortable. You can imagine how tempting that sounded to a little child.

"Those who live outside of Babylon, encamp outside its confines, but still interact with all the wonders within Babylon. They live alongside the security of Babylon's walls, the comfort of knowing if any travesty arose, they could join everyone else inside the city. They benefit from its wonderful commerce, its bustling social interactions, but still pay tribute to others.

"Those who live away from Babylon choose to find somewhere else. They don't disparage those living behind the towers and walls of the great city, nor those living near its walls, but they don't partake in the things which would have them pay tribute to others. They don't look back to the comfort of assurance or to the certainty of the established city. They're rarely comfortable and always in search. They have adventures, see the world, see all the mountains and valleys, deserts and oceans. Though the land isn't theirs, though they pay tribute to the earth and the oceans, to the animals and the storms, they're only confined by their own imagination and determination. Compared to the Babylon they left behind, the walls of their city encircles the entire planet."

"Your mother was a very wise and astute observer."

"Yes, she still is."

The brunch crowd appeared all at once, and as though they shared one medium-sized brain, they flooded the open standing spaces and vacant tables. The loud, unabated screams of little children reached a decibel level that scared dogs within a ten-mile radius. As the Adlers were finishing up their meal, they both observed what was most likely a four-year old child take a cup full of milk and pour it onto the shoe of a patron waiting to be seated. The man didn't notice the child, but the mother the perpetrator looked right at the little spawn. The brilliant mother resolved the issue by taking the cup from the wailing boy and refilling it, but this time with water. Apparently, she believed allowing her child to dump water on patron's shoes was more acceptable than milk.

The walk back to the apartment was enjoyable for both Miriam and Lennox. The Chicago air had not yet become imbued with suffocating humidity, and there was a light breeze flowing through the less traveled side streets. The community gardens were showing signs of promising growth and the new artwork popped with brilliant colors. Most of Wicker Park had not gotten up yet, giving way to a budding sense of calm within an ordinarily bustling part of the city. The day was ripe with possibility, and the two held hands as they slowly walked back to their apartment on Division Street.

3

"Lennox, this is Mom, please call me."

It was a rare occurrence when Lennox's mother called him on a Saturday, well knowing the weekend was his and Miriam's time to spend together, and an even rarer occasion when she left a voicemail. His mother had a knack for leaving cryptic messages which were fraught with an implied sense of urgency.

"Is everything okay? Who was that?"

"It was my mom. She wants me to call her back. Do you mind if I quickly call her?"

"Not at all."

This time didn't feel any different than the other times when his mother would call with a seemingly crucial message, imploring him to call back. His mother once texted him to immediately call her, only to find out she had purchased twenty chickens and four of them escaped the coup. She was devastated, he was annoyed. So, when Lennox did call his mother back, he perused through his mental index of past interactions, and wondered which reason it would be that day.

"Hi Mom, you called."

"Lennox, your Aunt Lena is dead."

The extended Adler family was massive. The last census bolstered an estimated one-hundred and ten cousins, and the last time they had a family reunion they occupied an entire city. Of the throng of relatives that faded from Lennox's life, Aunt Lena was not one of them. She always opened her home to guests and strangers alike, and when Lennox escaped to Portland during grad school, she insisted he stay with her. Whenever Alastor and Lennox visited, her face, on every other occasion full of pressing anxiety and perpetual sadness, noticeably brightened. She would say, "Here are the brothers of thunder. You two will be great men one day." Even though Aunt Lena had three children of her own, she saw something different within Alastor and Lennox. They never forgot her. They reminded each other every year of her birthday and each sent her a card with an absurd picture or message.

Aunt Lena had long battled cancer. It started off as breast cancer and quickly spread. Over the course of a year, she became bedridden and she isolated herself from everyone, including her own children. When Lennox first heard of her diagnosis, he called and insisted he go see her. She graciously explained what a waste of time it would be. She boasted, "I'll beat its decrepit ass." She had gone into remission twice, after which Lennox stopped hearing from her completely. He received a random letter when he was still in New York, shortly after he heard the news from his mother of her last remission. It was a fairly normal letter which included the state of affairs of her personal life, her upcoming hopes, and inquiries about Lennox's activities and life. Towards the end of the letter, she vaunted the fact that the last time she and Lennox saw each other was in the prime of their lives. Lennox had been in grad school, randomly travelling to other states, and she was succeeding with a new business venture while taking steps to make herself happy. She ended the letter by saying if she had a wish, it would be they remember each other as they were the last trip Lennox took to Portland.

"No one should go from life like she did. It's shameful."

"What do you mean, Mom?"

"She was alone. No one by her side. Her kids on vacation, husband flew away, and she was on hospice but no one was there. My sister died like no one, like no one deserves, in the most bad way. I'm sorry, Lennox. I wanted you to know. I wanted you to hear it from Mom. I hope I didn't mess your day, but maybe you wanted to know. I love you."

"I love you too, Mom. Wait, Mom, did you call Alastor?"

"I left a voicemail but no answer."

Lennox was accustomed to death. The Romanian immigrant community in the United States remained close knit since the early eighties. Having been part of such a large group of people, he attended more than a fair share of funerals. The first dead body he ever saw was his great uncle who died of a heart attack in an adjacent room. Lennox woke up to the sound of emergency crews trying to resuscitate a giant, motionless heap, slumped atop a wheeled gurney. The pallid complexion of a lifeless face defined death for Lennox: a cessation of motion. As a child, Lennox observed the wrinkles, the way the lips and eyes didn't move, and the way every part of the face was simply there. He formed a great appreciation for motion and life that day.

"What's wrong. What did your mom want to tell you this time?"

"My Aunt Lena died."

"The one who lives in Portland?"

"Yeah, that's the one. It feels odd in a way. I liked her a lot. Of all my relatives, I actually liked her. We weren't close, at least not in a way that would stop me cold in my tracks. I feel sad, but I'm not devastated. I remember her fondly, and again I'm sad she's gone, but....I feel like maybe I should be sadder than I am right now. Does that sound weird?"

"It's better to be honest with your reaction and feelings rather than try to fabricate a woeful disposition. Are you going to go to the funeral?"

"The only thing I'm sure of right now is, going forward, I can never anticipate what my mom is going to call me about. I now have to answer every time, and I don't know what I'm going to hear about. The gamut currently runs from her high blood pressure to the death of a family member. I thought I had it all figured out."

"That's what you're going to take away from all this? That's the life lesson you're going to tuck away in that brain of yours?"

"Miriam, we each deal with grief in our own way. I just happen to be a bit more demented than your run-of-the-mill inhabitant of this planet."

"I'm actually relieved you can joke about it. If someone were to overhear our conversation, they might think you were serious, and definitely demented, or maybe a little sociopathic."

"What can I say, my aunt Lena lived life with a shitty

family who cared more about her life insurance policy after she died than making sure she was comfortable in her final hours. Should I weep over the fact her husband probably thought it more important to get a nice tan at the beach than being there with ice chips? Everyone has their own shit. For all I know, her kids were by her side the entire time, through all the remissions and reappearances of the cancer, but just happened to decide to vacation when their mother took a turn for the worse. For all I know, maybe her husband couldn't see his wife go out like that and took off instead. I don't know. Everyone has their own side of the story."

"Would you leave my side if it were me? Would you need to get away to deal with my death? Would you need to make *my* disease *your* affliction? There is no excuse for him leaving her to die like that, all alone. They spent their entire lives together, had children together, shared so much together, and when it counted, he made it about him."

"Miriam, I didn't mean to bring anything up. I'm sorry, I completely forgot."

"It's okay, I've already learned my own life lesson. You have to make a decision and stick with it. No one is going to take care of you more than you would, or better than you would."

"Miriam, I'm not your father. It's me, Lennox."

They both sat in silence while the sun shone through all the windows in the living room. There was music wafting into their apartment from a nearby cookout that had an accordion and a trumpet playing the melody. There was indiscernible conversation going on in the apartment on the first floor. The two tenants who lived in the unit below used the weekend to let loose and smoke pot, coughing after every hit. Miriam silently took up her latest knitting project and Lennox put on his headphones to listen to Massenet's *Werther*. He was going to be covering the title role in a small production, slated to be produced that winter in St. Louis.

Lennox did not handle the tension quite as well as Miriam did. From the sofa, he would occasionally glance across the room at the golden-colored arm chair. There wasn't a discussion or official decree that Lennox would use the large sofa and Miriam the arm chair, but both organically drifted to those spots, gradually marking them as their own territory.

When Miriam and Lennox were putting together the guest list for their wedding, Lennox asked why she didn't invite her father. Miriam broke down and revealed her father left their mother a short time before she died. Her mother recognized what she wanted out of life, so when the doctors gave her the devastating diagnosis, she charged ahead with a potentially life ending surgery. Miriam's father begged she not have the surgery, pleading they still had time together. Her mother had already made the decision, and three months before her surgery, Miriam's father left. Neither Miriam nor Rachel knew about their mother's potentially fatal operation. All they discerned was their father left and their mother didn't seem phased in the least. They were informed of the details of their mother's diagnosis after her death, and learned of their father's justification for leaving considerably after the funeral, which he did not attend. Miriam and Rachel deified their mother and constantly paid homage to her in their conversations. It wasn't the case between Miriam and anyone else, not even Lennox, but between the two sisters their mother was a demi-god.

Miriam rarely spoke about her father. When obscurely referenced, he was a vague circumstance beneficial only in underlying the need for self-reliance in life. She didn't vilify him but she did not acknowledge him either. He was neither a father nor an existing person. She conceded Lennox's point that everyone possesses their own story, their own perspective of the main narrative, but she wasn't interested in hearing about or understanding her father's.

Lennox quietly took off his headphones and looked at Miriam as she sat knitting on the arm chair. She was immersed in her process and didn't notice as Lennox's gaze started to wander. The two windows behind her gave Lennox a clear view of the outside world.

"We don't have any plans tonight, do we?"

"No, not tonight, but remember Rich and Tereza are staying over after their concert on Thursday. No need for them to abstain from drinking or drive home drunk. Plus, the venue is three blocks from here."

"Where do you know them from?"

"Tereza went to Iowa with me. She was one year older, but we kept in touch after graduation. She was in New York for a little bit when I first moved in with Rachel, but then she met Rich and they moved to Indianapolis."

"And they were at the wedding?"

"Yes, you met them both. They left early from the reception because they were closing on their new house the next day. They were at the same table as Alastor and..."

"Now I remember. Got it."

The sun was beginning to set, and the reflections from

the windows of the apartments across the alley were blinding Lennox. Sunset was Miriam's prime time for knitting because there was adequate lighting.

"I think I might go lay down for a little bit. Are you okay to hold down the fort, Sergeant?

"I'll be just fine, Private. Are you going to sleep or just laying down?"

"I'm not sleepy just yet. I'm in dire need of a refreshing lay on the bed to revitalize these withering bones and rejuvenate this dwindling mind. Oh, that I may feel the welcoming thump of a pillow top mattress whose joyous purpose is to provide me with comfort. Aye, that I may lay where the essence of the fire sprite dwells, whose heart hath been set ablaze by this lowly squire. Alas, that I may seize the effervescence of serenity with these fickle hands, claiming it not unto myself but within my woeful shell."

"Are you soliloquizing?"

"Fair fire sprite, what harm doth mine sweet-less oozing honey serve to one such familiar with the ambrosia and elixir?"

"Have a nice rest. Hopefully the bed has a portal to bring you back into this world; this very grey and allergy-ridden world."

Lennox didn't want to fall asleep because he still had time cards to approve for Monday in addition to learning the recitatives for *Werther*. His remedy for needing rest without falling asleep was to lay with his head and neck hanging off one side of the bed and his legs off the other.

The bedroom was dark since the windows in the room faced an inside corridor and not the outside world. Lennox laid down facing the white box-fan that had mysteriously found its way back. He hated sleeping with the box-fan, but the noise drowned out his racing mind and his confusing thoughts—it also moved the flat air a little within the room, momentarily staving off the feeling of suffocation. He imagined the blades of the fan spinning, and he mentally composed the exact sound of the movement. It was a gentle buzzing noise mixed with symmetrical whooshes, altogether sounding like a swarm of bees caught in a non-undulating wind. He closed his eyes, focused his gaze on a single dot he imagined somewhere in the distance, and relegated the chaos to an indistinct, far-off static.

"Hey, hey, it's okay I'm right here. Shhh, it's okay, Lennox, I'm here."

"What?"

"You fell asleep and started screaming out."

"I was screaming out? What was I saying?"

"You kept saying, 'she isn't here' over and over. You were saying it this morning too, before I woke you up. Are you okay? Do you remember the dream?"

"No, I don't remember having any dream. I was watching the fan move and must've dozed off."

"But the fan isn't on. It hasn't been on since I brought it in from the other room this morning."

"Never mind. Sorry, I didn't mean to scare you. I have too much on my mind: work, the show, telling Alastor, making sure you're okay, the quick-escapists coming on Thursday; no wonder I yelled out."

"You're naming Rich and Tereza the *quick-escapists*?"

"Does *escape artists* sound better?"

"Infinitely better. Do you mind if I lay here with you?"

"Not at all."

"You know I love you right, Lennox? I'm fully aware

you're not like my dad. We've known each other for almost a decade; most people don't know another person for half that time. I'm asking you to bear with me, and please try to understand even if you don't. Even if I seem to you like I'm not myself, you have to know I love you. I always have and I always will, no matter what. Please don't forget that."

"How can I forget with such a heart-felt reminder? When, I ask, has such a pure-intentioned plea been reproduced to the ears of men? Where, I inquire, has more faithful a summation of love pristine been erected?"

"Just lay here with me, please."

It didn't take long for Miriam to fall asleep. Her schedule consisted of early nights and even earlier mornings. After readjusting her position on the bed and turning the box-fan on, Lennox escaped to the living room as was part of his routine. He utilized the time after Miriam went to bed to either read or sit silently on the couch. Considering the exceptional nature of the weekend though, Lennox considered it appropriate to partake in his high holy ritual.

The red lighter was his companion on the days of entering the highest of highs. Lennox kept two rolled up spliffs in the dry sink compartment that was used to house two decks of playing cards. They never used the cards, so it was a perfectly designated spot. The dry sink was a gift from Miriam's aunt who had bought the piece and ultimately stored it in a dank garage for several decades. At the time, it was an impulse buy with no sentimental value to anyone in Miriam's family, then being gifted to the Adlers by mere chance. The dank storage unit was Miriam's mother's garage.

It was Beethoven's late string quartets that served as processional to the sacred ceremony of the highest of highs. A click of the red lighter mimicked the starting breath, the uninterested audience scrambled to take their seats; the stage lights twinkled while the house lights softly dimmed. The strike of the downward moving bows released the shackles as the smoke of incense gently rolled before Lennox's eyes. Headphones disappeared and the bricks and mortar took over the playing of the music. The lights in the distance flickered on and off with each struck note, the skyscrapers became a magnified music score. No counterpoint was ever more elegantly conveyed than that of Beethoven's genius on the erected phalluses of the brimming skyline. Beethoven's melancholy jumped from the lowest floor of Michigan Ave to the highest expression on the top floor of the deafening cacophony at Jackson St; the legato line was never disrupted and the view never obstructed.

It was not an indulgence for Lennox to listen to Beethoven during his sacred ceremony. The sound of the strings was a dirge and Lennox stripped the violin bows and penitently whipped his back. The opening chords of the opus 127 screeched their overtones when they struck the unbending harshness of the skyscraper's metal frames, the solo violin of op. 131 was trampled underneath the disengaged soles of passersby steps, and the Grosse Fugue of op. 130 mingled with the dissenting voices of political fallout and morphed into a drowned plea. The Alla Marcia of op. 132 played as a city gleefully shook the hand of culture and respectability while embracing a blood-stained knife with their other hand, and the plucked finish to op. 135 stirred a lake of apathy into which the sick, impoverished, hungry, and lost could relinquish their sin, and a city would rejoice.

The city helped lash the entirety of Lennox's back.

The music came to its woeful conclusion, and the headphones throbbed loud enough to deafen the sound of Saturday night thrill-seekers. Lennox held the red lighter in his left hand and the extinguished flame of sacrifice in his right. He abhorred the sight of littered cigarette butts throughout the alleyways and the bus stops, but he couldn't fight the instinct to flick the remaining charred piece of rolled paper off the side of the balcony. It was as if hurling the means by which he welcomed the altered state also released him of the glinting amount of guilt which lingered after the spliff was tapped. The further he launched the remains, the quicker the ember of his hidden exploits would be snuffed. Both Miriam and Lennox smoked, but Miriam didn't know how often Lennox partook without her. The clock on his phone read 3:22 a.m. and his email inbox had one unread message.

Hi Lennox,

I know we never met, but Alastor and I knew each other back in college, and when we were able to rekindle our friendship, it made me extremely happy. I was very much looking forward to meeting you and Miriam sometime.

I didn't know whether or not I should reach out, and I'm still not sure an email is the right way to go about this. I'm writing because I'm genuinely concerned about your brother. I feel as though the abrupt ending of things between us, without the slightest warning, is cause for concern. I know he's gone through a lot with his divorce. I respect his decision to end things with me, but like I said, I wanted to convey my concern for him to you. He's sent me some long messages that have me worried about his overall well-being and safety. I just needed to let someone know because I seem to be the last person he wants to talk to. I care very much for your brother. I know he's in a bad place right now, but I want him to be happy because he deserves it. He really is an incredible guy.

    Sincerely,

    McKenzie

"Well, fuck."

4

Adler was the abbreviated and transposed form of the original family surname, Ardelescu. The unabridged version of the family history died in a small village house, in Arad Romania with Lennox and Alastor's paternal grandmother. The accounts which comprised the official, agreed upon family history were gathered from the tattered memories of Florin Adler, née Ardelescu, and his siblings.

The name Ardelescu was synonymous with wealth, power and generosity for many decades in the area surrounding, and including, Arad. Alexandru Ardelescu was an intelligent man who managed to purchase adjoining arable lands within the Western parts of Romania, and created an efficient network of goods-to-market transport. He was the only man to own multiple flocks of livestock, multiple tractors, and still have a reputation for paying his workers well and showing everyone he encountered a sincere form of human decency. His striking blue eyes were noticeable even within the black and white photographic technology of the time: a trait only one of his sons inherited. AnaMaria

Ardelescu gave birth to two sons and two daughters, Lazar, Gherasim, Daniela and Georgeta. Lazar died three weeks after birth, a tragedy which AnaMaria never fully recovered from and an impetus for Alexandru to share all his knowledge and wealth with his remaining children. Gherasim, with his inherited blue eyes, looked at the world with a passionate curiosity that kindled a fire within him which had the potential to consume everything in his path, including himself. He craved greatness and would walk to the ends of the Earth to find it. He absorbed everything his father tried to teach him, but would too soon try to implement his own vision while discrediting the sage advice of patience as whimsical shackles of an old man trying to restrain the fierce fecundity of his youth.

With the change of political regime in Romania, new formulations of wealth had to be addressed. Anyone owning more than one cow was considered too rich and had to "donate" their flocks to the ailing and needy government officials who considered themselves destitute and impoverished. The officials came on a Wednesday to the Ardelescu farm and took everything not hammered down, including their clothes, their jewelry, even their storage of hay for the winter. They also took Alexandru under the pretense he needed to sign over his wealth, officially and voluntarily. Alexandru Ardelescu walked down the neatly kept path from the house to the gates delineating their property with a gun pointed to his back. There was no sound of a gunshot and no sign of a struggle between detainee and detainers, but Alexandru never returned to his family nor to Arad ever again. AnaMaria did everything she could and incorporated every skill she had to keep her family alive. All the land except the house itself was reintegrated into the commonwealth; "common" meaning high ranking government officials, not to the common folk. Daniela died the next year of an infection which never subsided, and Georgeta moved to Valencia, Spain, with family friends. The communist government came back the following year and appropriated the last remaining cow from AnaMaria and Gherasim, claiming even one cow was too much wealth for only a mother and a son.

The two would wake up before the sun rose and spend the entire day in the fields, working alongside their former employees. It was the generosity and grace of the Ardelescu reputation that kept food on their table by means of donations from fellow workers and old acquaintances: a meager and humbling form of subsistence. AnaMaria died on a Wednesday, underneath the beating summer sun while hoeing the draught-hardened soil. Her death was not bookmarked by a ceremony nor did news of her death circulate. Gherasim survived on the merit and honor of the Ardelescu name long enough to meet Valentina, a modest daughter of a farming family that had fifteen children, all working the fields to ensure their own survival.

There were three Ardelescu boys born to Gherasim and Valentina Ardelescu: Florin the eldest, Ionel, then Stelu, and two daughters, Mirella and Ioana. The family lived in a small district of Arad. Gherasim died at the age of thirty-nine, when Florin was thirteen years old, placing undue responsibility and pressure on a scrawny, flimsy-framed boy barely able to maintain a C average in school.

As was customary in Romania, all males had to conscript into military service when coming of legal age.

During Florin's service, he was regarded as one of the most accurate and prominent sharp shooters the Romanian government enlisted. He was asked to take part in an official "game" which required him to shoot targets alongside the most respectable officers of the army. The prize was a marginal increase in government salary, an extended stay within the military, and the privilege of leaving behind all family connections. It was considered a distinct honor. In the time he spent within the army barracks, Florin fell in love with a feisty farm girl who lived ten kilometers away from his family home. For the sake of Mădălina, Florin had purposefully missed his final shot, the errant bullet striking a hay stack to the right of another shooter's target. His love for her had cost him more than the loss of a meager government prize and increase in rank. His superiors suspected foul play in his final round and decided behind closed doors that Florin Ardelescu was to be sent on a "special mission" to Siberia. There were ample stories among the natives of a knock heard on one's door in the middle of the night, never to see a father or son ever again. Florin either had to flee Romania or disappear into the labor camps of Siberia. With the help of Western-friendly connections, both he and Mădălina were able to enter the U.S. legally through a sponsorship of churches within the United States. Though Florin and Mădălina gained a life and future in a distant land, their heavy losses on the European front would haunt the Ardelescu family.

After Florin escaped the country, he entrusted the day-to-day responsibilities to Ionel, a care-free and antagonistically inclined teenager, who preferred to spend his days boiling up a batch of homemade vodka in his best friend's barn than attend to the needs of five needy beings. Ionel did not set himself up with a job that would provide the basic needs for his siblings and mother. Instead, he stole cartons of cigarettes from cargos coming into the country and used the booty to bribe government officials into providing the family with, what turned out to be, substandard provisions. When Ionel met Mariana, his eventual wife, she insisted the two escape the communist country and throw off the yoke of family responsibility. The absurd lovers illegally crossed the border into what used to be called Yugoslavia, and then miraculously found their way into the United States. It wasn't until Ionel made his first million dollars, bribing city officials for state construction contracts, that the U.S. government recognized his worth and issued him the necessary paperwork for legal status in the country.

Stelu Ardelescu was a railroad engineer, working as a cog in a massively disorganized communist system which forced him to retire from his post at the age of forty-five. He was the only Ardelescu boy to remain in Romania, tending to the needs of the family farm and their aging mother. For his loyalty and devotion, both Florin and Ionel would send care packages from the United States containing clothes, American delicacies, and most importantly, money. At the end of her life, Valentina Ardelescu bequeathed her final wishes onto Stelu and asked he transmit her last words to all of the remaining children.

To Stelu was left all the scraps of Ardelescu farmland that had remained in the family's possession after the government re-balancing; that which was not transferred to the communist government as an exorbitant tax. It was at the end of Stelu's stress-ridden life that Ionel decided to sue the Ardelescu estate for wrongful transference and collusion to benefit himself, Stelu, above the rest of the children. The legal proceedings lasted only one month, in which time Ionel had bribed enough of the Romanian officials into seizing the land and redistributing it back with Ionel's name on the title. Within the same month, Stelu died of a heart attack and his remaining wife and children were left destitute. Feeling a sense of familial duty, Ionel offered them the opportunity to live on his land at an "acceptable" amount of rent.

Mirella and Ioana, the two Ardelescu girls, never married and never had any children of their own. All the earnings they made, they shared, and all the success and failures, they experienced together. When Stelu's family had nowhere to turn, it was the two faithful sisters who welcomed them. The now three Ardelescu sisters, as they were well known to many in the city of Arad, amassed wealth and influence, and sent the children, which they all considered as their own, to the greatest universities around the world.

Though coming from the same ancestral line and shared history, there was a great schism between the Ardelescu family of Romania and the Adlers of the United States. The Ardelescu siblings that remained in Romanian did not envy the exodus of their brothers to fabled greener pastures, yet they attributed the distancing and growing apart between the siblings to an impetuous decision on the boy's behalf. Any money sent to either Mirella or Ioana from the States was redistributed to Stelu's four children. The sisters would not accept recompense they deemed as coward's money.

Ionel was eventually granted ownership of the Ardelescu farm but ended up paying more in both international taxes and State taxes than the cumulative value of the land. He had a fire sale of the property in the province of Dud, just outside of Arad, at a fraction of the price he paid. The details of the buyers of the property were not made public in the available court documents, but there is a placard outside the farm in Dud that still reads, "Ardelescu farm".

During early childhood, Graham, Katelyn, Lennox and Alastor spent every other weekend at their Uncle Ionel's house in a ritzy mansion located in a Northern Suburb of Chicago. Constance and Darius, their two cousins, loved to show them around the house and the unused treasure trove of toys that were always scattered on the floors of their rooms. After Graham turned ten, the two sides of the Adlers firmly established their territories and rarely, if ever, deviated from their boundaries. No clarifying reason was offered to any of the children as to why the weekend trips ceased, but the cause was assumed to be a natural growing apart of families who lived on opposite sides of the city. The Adlers of the North added two other children to their brood, cousins the Adlers of the South did not even hear about until chance meetings had them crossing paths.

The demarcations of North and South gave each fractured side of the Adler family a chance to create and foster an identity of their own choosing. From the day Ionel and Mariana had arrived in the United States, they settled North of the city with a sponsorship from a wealthy Romanian church. Though legal papers could not be obtained by those means, considering their initial illegal status, the fidelity of Ionel and Mariana remained with the haute couture of the North. They willingly and eagerly offered their name and cash flow to the wealthy sect of the Romanian Chicago population. Eventually, that same city, which was at first reluctant to even acknowledge the North Adler's existence, sent them a manila folder with all legal documents entitling them to the freedoms of the country and also tax obligations.

The South Adlers had, from their legal introduction into the States, humble beginnings. Florin and Mădălina were sponsored by a small Romanian church in the Southwest suburbs of Chicago. The first house they purchased was a modest two floor on the city's South side, and after employing financial restraint for several years, eventually relocated to their second house in a more affluent Southwest suburb. The South Adlers were never lacking in basic necessities, nor denied an occasional splurge or frivolous expense.

The Adlers of the North and South were in the same location on only a few occasions during the children's teenage and young adult lives, and only twice in their adult lives. After the immediate shell shock of Graham's astonishing proclamation he was inviting the North Adlers to his wedding, there was a budding hope the two sides of the family would be able to mend their kinship and perhaps even communicate regularly. The optimism grew even stronger when the North Adlers acquiesced to the invitation. It was an incredibly joyous occasion for both sides of the families as Graham was the first member of the Adler clan to get married in the United States. All the cousins rekindled the friendship they once shared as little children and even began to lay the groundwork for a future blossoming of family loyalty. It was at Graham's wedding the South Adlers first met their two new cousins. For no other reasons than negligence and lack of effort, after the wedding, the Adlers again became estranged of their opposite-direction counterparts.

* * *

Light from two floor lamps mingled with the gloom of an overcast sky, giving life to frolicking shadows on top of the hardwood floors of the Adler apartment. Blankets were strewn about the sofa and the luminescence from the lamps revealed hundreds of salt crystals hiding in the crevices of the coffee table. Lennox peered through the two windows across from him, noticing the lethargic movement of the clouds, and a dull glow emanating from his phone.

"Graham keeps calling and insisting we meet up with my Uncle Ionel. He persistently flings about these accusations that I'm not making an effort to keep the communication lines open between us. Just because he found a new shiny play thing doesn't mean I'm interested, or willing to see what the fuss is about."

"It's Sunday morning, shouldn't he be in church right now?"

"Maybe he and Camelia decided to purge their sins at home."

"Gross. Doesn't he realize we don't have a car? It would take us an hour and a half to get there by train."

"He supposes everything on the North side is within walking distance."

"Humboldt Park is not close to Skokie, especially without a car."

"Graham wants to convince me to give him the benefit of the doubt. He feels indebted because Uncle Ionel's family came to his wedding. Graham conveniently forgets the fact they brought along four uninvited guests which forced Graham to pay a lot of money to accommodate them. Who the hell does that? I swear, they walked into the reception hall like they were part of an entourage: sunglasses, over-sized purses, walking in with a haughty swagger and smelling like they partook in an Ancient Egyptian essential-oil bath. I found out later the guests weren't even directly related to us."

"Four extra people? Why four?"

"I don't know how they found out, but the tables at the reception only sat eight people. If they had to attend the wedding, their triumphal presence would not be wasted sitting with lowly bred Southerners. They needed to surround themselves with a buffer, people of noble blood and authorized aristocratic ties. They needed to take up an entire table all to themselves."

"Who got booted from the table?"

"Technically, no one got booted. My dad offered his seat, my mom did the same, and the pastor and his wife followed. My dad was overjoyed to finally see his brother, so he didn't mind having another table setup in the back of the reception hall. I think the only interaction between them was when my dad gave up his seat."

"And Graham wants to give your uncle a chance? I can't believe he would consent to even be in the same room as him, let alone try to get you on his side."

"I don't know if Graham is aware of what happened. He never brought it up and none of us ever mentioned it to him. If I'm being completely honest with myself, this makes sense for Graham. He's had to work the hardest out of the siblings and he's painstakingly earned everything he has. My parents had no idea what this country was about, and in many ways, Graham paved the road for the rest of us. He's at a place in his life where he feels he could compete with anyone. He has an awesome job, he's making a ton of money, his kids are fairly grown, and he probably feels the impulse to climb up the next rung. It just so happens my uncle is on that very rung he is trying to get to. It doesn't bode well for Graham, but if he chooses to shake hands with him and join that circle of people, then that's his prerogative. Me, on the other hand, I'm fine associating with the lowly people."

"I just don't get it. Graham has never been this interested in your life or what you do, at least not since I've known you, which in case you forgot has been a very long time."

"Ever since I let it slip I was promoted at work, he's been making an effort to connect with me again. Graham finally sees something we have in common, something I happen to abhor but something his life revolves around— work. I don't think the two of us have ever shared a common interest, well, except one summer when all we did was play video games and yell at each other. That was probably the closest we've ever been. Now, he has someone to commiserate with over the ineptitude of work subordinates and the ineffectiveness of clumsy, heavy-handed upper management. The other day he texted me about fiscal year-end summaries. I nearly punched him through the phone."

"It's great he's reaching out to you. It may not be the way you expected, or even like, but I don't think you want your relationship with Graham to end up like your dad and uncle's."

"But it's not just Graham, because if it was, I wouldn't be so torn about it. I've come to realize the expectation of maintaining a relationship with him means I have to form and nurture a connection with his entire family. I don't have that many cumulative friends in real life. I'm expected to be best friends with his wife, a best friend to my niece and nephew, and a marvelous brother. I also have a swell uncle who wants to be buds too as an added non-negotiable stipulation in my contractual affiliation with Graham. You know it will eventually lead to me having to rekindle attachments with cousins, aunts that are as wily as any coyote, and other acquaintances I absolutely must meet out of filial obligation. Hopefully you can see why I have my reservations about friendships. Putting an effort into strengthening bonds and dealings with family supersedes the illusory effort of making connections outside the household. At one point or another, I was best friends with each of my siblings. My mom told me Graham and I were inseparable when I was a newborn, Katelyn and I were pretty much conjoined from grade school until I started college, and now Alastor and I are taking over the world. Those are never forgotten or erased, but they're also relegated to memories; there's no hope for them to be resuscitated into something vibrant or even temporally tangible."

"Are you implying you couldn't be best friends as a result of them getting married and starting families of their own? That seems like a revival of the archaic concept of 'a man shall leave his family and start a new herd'. I'm paraphrasing of course."

"That sounds odd coming from you, Miriam."

"Maybe it's because I have vested interest in it not being true. Maybe it's because a little effort goes a long way into making the impossible more feasible. Yes, relationships change over time but it doesn't necessarily mean they become a festering pile of expired potential. Do I think you can go back to having the same type of bond with Graham, or Katelyn, or whomever? No, but I also think the memory of what you had should be respected enough to warrant an occasional dusting-off, however perfunctory."

"What happens when the expectation of reciprocity is greater than what the other can give?"

"Are you referring to Rachel, because it isn't too much to ask for you to at least try to get along with her. Of course, I want my sister and my husband to be friends, but at this point I would settle for cordial acquaintances who shake hands, hug, and at the very least not bicker about pointless dribble at dinner. Is it futile to expect both of you be in the same room without one of you making an attempt on the other's life?"

"Do you get along with every one of my siblings? I have absolutely no expectation of you being friends with any of them, because when it's all reduced down, they are *my* family. I married you and you married me. You didn't espouse my family or sign an agreement to become bosom buddies with anyone in my life. How long did it take us to find each other, for each of us to find someone else we wanted to spend the rest of our lives with? Now, you're telling me since we've found that one person, we have to include a village of strangers into our lives, incorporating the same trust and openness in those relationships as well? Miriam, after a while the well gets tapped, and there isn't enough in one person to dole out that much love, trust and parts of themselves to so many different people. I can't shatter myself into sufficient pieces for everyone to be satisfied with how much of me they get and still have enough left to motivate myself into living."

"I have one sister; that's it. I'm not asking you to create horcruxes to cover the spread."

Family was the reason Lennox and Miriam moved to Chicago. Over countless cups of coffee at 33rd street and Ditmars Avenue in Astoria, they discussed the prospect of starting their own family and the shared desire for future children to have as much exposure to grandparents, cousins, aunts and uncles as possible. The final decision to move out of NYC was made on a sunny winter day, the layers of snow melting atop mounds of garbage and refuse. It was the first time both Miriam and Lennox were in the same headspace; ready and willing to move out of indentured servitude, allowing their youthful dreams to take a back seat, and primed to move closer to an ancestral stronghold. Family was also, by far, the most prominent impetus for arguments between the two. Miriam had only Rachel left, and she had moved to London to marry a man Miriam had never met. The people the Adlers referred to as *their people* consisted of Lennox's side, several friendships subsisting from their undergrad days, and the looming memory of Miriam's mother, who'd spent most of her life in Chicago. Miriam wasn't particularly superstitious, but she was familiar with Chicago, and she believed her mother was somehow still there. Even though Miriam had to rely on memories, experiences, sensations and stories, she felt as connected to her mother in Chicago as she did during childhood.

"It's Graham again. He senses we're talking about him."

"Lennox, it's time you realize we're here. This is where we're supposed to be. This is where we agreed we are supposed to be. Your family is here, we know this city, we love this city, we have jobs, we have friends. We can't keep doing this. We can't keep looking for an out when this place is here and we're here—we're in it. I know it will never be perfect and it probably won't be your concept of a home that's unsullied, and has dutifully waited for you all this time. You're not out slaying dragons or deposing forces that are set on disrupting the pivotal balance of humanity. You deserve to rest. You deserve something real and tangible. You deserve more than fanciful illusions of greatness in a world completely comprised of ungreat things, whose core is built up from things that are innately unsavory and without worth. Great soil has no intrinsic value; it's worthless, yet great cities are built on top of mounds of it. Sure, farmers use it and covet it, but not by itself. It's what comes from it, what it's used for, and inevitably how successful it is in aiding the final product, the outcome, not what it merely is by itself.

"If you insist on searching for fabled lands and pristine homelands, you are doomed to find nothing. Because even if you found something close to what you're looking for, it will never be exactly what you imagined. I know you, Lennox Adler; you'll never be satisfied. Please, we have a place here, we have a home right here. Look around you. All this furniture we have, all of it has a legacy that enriches our existence. We had nothing when we came to Chicago, but now we have this table, this dry sink, this desk, this armoire, even this chest of drawers; all of it is our inheritance. Our children will have a story to tell here, in this city and this place, with this furniture, and with us right beside them. When Rachel and I were younger, we used to eat at that rickety table every night together as a family and now we have a chance to do the same. My great aunt bought that desk and wrote letters to her lovers every night on it, and now we have that history to share with each other. We are building a home. We are taking what has been given to us along with what we've earned, and together we are fortifying this place.

We've arrived, Lennox, we're here. Please, stay with me."

"Miriam, I'm here, I promise, but it isn't enough to stop me from getting lost. It feels like we're back in that shithole in Queens, in the basement apartment, sinking further and further into the ground. The stairs out of the basement keep getting longer and longer, and the building is coming down on us. That neighborhood gave us so many memories but also took away so much from us. Now this place. We have everything that isn't ours, and I'm not just talking about our belongings. This spot, this city, can and will always go on without us. Nothing here is uniquely ours. We are at the mercy of the city, we are assimilated into its history, into its culture, into its directional velocity. Chicago is growing upward, it's reaching towards a place where there's no life, no oxygen, no humanity. There's no ground floor. Everyone lives at least two stories above the ground, looking down on passersby and then looking up to a sky that is getting closer every day. Astoria keeps digging deeper into the ground, trying to establish profound roots, making a place for its inhabitants beneath it where no light can reach, burying everyone underneath its progress. Chicago reaches for the sky, hoisting up its peoples to where the oxygen is thin, exalting them to the status of gods where they eventually hallucinate and see themselves above progress. We were buried alive in Queens and now we're being strung up in Chicago."

"And where do you expect you'll find a place that'll fulfill all of your criteria? Will the mountains of Colorado do, or maybe a hut in the Gobi Desert, or a deserted log cabin in Iceland, or a tree house in Saskatchewan? Maybe you're more of a cave-in-Tennessee person where you can write a tome of your learned ways that will grace the minds of all future generations. Or maybe, just maybe, all the energy you've put into looking for a site, all the thinking and hoping, actually has created a somewhere that resembles your true *home*. Perhaps it's somewhere near Mars or further outside of our galaxy. Maybe if you close your eyes really tight, I mean really tight, and hold your breath at the exact moment that Mars passes gas, you might be able to see a glimpse of your far-fetched land."

The coughing that emanated from the unit beneath the Adler's apartment increased in frequency and intensity. To anyone not accustomed to the neighbor's weekend smoking ritual, they would have thought someone needed medical attention. The volume of the coughing coupled with the intensifying smell of the smoke did little to drown out the argument between Miriam and Lennox. There was little patience left between them, let alone for what sounded like smoking amateurs.

Miriam hoisted herself off the yellow arm chair and took hold of the back of one of the wooden chairs that, together with five other chairs and the large wooden table, made up her mother's prized dinner table set. She slammed the chair up and down against the hardwood floor, hoping to gain the attention of the hoodlums whom she was addressing.

"Shut the hell up. If you can't take a measly hit without coughing your lungs out your ass, then you shouldn't be smoking."

As Miriam turned back to retake her seat after spewing fiery justice, she caught Lennox's gaze and the two slowly smiled at each other and started chuckling quietly. The coughing continued in the downstairs unit as Miriam made her way to the sofa. She sat next to Lennox on the sofa, leaned up against him, closed her eyes and squeezed him harder than she ever had before.

* * *

Sunday night ushered in one of Miriam and Lennox's favorite rituals. They agreed they needed an activity that would have sufficient inertia to keep them enlivened through the beginning of the work week and plenty of excitement to carry through to the next Sunday night. From March until late October, a local gelato shop supplied them with the perfect Sunday night activity.

It was only a half-mile stretch down Division street that separated Humboldt Park from Wicker Park, but it seemed like a different world after the intersection of Division and Leavitt. Humboldt Park, from California Ave to Western Ave, is a thriving Puerto Rican neighborhood which sustains some of the greatest cultural traditions of PR, including a yearly parade that closes down a part of the city for a whole day. The commissioned murals which line the buildings down the section of Division Street offer a glimpse into the concentrated effort of the local people to keep the traditions of their homeland thriving and vibrant for future generations. The store fronts maintain a sense of cultural flair, lacking the homogeny most of the thriving hipster movement within the city vomits onto every inch of small cultural neighborhoods. After Leavitt, though, Wicker Park takes over and both sides of Division Street are lined with smoke shops, swanky bars, shops selling Chicago knick-knacks to tourists, and sky risers full of vacant condos.

The Adlers would walk to and from the gelato shop every Sunday night during the open season. It was not a tradition they had inherited from childhood, both families having lacked the disposable income to spend on what was considered frivolity, but it was a custom they had implemented out of necessity; it was for the sake of their shared sanity. They considered it an adaptation to a new and foreign land, and cherished it as an inheritance of practice they could bequeath onto their progeny.

"What does your week look like?"

"I have a meeting on Tuesday and Wednesday, inventory on Friday, and I'm meeting with my boss for a one-on-one somewhere in there. He's still trying to learn his new job and teach me mine at the same time."

"Don't forget Tereza and Rich are staying over on Thursday night."

"Who goes to a concert on a Thursday night? Better yet, who performs a concert on a Thursday night?"

"Lennox, just because you've come to terms with your inner old man doesn't mean everyone else has let go of their youthful aspirations. It's great they're deciding to try and keep up with the twenty-somethings; it's very brave of them. Even if they'll probably end up deaf, drunk, and exhausted."

"Who's the old man now?"

"That'd still be you. The difference is I can perceive some marginal value in their adventure seeking even though I wouldn't myself partake. You on the other hand probably think less of them because of it. What do you like to say, 'only the riffraff stay out past eleven'? Did I get that right? I don't want to misquote you."

"I've partaken in more than my fair share of tomfoolery over the years. It's a young person's game."

"You're barely thirty-two years old."

"Old enough to know better."

"Oh, I also have an appointment this week with the doctor. It's a routine physical and a first check-up, nothing special or important."

"Miriam, why didn't you tell me earlier? I want to be there with you."

"Really, it's okay. I knew you would want to take off work unnecessarily. Honestly, it's just a routine physical and consultation. If it were more important, I promise, I would've told you well in advance. You have a lot going on right now, so focus on that and when the time comes, you can exclusively focus on me."

"When's your appointment?"

"Tuesday at ten-thirty in the morning. I already spoke to the daycare and told them I will be unavailable for the first half of the day. I should be able to get back to work after noon and then be home at the normal time."

"Are you going to take the train or a cab?"

"It's a few stops away from the daycare, so I'm just going to take the train. Plus, I enjoy the walk to Ashland in the morning. It gives me some valuable time before the day really starts with elbows in the face and screaming children."

"Tonight really is just a perfect night for a walk. Makes it that much harder to go home and get into the Monday mindset."

"So then, let's not. You don't have meetings tomorrow, right? Let's both call off of work and spend the day together. We can go to the Field Museum, or the Shedd, or maybe even the Museum of Science and Industry. I haven't been to any of those since I was in grade school. Two years back in this city and we haven't taken the time to savor the real Chicago, the Chicago painted with vibrant colors and embroidered with gold."

"I need to put in my ordering for the rest of week. If I don't do it tomorrow, it'll screw up the inventory for Friday."

"So, you have managers who can do that, right? You can't live in this city and not experience what it means to really live here. Let's forget work and responsibility for one day, one meager, itty-bitty day. The world won't stop turning without us. Like you said, it keeps going with or without us."

"I like this enthusiasm. Let me text my boss and the manager-on-duty tomorrow."

The walk back to the apartment was habitually marked with a slower place and an array of conversation. However, there was an electricity of enthusiasm running through their ritual that Sunday night, catapulting them forward to their apartment with an eagerness that vibrated through them. Their conversation about Monday held open the door to an infinite realm of possibility. The Adlers were practically skipping back to their apartment; melted drops of gelato flew through the air as they spoke with their hands as much as with their mouths.

5

"Good morning, lovely, are you awake yet?"

"I'm either awake or I'm being tortured and have fallen into a state of semi-awareness. It's difficult to decipher which one is reality considering the ungodly earliness of the hour."

"Has anyone ever mentioned you speak too elegantly and cohesively for someone who is instinctively crotchety and a curmudgeon in the morning?"

"I believe my wife has mentioned such a sentiment on several unsolicited occasions."

"Then you should heed her observation and take steps to implement corrective action."

"I feel like I'm at work right now. Did I sleep all the way through Monday? Am I in a meeting with no pants on? This is my nightmare."

"Do you want coffee, Mr. Operations Manager, boss man?"

"Yes, please."

Lennox heard the comforting sound of the coffee grinder, the electric kettle and the clanking of the coffee mugs. Neither Miriam nor Lennox had taken a day off from work since they arrived in Chicago, foregoing that comfort in hopes of accruing enough savings to eventually buy a house. This Monday felt sublime.

"Let's make a deal, you can pick where we go first, but then I pick what we do after. Sound good?"

"Do I get to know what your choice of activity is beforehand?"

"Lennox, where have you decided for us to go this brimming morning?"

"Let me think about it. Actually, let me wake up first and then I'll think about it."

Lennox stumbled his way out of the room, eyes still closed, his feet dragging across the hardwood floors. The sound of the boiling kettle and the clanking cups concealed the sound of his lethargy plopping across the apartment. He peripherally saw Miriam, a blur he interpreted as being human, putting together their morning coffee before he disappeared into the miniature space called a bathroom. The light fixture was automatically connected to the exhaust fan; when the light went on, the deafening sound of the decade-old blades cut off any communication. Quietude was replaced with a deafening hum. Lennox hated the taste of toothpaste with his morning coffee but he abhorred the layer of film on his teeth even more. He didn't mind the coating of dried toothpaste or month-old food remnants propelled onto the mirror above the sink, but the smudge on the glass that morning made it seem as though he had slept on a blotch of toothpaste which smeared onto his face in the shape of a crescent moon. He moved his right thumb from underneath the faucet and wiped away the spot on the mirror. The dried substance instantaneously mixed with the liquid and dripped down into the sink.

"What about the Field Museum?"

"What? I can't hear you over the fan."

Lennox stepped outside of the bathroom, light and fan still on, and observed Miriam as she stood over the counter pouring clove honey into his cup. She assumed Lennox was still in the bathroom as the sound of the fan continued to buzz. He watched her as he always did, aware of everything she was for him yet failing to realize what she was thinking. Lennox's mind took a breath and ruminated.

"I say we go to the Field Museum."

"Alright, Field Museum it is."

"I assume I'll eventually know what comes after?"

"You'll know when I do."

The two savored the beginning sips of their coffee in bed, per their routine, but soon consigned to taking intermittent sips between getting dressed and preparing for the day ahead. There was a newness, a flurry of thrill mixed in with the jittery effects of the caffeine, which compelled Miriam and Lennox to see each other as though they had been apart for a year. Their undressed bodies seemed different to each other as though rediscovered in the glow of a frantic exhilaration. They were giddy and childlike, groping each other with the shyness and zeal they had exhibited the night they'd first almost had sex on the second floor of a frat house. They hurriedly worked through the effort of dressing, foregoing the vestments of their typical work day, and focused on racing down the yellow painted hallway, down the mountain of stairs, and onto Division Street.

There was no point in taking a cab and rushing the day they had together. Every passing second would be absorbed as through a semi-permeable filter; time would have to work with them and not against them. Miriam's sun dress danced along with the quivering of the erratic gusts of the city wind; Lennox's heart cracked under the pressure of her enchantment. Four number 70 Division buses had passed them by the time they arrived at Damen—they scoffed at the city desperately trying to take possession of what the Adlers would not relinquish. Miriam peeked into the wine shop where they'd commemorated their second wedding anniversary; they purchased a French Malbec that night and kept the cork with the message, '2nd anniversary. Two down...' written in black marker.

Division street was sprinkled with their memories. A homeless man once threw a pot of flowers at Miriam on her walk to the Blue Line. Though both Miriam and Lennox avoided interacting with the screaming homeless man, they endeavored to think the best of him and his life. There was a stray dog that didn't move from the corner of Wolcott and Division. Neither of them ever saw the dog eat food or drink water, or heard it bark. Eventually, the Adlers felt the compulsion to create a myth explaining the origin of the dog and its peculiar behavior. The myth posited the soul of the dog was the reincarnated twin of the Dalai Lama, passed up for the prestigious position and mandated to be reborn on the corner of Wolcott and Division. Its purpose was to overcome its nature and the tendency to rely on food, water, and shelter. Everyone on Division Street was trying to get along as best they could.

During non-peak hours, the Blue Line was forsaken compared to the circus-like throngs that took stage during weekday rush hour commutes. The smell of urine, both animal and human, was still unmistakably present and periodically stimulated the olfactory system with flashes of variably strengthened wafts. The Blue Line sunk underground after the Damen stop heading into the Loop, and by Ashland had already cloaked itself in the all too familiar mantle of dank hopelessness. The train wandered through crudely dug tunnels underneath the dragging feet of the homeless and the scurrying patter of misanthropes, delaying its emergence back into the spotlight of the city until its wearied resurgence around O'Hare.

The ride into the Loop was never devoid of drunken prophets, silent mystics or poorly disguised changelings, regardless of the time of day. Neither was there a "kid friendly" window of time when parents could safely take infants or toddlers to ride the Blue Line without exposure to the crude nature of destitute humanity. The best anyone could wish for was an overcrowded train that tipped the scale in favor of sanity based purely on the numbers; the more caffeine-fueled, stoic city dwellers there were on the train, the less the crazy outliers stood out in the grand scheme of it all; a method into silencing the undesirable voices and fading out the lamentable presence of the homeless.

"The next stop is, Jackson. Doors open on the left at Jackson."

That Monday morning commute was unlike any other, lacking the stream-like current of farm-raised fish all pushing and nudging to be the first to arrive to their own demise. The suits were already at their offices, cozying themselves with conversations of their weekend exploits while sharpening their talons for the rest of the workweek. The next wave of work force was fifteen minutes away from standing on the train station's platforms, staving off saturnine thoughts of their existence and fueling themselves with dollar thirty-five coffee. When the doors of the Blue Line opened for the Adlers, there was a clear path to the stairs going up to Jackson Boulevard; no clicking of seventeen-hundred-dollar soles or shuffling backpacks.

From the musty enclosure of the underground, Miriam and Lennox jetted out with renewed spirits. The doors closed behind them and the screeching of the city serpent echoed into the cavernous continuation of progress. The two passed the escalator and walked the thirty steps up to civilization. Every step needed to be accounted for, appreciated and deemed an appropriate countermeasure for the taunting and teasing of time.

In the twenty minutes from Ashland to Jackson, the city brightened even further, allowing the eyes to consider the possibility that the buildings expanded outward toward the lake. The reflections of the light thrashing against the windows and doors of the skyscrapers made enough room for a deepened, relaxed breath. The sidewalks stretched, cracking the cemented confines and dispersing the illusion of confinement even more. The street lamps gained life under the renewing sun and outstretched their blackened metallic limbs above the pedestrian crosswalks. Though both the Adlers worked in the city proper, often commuting during the treacherous hours which hosted the appearances of the beasts from the bowels, they climbed up to the metropolis' center unlike any preceding occasion. The couple walked north to Jackson Boulevard and then east to Michigan Avenue under the guise of a triumphal return through the city gates.

The consensus to forego a morning meal was a precarious one given both their dispositions to unprovoked cruelty and anger brought upon by lack of immediate nourishment. The agreement was they would break their fast at the Field Museum cafeteria if the intensity of their unrelenting hunger would outweigh the enjoyment of each other's company. Even if they had wanted to quickly grab something before the doors of the museum opened, options were limited to a pretzel cart, scones doused in sugar, or a swig from a flask Miriam had forgotten in her purse. Both agreed a cup of morning coffee sufficed to stave off the onslaught of stomach rumblings, and given the limited meal selections, a slight morning fast might do some good. Apart from the temporary nourishment dilemma, Miriam and Lennox also mistimed their arrival to the museum. The doors were not set to open for another fifteen minutes, leaving the two outside on the steps in front of the towering pillars: a pair of seemingly overambitious and overzealous admirers. As they sat on the eighth step leading to the entrance, Miriam leaned into Lennox and the two blankly perused the museum campus lawn and the proximate skyline. The sun melded their shadows together and the stone stairs bent and projected their merged, misshapen bodies onto the concrete landing. Their amalgamated body was absorbed into the cement, temporarily leaving a shadow imprint atop the heated cracked surface. They were alone. No sole trotted upon their fleeting inscription, and for a hastening fragment of a moment, while the sun splattered a contour in front of them, their eyes strayed from the marks of modernity and they visualized themselves magnified amidst a forest of columns and a horizon of frieze. The joined forms blended into a shadow story refracted onto the steps and landing before them; the entirety of the divertissement briefly eclipsed the looming rectitude of a bragging city skyline and the proud glimmer of a sultry lake.

The deformed beauty of their conjoined selves moved with the sun's flicker. Every passing insect or leaf that neared the shadow disappeared within the darkened blob, absorbed into the amalgamation. Everything that was static and motionless in the reality of the modern, everything born without life or breath became animated and fluid in their projected shadow. The new world danced and moved with reckless abandon. It was a place more alive and more purposeful than the one providing their seats. It was energized and motivated by a clarity and brilliance they couldn't see, emanating somewhere behind and above. The small space between them, even as they leaned into one another, periodically reformed the story—their unified shadow fractured and displayed two separate entities, each formed with its own darkened hue. Within those moments of disunity and separateness, the shadow story unfolded uniquely and diversely. Leaves that flew by them in the unfurling wind no longer disappeared within the magnetism of an integrated shadow, but rather momentarily appeared between the shadows of Lennox and Miriam. As each spectator observed the entering character, each for themselves determined whether it was ingénue, Petrushka, shrew or hag. Lennox saw the outline of someone he thought he had forgotten, a flash of green, and Miriam slowly smiled.

Miriam had three relationships, but two loves during

the intermission. She fully resigned to the certainty she would never see Lennox again. She opened her heart entirely and without reservation, forcing herself to close the door on her past and the hurt that accompanied it. She met a former undergraduate classmate of hers while at the University of Iowa. His name was Collin Talley and he played oboe in the Civic Orchestra. He was a country boy, born and raised in Southern Illinois with a sensibility for haute culture but a base humor that would make the most ignoble of individuals blush and cringe. Collin stood tall, regardless of social situation or circumstance, which fed into his aggrandized status among his classmates, especially lowerclassmen. Miriam had first seen him in the orchestra pit carrying around a copy of *Beowulf* hidden underneath two textbooks on oboe technique. She never asked Collin if he purposefully left the title of *Beowulf* visible among the other books, or whether it was unintentional.

During their short time together, Miriam and Collin reminisced a great deal about their undergraduate years, and especially focused on the *what if* of their potentiality: "What if we had dated back then?", "What if we had met sooner?", "What if we had given into our urges and said, "screw the rest?" It was also the *what if* of their tryst which led to their demise. Collin formulated his life within the bindings of the great epics and beneath the shadows of fortified heroes. He fancied he was simultaneously Roland, Gilgamesh, Beowulf, and Odysseus but realistically created a new level of hell unforeseen and undocumented by even Dante. Miriam cared for him greatly. With him, she was given an illusory chance to alter her past choices and make amends with a future which seemed brighter and more promising. Lennox's face slowly blended into the face of Collin, a man whose hope elevated him to the heights of the demi-gods. But the *what if* between Miriam and Collin created a gulf as one between the mere mortals and those destined for a higher calling. Collin was stuck in the clouds of his epics and Miriam was continually tripping over the rocky terrain. She recognized Collin's status atop mere mortals was imagined. He was denigrated to a level of misunderstanding of his own shortcomings and inability to surpass the written accounts of fabled men that were all doomed to collect dust on the shelves. Collin faded into the number of forgotten stories within Miriam's cache.

Miriam met Alessandro Jiménez, Alex for short, on the fading end of the Collin glory days. It started off as a connection based on mutual friendship and common interests which included drinking heavily and causing havoc. Miriam shared her insecurities and misgivings about Collin, who was completing his doctoral studies at the University of Missouri, and the hardships of sustaining a relationship over such distances. Miriam and Alex visited the Iowa ped-mall every night in search of means to suppress their woes. Unknowingly, Miriam began to open herself up to someone who was the complete opposite of Collin. Alex cared little for the illusion of grandeur and even less for the fulfillment of a life's purpose. Miriam was unrelentingly uncaring about everything when she was with Alex. She delighted in using every curse word imaginable as often as she wanted, drinking to the point of peril, and releasing the shackles of friendships which did not adhere to her new-found mantra. She felt alive and uninhibited when she was with Alex. Miriam was finding out how far she could search within herself, how deep she could dig, how many walls she could knock down that held her motionless in an era she desperately tried to escape. She dated anyone she found slightly attractive and Alex would do the same. They divulged every detail to each other, their impassioned feelings, their cravings, their yearnings, their urges, and fueled the bliss of their forgetfulness together. They screamed out other names while tearing at each other, somehow hoping the person underneath or on top of them could simultaneously be everyone and no one. The more intensely Miriam studied, memorized, wrote, researched, the more she hungered for the arrested development of a one-night stand followed by a week-long frenzy fuck, revealing the intricacies of her conquests to a man who saw through her and beneath her.

Miriam first saw Tereza Elezi at an end-of-semester grad house party after two strenuous weeks of studying sixteenth century counterpoint and two physically taxing weeks on her back with Alex. Tereza was sitting on a Barcelona chair; her raven-colored hair draped over the back of it. Miriam felt an instantaneous draw to Tereza. They spent the entirety of the party drinking tequila, foregoing socially acceptable topics of discussion, and absorbing all the intimate details of each other's lives. They signed up for all the same classes the following semester and were both cast in the opera chorus. The two would sing to each other during their scenes on stage and utterly alienate the audience. It was just the two of them. They were inseparable. Whatever depth was missing from Miriam's interactions with Alex was offered in abundance with Tereza. Miriam felt a profound strength in Tereza; a force which encouraged her to find mystical wells within herself that had been discounted for far too long. No one in Miriam's life had seen her cry more than Tereza had.

Miriam felt satiated having both Alex and Tereza, and sincerely loved them both. She held onto them tightly. Remembrances of previous pain and affliction floated to a galaxy far apart. Even though Miriam lovingly and eagerly offered her time and affection to both, they all only nearly met once. It was at a party in Tereza's last semester at Iowa. As the night progressed, and the emancipating effects of inebriation took hold of the grad students, Miriam, employing her lessons learned from her relationship with Alex, took Tereza's hand and guided her upstairs.

Miriam opened a door, found Alex on the floor of an unknown house, next to an empty bottle and a bloodied razor blade. Tereza hadn't entered the room yet, and at the sight of Alex's hacked up arms, Miriam squeezed Tereza's hand so tight she shrieked in pain. She averted Tereza from seeing what was in the room. Miriam desperately wanted to spare her, to shield her, and to hide her from Alex. Miriam lovingly looked at Tereza, kissed her, and asked her to call an ambulance without letting her see the carnage in that foreign room. She would not disregard her love for Tereza.

Alex plummeted from his wistful sojourn in the realm of the uncaring. He had fallen with such gravitas and uncontrolled vigor that his lucid moments became fewer and fewer with the lack of oxygen on his way down. Miriam lingered by his hospital bed until he awoke from his hard landing. After that night, Miriam sought to take care of Alex and offer him someone who would nourish, nurture, and sustain him throughout a new sobering path.

He refused the proposition, and for the next two months he became violent in tone and demeanor. Miriam could not save Alex from himself. He refused to relent from his determination to free himself from all things, which Miriam comprehended included life itself.

Miriam Lehr rarely thought of those two loves. In the moment when an obscure shadow passed in between the ridges of her body's shadow and that of Lennox, she did not reminisce of the lovers she'd had, nor their faces, nor their aspiring ascents and inevitable downfalls. She didn't gush over the *what if* or immeasurable pit she dug within herself over the course of heroic and tragic eras. She thought of the walls she rebuilt around herself. She thought of the pain and suffering it took to reorganize each boundary around her inner self and her life. She remembered with a sense of accomplishment and fulfilment that it was her, no one else, who took everything down and built it back up again. She wrecked her psyche, her relationships, her desires, her identity, and found who she was, what she wanted, who she wanted, and how she wanted it all to be. She slowly smiled because she knew Miriam.

Lennox did not fall in love during the intermission. The splintering effect on his mind from the parting of ways was fully evident for the first few months. He closed himself off from the world, from his studies, from any form of social interaction, from opera, and from reality. He sought solace in religious texts, hoping somehow a higher purpose could be found in the blank spaces between the words. He knew all too well the teachings and implications of the written word of spiritual sects and dogmas, but hoped a pure purpose would make itself known through an ascetic reinvention of his mind. Lennox absorbed and discovered many things about himself and the world he crafted for himself during that time, but alienation of woe was not one of them. His reconciliation with reality and the outside world mixed intensely and ferociously spluttered, much like a pressurized water cannon used to suppress the upheaval of an angry mob. Neither the written word nor the obfuscated purpose in between the spaces could have cleansed or enlightened the deluge of desecration which Lennox unleashed upon his re-admittance into the world of the unrighteous.

Caroline Freely played the role of Amore to Lennox's Lucano in Monteverdi's *Coronation of Poppea*. At the time, Lennox was feeling the full brunt of the poetically inclined Lucano, though Caroline's Amore obtained all the power and influence over his yearnings. Lennox was unresponsive to the fact she was seeing someone else, and she herself couldn't refuse the ardent worship of a storm-trodden castaway. To Lennox, the effort of constantly putting himself within harm's way with Caroline was a form of self-flagellation. In the days and moments when his passion for Caroline would wane, she would craftily reel him back with such gossamer threads as "My heat isn't working, could you come fix it?" or "Can you meet me in the practice room to hear my aria?" Onlookers saw the peril and often warned Lennox the game was fixed, but he relished the stinging sensation of the pain. One night, while walking back to her dorm, he declared his want to kiss her. She warded off his advance and never spoke to him again. Amore had one arrow left in her quiver and that was intended for an accountant unaware of his own beloved's wayward tendencies and inner strife.

Mandy Pierce was the stage manager for *Poppea*, but Lennox did not meet her until the following semester during rehearsals for Mozart's *Don Giovanni*. The attraction was purely sexual for both Mandy and Lennox. The depth and profundity which accompanies most interactions between humans was severely lacking between them. The like-minded duo shared an animalistic quality in their exchanges, forcing propriety and decorum to beg the universe for the cessation of such an unholy union. Lennox and Mandy shared un unbridled potential for lewdness. The last they saw of each other was the night after *Don Giovanni* closed. Lennox, reaching the nadir of his woe and discomfort, walked Mandy back to her car. On the sidewalk in front of the music building, campus building on one side and residential houses on the other, he threw down his backpack, laid Mandy's head down on it and pleasured her, heedless of being caught. Lennox walked to his car, Mandy walked to hers and they never spoke again. Lennox cared very little of what anyone thought at that point in time. He had no qualms about Mandy realizing his debased state of mind. He cared even less whether or not the neighborhood watched in disgust as his head disappeared between her legs.

Peyton Harper sang the role of Poppea in the *Coronation*, but several trysts separated Lennox from meeting her. Even while he was preoccupied with bending Amore's arrow for his own increasingly caustic desires, Lennox always took the time backstage to watch and listen to Peyton sing. Peyton was beautiful, eyes ablaze with a blue tinge that scorched the world around her. Many would remark about the icy quality of her demeanor and logically, they believed, attributed the blueness of her eyes to the paralleling of her intrinsic frostiness. Lennox, however, saw a flame which burned too blistering and intense in those eyes. Everything melted around him when he saw her perform. She stood up tall, proud to the rest of the world, but it felt feigned to Lennox. At any moment, she could implode and destroy everything around her were it not for her attempts to seem collected and poised. She burned so bright that no one noticed the real volatility of her inner self; a precariousness that would rip through sheet metal. At least that is what Lennox saw when he watched Peyton on stage.

Peyton Harper and Lennox Adler met on a walk back from The Library, the bar, not the academic institution, on Boyd Street in Norman. All their friends gradually went their own ways, leaving the two alone in front of her house. They decided to extend their walk as long as they were ensconced in conversation, with the added contingency that the sidewalk didn't end. Lightning streaked across the darkened sky, a perennial occurrence in Norman, but no rain fell. Conversation continued unabated, and sauntered alongside them to a park playground a few blocks from the house. They both sat on a swing and talked while the lightning skated across the Oklahoma sky. Lennox had grown accustomed to his spot at the bottom of the River when he met Peyton; he was still learning to breathe normally while clearing the murky water from his lungs. He went from being lost within a current of non-normalcy, confusion, and disassociation, to a current of emotions that he began to feel for Peyton. She was also recovering from her own distortion. She was still in a battling relationship which lasted on and off again for several years. Peyton loved someone else and would always go back.

None of it mattered when they kissed. Peyton's eyes closed and the unbearable heat of her existence momentarily ceased. She no longer burned everything around her. Lennox closed his mind and no longer cared about anything. They sat on the swing set all night long, sharing in the ubiquitous presence of forgetting and relishing in the sensation of each other's lips.

The end of the semester was Peyton's farewell to an Oklahoma that didn't understand her, lacked any compassion for her, and didn't show any sign of remorse for not getting to know her. All the grad students went to Blackbird, the common hangout for opera fellows and grad assistants to drink heavily at cheap prices, to offer their farewells to the graduating class. Peyton rarely made appearances outside of rehearsals or practice rooms, but promised Lennox she would try. Lennox had an entire year left of his graduate tenure, and so once again joined the legions of students who found their way to the bottom side of despair. He was four scotches in when Peyton showed up to the farewell jamboree. They each drank one last glass of Oban 14, then left the party to offer their own farewells they'd reserved for each other. Lennox threw up all over his shoes, jeans, and on every lawn from Blackbird to Peyton's house. The world around Lennox shifted and swerved, always alluding stabilization and never standing still long enough to make sense.

Peyton undressed Lennox of his clothes. She turned on the water in the shower, waited for the temperature to be bearable, and asked Lennox if he would like to get in. She took his clothes and put them in the washer. As Lennox sat in the large shower, the hot water hitting his head with the ideal amount of pressure to be a comfort to him, his knees to his chest, arms wrapped around himself, he saw Peyton. It wasn't the Peyton who was performing on the stage, her eyes setting fire to everything around her. It wasn't the Peyton who stood tall so no one besides herself could bring her down. It wasn't the icy Peyton or the fiery Peyton. It was Peyton Harper.

She closed the bathroom door behind her, the steam of the shower clouded the room. Lennox watched her as though it were a dream. Peyton undressed herself and unveiled a body that seemed remarkable to Lennox. He had never seen a body like Peyton's. It was tall and slender, but more than that, it was exposed. He had never seen Peyton without fear, without hiding, without standing tall, without burning, without freezing. He had never *seen* like this. Lennox didn't perceive her as a feigned someone. She was beautiful and magnificent. Peyton walked towards him, her body swaying gently, a true representation of Augustine splendor. It appeared her eyes were hazel in that moment. She bent down and sat next to Lennox. Peyton draped her arms around Lennox and the two found relief and shelter under the constant pittering of the water. She held him zealously and sincerely.

When an obscure shadow passed in between the ridges of Lennox's body's shadow and Miriam's, he identified every remnant which haunted his memories and heard the oeuvre of nostalgic overtures. He contemplated how people change. He recognized everyone he had ever met, how they morphed before his eyes, how even his eyes altered before his awareness and consciousness.

The shuffling throng waiting to get into the Field Museums dissipated the divertissement from atop the concrete steps. Lennox was the first to be cognizant of their presence and flinched with unexpectedness, causing Miriam's smile to vanish. The two rejoined reality on the eighth step of the entrance to the Field Museum. They stood up, held hands, and merged into the invading swarm at the front gates. The pinnacle of Lennox's excitement for the Field Museum was the Ancient Egyptian exhibit. Miriam preferred the Museum of Science and Industry, but she acquiesced to Lennox's childlike enthusiasm for antiquated relics.

The staircase down into the Ancient Egyptian tomb was a haunting thrill for Lennox. The coloring of the walls flawlessly matched what he imagined would be the innards of the Earth, the accuracy of the texture of the floors and walls, the jagged appearance of the freshly sculpted graves, the scarcity of air circulation, the small spaces, the impression that this was as intimately acquainted as he would ever be to Ancient Egypt. It exhilarated and disheartened him all at once. It never changed for him, regardless of how much time had passed since he last visited. It was the awe of the unknown that comforted him, the prospect there was something more than what was epitomized in the exhibit. He would ask his classmates as a child, "If this is how they *think* it was back then, imagine how much more amazing it actually was." To Lennox, Ancient Egypt was shrouded in a mask of mystery and glory. No matter how much he read, learned, observed, no information could ever accurately recreate the feeling of home within the glorious empire. He felt safe and cozy in Ancient Egypt, a home which could never be truthfully recreated in any era but its own.

"Are you hungry yet?" Miriam had a way of asking

Lennox whether or not he was hungry with the pretext that she herself was the one who was hungry.

"I could eat. What did you have in mind?"

"I don't mean to take you away from your one true love. I know how much you long for and lust after that sand-ridden era of wonderment. I know how you ponder what those queens were wearing underneath all that garb when it was so hot."

"You do know there were a lot of fleas and lice, right? I mean, a lot of fleas and a lot of lice. They had to shave their heads and wear wigs for crying out loud. I don't think they fared any better down below."

"Do you think they wore a merkin to add a bit of spice to the bedroom? I mean, if they were so self-conscious about adding a wig to their heads, doesn't it stand to reason they felt naked without a hairpiece everywhere they shaved?"

"Miriam, you ask the truly insightful questions of our age. I don't know, maybe they left a landing strip for the fleas to attach to and the men to stay away from. And now that we've resolved that, do you know what you want to eat?"

"How about we have a picnic in Grant Park? You can grab some cheese, wine, and accoutrements from work, right?"

"I can, but I would rather not go in there today considering I took the day off."

"What excuse did you give them?"

"I simply said I wasn't coming in today. I left it fairly vague. I mean, does it really matter why I'm not coming into work as long as I make sure everything is covered? If you really want a picnic, we can go pick some stuff up."

"Yes please, I want that."

The two emerged from the depths of the exhibit and made their way out into the sun-filled plane of the living. By early afternoon, the streets of the city had become infested with the fast-paced phantoms of the business elite and the posh gaggle of city mothers, deliberately running over pedestrians with their emptied strollers. The hour of caffeine witchcraft descended upon the city, fueling mindless drones and invigorating the zeal and ardor of the eccentric. Taxis honked with resolute determination. Both Lennox and Miriam thought the Egyptian tomb was preferable to the surface city during the caffeine witchcraft hour. The mummies and sarcophagi were more respectful and had immeasurable more insight into the human condition. As opposed to city folk, they comported themselves with a demeanor fit for an enlightened civilization.

It wasn't too far of a walk to Urban Whey, a small cheese and wine shop in the heart of the Chicago Loop. The sound of the bell as the door opened triggered a visceral response within Lennox.

"Hey, Lennox, I thought you weren't coming in today?"

"I just stopped in to grab a few things and then I'll be going back the way I came."

"Don't know why you would want to stop by on your day off."

"Me neither, Sean."

Lennox hurriedly grabbed a bottle of Nadler rosé, a piece of Jasper Hills Harbison, a piece of Kenny's Farmhouse Kentucky Rose, a piece of Pleasant Ridge Reserve, Smoking Goose Gin and Juice Lamb salame, a ramekin of olives and a bag of spiced almonds. It was enough to tide them over until dinnertime, or at least until Miriam needed to eat again.

"Please put this all on my tab."

"No problem, see you tomorrow."

"Don't remind me."

It wasn't the anxiety of getting caught in the store that had Lennox on edge, it was the location itself. Everyone in the company whimsically joked that the Wabash location was haunted, but Lennox had been Operations Manager for more than a year so he was less inclined to believe it a ruse. There were circulating rumors the building once housed a hospital, and the victims of malpractice lingered to remind the residents of their own fate. There were too many mishaps and inexplicable occurrences for even the most ardent skeptic to negate the possibility of hauntings. Of course, Lennox didn't allow the inkling of belief to grow beyond its well confined storage within his imagination. He hated being at work on his days off, something that happened with more frequency than should ever be allowed within an advanced society. Miriam understood completely. When Lennox looked like he was going to bolt out the door after he was done, she was right by his side waiting to sprint alongside him.

Fleeing the scene of the countless work-related hardships and misgivings had a laxative effect on Lennox's soul. He didn't say much to Miriam after they exited the shop, but the aura of irritation rapidly dissolved as the two arrived at Grant Park.

Millennium Park hosted a myriad of events during the summer. Mostly it held events whose primary aim was to attract the bougiest audience willing to invest in the restaurant, food, and drink scene of the surrounding area. On Fridays, Saturdays and Sundays, troves of Northern suburbanite families drove down to the city for a brief getaway from the hardships of financial security and posh humdrum which adorned their grueling daily lives. Children would be dressed in the most uncomfortably spectacular outfits, husbands would gawk at their phones the entire time, occasionally lifting their eyes to mentally lift the skirts of the passing twenty-year olds, and wives would peruse the surrounding area on the lookout for potential friends who decided to getaway without the courtesy of having informed them of their plans. It was the idyllic playground for those who lost their sense of playfulness and adventure with the accumulation of their Scrooge McDuck-sized fortunes.

Grant Park events also emboldened the enchantment of a younger generation who inadvertently recreated the plotline to Puccini's *La Boheme* without having heard or seen any scene from it. They were all stock characters on a lawn, minds stuck somewhere between fantasy in their sky castles, woe in their pastoral purgatory, and a victim's attitude in the brazen and condemning feel of the everyday. Enchanting Musettas with their décolletage were on display, Rodolfos poetically rapping, Marcellos painting with their spray cans, and the often forgotten Parpignols selling goods in the city alleys to avoid being discovered by local law enforcement. Both the *Boheme* troupe and the migrating Northerners coveted a moment of ephemeral repose from the buzzing atmosphere of e-cigarettes, craft beer, and coffee scooped from the dung of the African elephant.

On the far edges of the park were the homeless and

impoverished who simply sought out a temporary abode where they could uneasily lay down on the lawn and sleep, but instead were obliged to seek reprieve on trash bins, broken benches, and wherever else the others dared not approach. The music in Millennium Park was neither comforting nor gratifying for them because they discerned the alleged power it had to allay the hatred of humanity was merely a myth. To them, those to whom the fewest words were allotted, the music was noise keeping them awake.

Miriam and Lennox had no trouble finding a spot on the lawn to have their picnic on a partially cloudy Monday afternoon. There was no crowd of suburban families or stock characters congregating in the park because there was no spectacle worthy of attendance nor a worthwhile occasion to grace society with their presence. The Adlers had no blanket to sit on, no cups for the wine, no utensils, no basket, just a bag full of their purchased goods and a willingness to enjoy the day.

"This is as good a place as any, don't you think?" Miriam had already been seated when she posed the question to Lennox. He didn't even bother looking around for other options, but rather nodded and sat down next to her on a shaded part of the lawn.

"Thank goodness for twist off wine tops, am I right? Do you want some?"

"I just want to smell it."

"You asked me to get a whole bottle of rosé so you can smell it?"

"Lennox, don't argue with my sensibilities. If a woman wants to merely smell the delightful and fruitful aroma of a bottle of rosé, then she should be granted the opportunity to do so."

"Your sensibilities are not under scrutiny here, my dear, but you not partaking means I'm going to drink the whole bottle by myself. I mean, I figured you wouldn't down the whole bottle, but I expected you to at least have a little bit."

"Are you afraid of excellence?"

"It's not excellence I'm afraid of. It's going into work tomorrow with a hangover."

Miriam seized the opened bottle, smelled the rosé, put the opening of the bottle to her lips and tilted the bottle. The chilled liquid touched her lips and sent sensations from the back of her neck down to her toes. It was the mixture of the cold pink liquid on a summer day which was beginning to show its heat and the nostalgic quality of rosé that stretched the corners of her mouth into a smile. She handed the bottle back to Lennox, the smile persisting on her face, tilted her head to the left, raised her eyebrows, and pursed her lips as though to say, "Show me what you got." Lennox looked into her squinting eyes, her left arm stretched towards him with the bottle offering, and he smiled back at her. He loved her.

"Alright Lehr, but let it be known you are the instigator in this instance."

"Shut up and show me the man I fell in love with."

The smiles shared between Miriam and Lennox were laden with flashes of past exploits, stories of drunken debauchery, streaking through the quad, watching lightning storms while drinking Sangria spiked with Cognac; filaments of experience, thin and brittle, surviving the years and connecting them through the undulation of every second. Miriam loved his enthusiasm for adventure when he drank. She had watched in delight during their undergrad years as he concocted the most god-awful and unpalatable mixed drinks, and then danced all night even if no one else was dancing with him. Lennox dubbed it *dance synergy*. He would prance and wiggle until he sweated through every inch of his clothes and when his legs gave out, he would gyrate up and down as he lay on his back. Miriam loved the story of when he climbed an art installation of a horse in grad school during a night of festivities. He couldn't recall how he defiled it, but the school took down the installation the same week. It could have been mere coincidence, but both Lennox and Miriam enjoyed to think he desecrated the horse beyond recognition, forcing the school to retire the installation and send it to the equivalent of a glue factory.

Miriam marveled at Lennox as he started taking larger and larger gulps of rosé. She was familiar with his disdain for drinking any type of wine that quickly, but she was certain he would do anything to make her happy, even if it meant an excruciating headache the next day. The cheeses were exceptional, the olives perfectly briny, the almonds impeccably seasoned, and neither of them minded eating everything with their hands. Miriam could hear the wonder and electricity come through Lennox's voice as he soliloquized halfway through the bottle. She beheld him as though seeing him anew. She loved him so enlivened, roused, and carefree, even if it meant his pretentiousness would invariably seep through. She was eighteen again and in love with the Wanderer above the Sea Fog. Back then, the prospect of seeking, exploring, rummaging, with the stimulus of his inquisitiveness at the helm was captivating to her; it transported Miriam outside somewhere, in the vast expansiveness of possibilities. She trusted she could be anywhere and still be close to Lennox, as long as they would be searching together. It was warming to have a glimpse of it again, but Miriam resolutely grasped she was already home. She was within the dwelling she had painstakingly created and built for herself; brick and mortar from the tattered remains of crisis—a home built to sustain her. Lennox, however, was still the Wanderer above the Sea Fog. She was home, but he was not.

"I have an idea! Let's grab a cab."

"Miriam, I'm about to finish this bottle of wine. It would be rueful to allow the liquid of the gods to be splattered among the refuse of mortals."

"Lennox, chug the rest and throw the bottle out. Come on."

While Lennox was finishing the remaining rosé, Miriam was on the phone solidifying plans for the conclusion of their day. Lennox held his liquor surprisingly well for a curmudgeon, and at times his temperament and mood were vastly improved by a few drinks.

"1935 North Avenue, please." Miriam hailed the cab and Lennox asked no questions. When they were ten minutes into the cab ride, Lennox could no longer stifle his curiosity.

"Okay, I'm assuming you now are privy to the conclusion, and as you promised this morning, you said I would know when you do."

"I have a friend who owes me a favor and I just called it in. I can't tell you what it is just yet; you have to be patient until we get there. Also, I need you to be very open minded, okay Lennox? No questions yet, and please do this for me."

Lennox frowned at Miriam yet acquiesced to her demands. The light posts, bridges, sidewalks, and buildings smeared together in a haze for Lennox, but Miriam absorbed every detail of the cab ride. She clasped Lennox's hand and squeezed it with deliberate emphasis. When the cab arrived, there was still no immediate dispelling of the mystery for Lennox as the façade of the building gave no indication as to what the final act included. Up the stairs they went to a door that read, "Speakeasy Custom Tattoo". Lennox pulled back and stood immobile in front of the entrance. Miriam turned towards him.

"You promised me you would be open-minded. This is the perfect end to the day. Please."

Lennox planned to eventually get a tattoo, but he could never settle on a concept that would warrant a permanent staining.

"Do I get to pick the tattoo?"

"No Lennox, I already have one picked for you."

"Do I get to consent to what it is or at least see it before it's on me forever?"

"You'll see it when it's finished. Where is the spirit of adventure I know is in there? What a perfect day to finally take the plunge and get a tattoo. Who better to pick it out than your true love, the magnificent embodiment of grace and beauty? Who better to brand you than the person who knows you best, well, second best—that squeaky voice in your head thinks he's got one up on me."

It didn't take long once Lennox was in the chair. He leaned back, head still spinning from the picnic, and turned his gaze to the side so as not to ruin the surprise Miriam had assured him of. The day rolled onto a continuous reel with the buzzing sound of the needle. Miriam scribbled a design onto a piece of paper and handed it to the tattoo artist. She was fairly prolific at drawing and at times displayed flashes of creative brilliance. It was that fact which kept Lennox from calling off the whole adventure. Lennox managed to keep from ruining Miriam's surprise throughout all the discomfort of laying on the chair, and kept a resilient focus and ascetic spirit all the way back to their apartment.

The stairs up to the Adler apartment were not as difficult to maneuver for Miriam as they were for Lennox. The city night ushered in the coolness of the dark; a refreshing incentive to get up to the apartment and revel in the rest of their night. Miriam helped Lennox to the front door, pressed him up against the yellow wall, fastened her hands around his neck, and kissed him as though she had never met him before. Her hands surveyed then groped his entire body with reckless prowess.

Miriam paused, inhaled all the oxygen in between them, unsealed the door, helped Lennox into the bathroom, turned on the light, and tenderly took off his shirt as she peered into his darkened and glossy eyes. The fan immediately began its deafening process. Miriam steadily touched Lennox's bare arms and chest, making sure to only make contact around the inked area. She gently lifted the gauze, smiled at her work, and then beamed at Lennox.

"Take a look." Miriam moved to the side, almost having to get into the shower to make room for the two of them in front of the streaky mirror.

"It's five letters from Linear A. I wanted you to have a reminder there is still something out there, unknown and undiscovered. There is something in existence we haven't explained, that we still can't explain. There is a place you can search for with a language that hasn't been deciphered. It's for you, it's on your body, and you can reference it to find your way there."

"What if they decipher Linear A in the next decade and the symbols together mean tofurkey turd, or boy who steals squirrels, or follow me I'm lost, or..."

"Then at least you'll know if there was once something, or someplace, we couldn't explain, there will inevitably be another. You can always look at your chest and know mystery is always out there, somewhere."

The Adlers cozied in for the remaining hours of their day together on the sofa. Miriam did not sit on her usual yellow arm chair, but instead laid across the sofa on top of an inked and dazed Lennox. They both fell asleep on the sofa for a few peaceful hours, at least until Lennox woke up at 2 a.m. and convinced Miriam to occupy the bed instead of the uncomfortable couch.

"Goodnight, lovely." Lennox laid down next to Miriam and yearned to fall back asleep. Miriam fell into an exhausted deep slumber while quietly laughing. Lennox gawked intently at the ceiling until the darkness around him convinced his eyes they were closed. They were not, but at least he couldn't tell.

6

"You have to be productive and useful in this country. You have to be fast, efficient, and good in everything you do. I came to this country with forty dollars in my pocket, no English, no connections. You have to be better. You have to do good."

It was impossible for any one of the children to forget the words of Florin Adler because he wouldn't let them. Every Adler gathering, even well after the children were married and living far from their parental home, mandated that Florin be allotted a few minutes to reiterate his famous words. It was an unspoken understanding between every member, a sign of respect from the children and a duty not taken lightly by Florin. Mădălina would regard each child as a priest his flock, blessing them with eyes full of empathy, pity, and hope, while Florin iterated the wisdom forged by decades of hardships in a foreign land.

Florin was proud of his children when they succeeded but did not sputter out mellifluous words of encouragement to them. It was a requirement for his children to succeed, especially financially, in this foreign land because he had accomplished a great deal with more hurdles, disadvantages and prejudices than they ever had. Success to Florin was an obligation for his family and not a deed needing constant verbal encouragement or patting on the back.

Mădălina Adler had her own apprehensions about the children; she was constantly worried about her children's spiritual well-being.

"And remember to forever pray. No matter where you are, no matter how bad, pray. Don't lose your way, don't lose your soul in this place. God listens."

Graham Adler was a contract lawyer who worked in commercial litigation and attended church every Sunday. Katelyn Adler was a marketing specialist for a small nonprofit organization and attended church every Sunday. Alastor Adler was a lab technician who worked in Research and Development and went to church by word of mouth. When asked, "Alastor, do you go to church?" the response, "How could I not?" was an efficient sidestepping maneuver he utilized, well-knowing his mother's wobbly grip of the English language.

It took several years, countless detours, and innumerable conversations between Lennox and his parents for him to be downgraded to Defcon 4 on the parental worry chart. His final decision to take the job as Operations Manager was an enormous relief to his father and Lennox's habitual conversations about religion were a glimmer of hope for Mădălina. Perhaps it was Florin's soliloquy that worked on some deeper level within Lennox's mind to convince him to take the job at Urban Whey, or perhaps it was the ideal time for genetics and parental conditioning to finally meld together and reprogram Lennox into a younger and shinier version of his father.

The common good was a concept adopted from a history, country, and mindset which was foreign to all four Adler children. They had heard the stories of a time and place where all that was individually earned was reallocated to the State so the goods could be utilized to their maximum efficiency. In reality, the government did not use the redistribution of goods and services to stabilize the well-being of all its citizens. It used the stolen goods, seized from the beaten hands of the workers, to play politics. If one supported the Party, they would see their wealth increase. Even though Romania was a distant echo for the Adler family, Florin and Mădălina took the lessons they learned under the communist regime and applied them to the children's upbringing. They provided their children with an authentic reality even if the new land would often try to marginalize their worldview as passé, unfounded, foreign, or mistaken.

The common good for the Adlers was *family*. All one did, all one could strive to achieve was a family unit which was bound together with threads of loyalty, devotion, support, love, understanding, and respect. The relentless lectures and admonitions against bickering and divisive opinions within the family became the platform by which Florin and Mădălina molded the minds of the four Adler adolescents. It was a sentiment of *us* and *them*; there was a distinct parlance of *the others*. At all times, it was *us* in terms of the South Adler family that strove to strengthen their bonds within a country which offered an array of culture, education, and social constructs which taught the importance of self-destiny and self-identification.

"They can talk what they want. They can believe anything they want. But you, you all have to be together. Me and mom won't be here always, you know that. You have to keep to one another like family." Florin's index finger never pointed to any person, but when he implored his children to stick together, he pointed his right index finger upwards as though uttering a prayer to the heavens.

"My father died when I was thirteen. I didn't have a father to teach me and show me what to do in this life. I had to find a way. I had to make a way for me, Mommy, and you kids. You kids are not alone. You have each other. Talk, understand, respect each other. When you fight, it's okay; nothing is enough to break you apart. You have to communicate with each other, help each another."

There weren't many occasions when Florin's speeches were needed as guidance to resolve a serious issue between the four children, but there were nonetheless a few noteworthy meetings of the minds. When the need arose, the four Adler kids gathered at their parent's house, each sitting in their designated seat at the dinner table. Lennox sat to the right of Florin, Graham to the right of Lennox at the foot of the table as firstborn, Katelyn to the right of Graham, and Alastor to the right of Katelyn and to the left of Mădălina, who sat at the head of the table. When the children gathered to discuss the state of affairs, Florin's and Mădălina's seats were left empty. The parents would retire to the living room, allowing the children to talk amongst themselves without parental interference, only resurfacing when guidance was needed.

As the lineage extended through marriage, the chairs reserved for Florin and Mădălina were gradually occupied by spouses, and the counsel of wise parents was seldom solicited. It wasn't the introduction of unfamiliar spouses that destabilized the consonant pact between the Adler children, but rather the relinquishing of understanding between each other that had been harnessed and strengthened through years of shared experiences and instruction. Graham forgot how Alastor rushed to get help when he fell through a faulty sewer covering, but remembered how hard he used to hit Lennox when they were younger. Lennox disregarded how he and Katelyn used to be best friends, but recalled the day when Alastor blabbed to their parents about his unsupervised and dangerous scientific projects. Katelyn overlooked how Graham paved the way for her acceptance into a college honors program, but vividly recollected the pain she felt when Lennox shoved her into a table. Alastor blocked out Katelyn's generosity when he couldn't make rent, but held onto when Graham used to throw tennis balls at him.

Eventually, spite grew within them: a spite neither immediately checked or thwarted, nor covertly encouraged or allowed to flourish straightaway. It was a malice passively ignored, finding means to subsist in the darkest parts of their minds and hearts until their words and glances spoke their innermost sentiments. That enmity churned and fermented within them, birthing new grotesque spawns. Graham considered himself the inevitable head of the siblings: a prestige allotted to him as birthright. At his side, his queen would inherit the title of matriarch and together they would command a respect from even the mouth of babes. Katelyn was the spurned sheep, or so she believed; a sole daughter alienated from a family that did not understand her and irreparably damaged her psyche during childhood. By her side, she would persuade her spouse to join her flight from a household that caused her to unduly suffer. Lennox became the recluse, hiding amongst thieves and harlots to warrant the family to shun him further into the depths with which he had become accustomed. Alastor was his own and would not be held by familial bonds which he considered shackles. If the sound of the metal restraints did not suit him, without the slightest delay he would cast each fetter off a cliff.

Each of the four children had, in their own minds, justifiable reasons for acting and speaking against each other. Unintentional slights became unforgivable treasons. A lack of response to a text or phone call was broadcast as a declaration of war. Over the course of years and marriages, the Alder children rarely met altogether at Florin and Mădălina's house. Excuses and justifications for absences were bountiful.

It wasn't Alastor's divorce which set the remaining diaphanous thread of familial cooperation ablaze, nor the ensuing texts and adroitly placed misinformation that emanated from Alina Kovaci, his ex-wife. It was Graham's, Katelyn's and Lennox's own inclinations to either believe or discredit any received information, and then ascertain the truth based on what they believed in their own minds to be gospel. Each of the three children chose their side well before they sat down for one final meeting. Some of them identified as victims in the situation, lamenting how their own reputations would be tarnished, while others used the occasion to validate their misgivings about Alastor's life choices, his history of erratic behavior, and the inescapability of the outcome.

Alastor's decision was his alone and the final meeting at Florin and Mădălina's house was pointless, unfruitful and schismatic. Graham, Katelyn, Lennox and all their spouses met on a muggy Chicago-night apart from the inquisitive ears of the Adler nieces and nephews. News of the divorce, an event unprecedented and unfathomed in the Adler world, stigmatized the elder Adlers in the Chicago Romanian community. They said nothing and would not sit at the kitchen table even if summoned. Florin and Mădălina Adler sat on the green fabric sofa in the living room, holding hands, slowly wiping away their tears, and stared past the wooden deck into their blossoming garden. Graham sat at the head of the table, his wife, Camelia, added a chair next to his. Alastor's seat was left unoccupied. To the left of the absconded chair sat Katelyn and to her left was her husband, Brandon. Lennox sat in his usual seat with Miriam to his left.

"This is all so shocking. I can't believe this is happening."

"Does anyone know why? Has Alastor talked to any of you?"

"I tried calling him, I don't know how many times, but he never answers. He's just hiding. I don't know why he won't just tell us what happened."

"I mean, I talked to Alina and I know her side. I think it's only fair that Alastor give us his side."

Of all the people seated at the Adler kitchen table, only Brandon had any first-hand experience with divorce. He never said anything. He kept a distance from them. He spent hours at that table looking and examining his fingernails.

"My kids looked up to him. I can't believe he's being so

selfish and not considering the impact this will have on them. He has to grow up. Graham and I knew he was lying, we just felt it. We knew something was wrong. We had to have a conversation with our kids that no parents should have to have. I hope my kids are nothing like him when they grow up."

"I don't understand why he doesn't want us to know the truth. Alina is telling everyone what happened, and it sounds like it's all Alastor's fault. Doesn't he want us to defend him? Don't we deserve to know the truth?"

"What the fuck Katelyn?"

"Lennox! This is Mom's house. What's wrong with you? Don't swear."

"Alastor doesn't owe us anything. Did you marry him? Did you live with Alina?"

"Gross! No, but I'm his sister and when people ask me what happened, I want to tell the truth."

"Truth of what? He got divorced. He didn't kill anyone, did he? I'll tell you all something though, if he did kill someone, I would help him bury the body and not tell any of you what happened. Or better yet, I would pull the trigger for him. I wouldn't tell Camelia what happened because her kids would have nightmares. I wouldn't tell you, Katelyn, because you would sell us out as soon as there was a pause in the conversation. You're all full of shit."

"Lennox, what's wrong with you? Have respect for Mom and Dad's house and for your brother and sister. Don't blame my wife for this."

"Thank god, Graham, I thought you had your tongue removed this entire time. You and the French manicurist."

"What? Who?"

"Let me guess, Graham, you're sitting there all silent, praying to god for guidance when what you really should be doing is defending your brother."

"My brother decided to get divorced."

"What does that have to do with anything?"

"It isn't right. God created marriage as an *eternal* bond between man and wife."

"Eternal bond my ass."

"Lennox, if you swear one more time, Camelia and I are leaving."

"Forgive me, I forgot about the virgin ears. Look, Graham, I don't know what beef you have with Alastor. Katelyn, I don't know what you have against him either. You of all people should sympathize with what he's going through. Dare I even mention your wedding and how you were treated?"

"Lennox, don't bring that up. That's none of your..."

"Before you all feed me your party lines again, let me say this; he's our brother. It shouldn't matter. None of it should matter. He's our brother."

"Alastor didn't take us into consideration when he got divorced. He didn't ask us for help, he didn't even let us know he was getting divorced. You want to know how Camelia and I found out? Someone at church came up to us and asked if it was true my brother was getting divorced. You can't even imagine how embarrassing it was, in church of all places."

"I would think there would be understanding in a church of all places."

"Oh, get off it, Lennox. You know that..."

"I know plenty, and I especially know a stranger would have more compassion for Alastor than you would."

"Don't make me out to be a villain. I love him, I'm his older brother. But I can't accept what he's doing."

"Who are you to have to accept? Is the Torah physically written on your heart? Is the good news always spilling from your guts? Are your eyes so impeccable you only see a pile of *poop* when you see your brother? Made sure to clean that phrase up, special for you Camelia."

"Don't speak to my wife like that."

"If she wants to dish on what is happening in this house and fling mounds of brown judgment at people sitting across the table, she better be ready to have judgment thrown right back at her."

"You're a little shit and you don't know what you're talking about. We don't need you to be the voice of reason. We're firmly reassured in what we believe and we know in our hearts that Alastor is wrong in what he's doing."

"Well, then I'm wrong too."

Miriam gently squeezed Lennox's leg underneath the table. He had crossed into the intersection; he was at the point of no return. Inadvertently, Lennox had abandoned reserve and insulted everyone at that table. He did murder for Alastor. Lennox assassinated his relationships with all of his siblings in the rage of the moment. After that night, it was all different. He drowned out all the good memories of Graham and Katelyn and supplanted them with images from the night at the kitchen table.

The assemblage sat quietly. Graham tightly rolled a napkin that was laying on the table, Katelyn scratched the etched needlework of the tablecloth, Camelia had her hands rigidly folded and her chair pulled out a foot from the table. Brandon continued to polish and coiffure his nails, Miriam clasped Lennox's hand underneath the table, and Lennox glanced at each of them. When the silence faded into an unbearably high-pitched screech, Florin and Mădălina got up from the sofa, held hands, and walked up to their room.

After that night, there were a series of group texts sent from Camelia and Katelyn to the fellowship of the kitchen table; Alastor the Absconder was added to the guest list. They berated Alastor for his ludicrous behavior and divulged the apparent truth of what transpired as relayed by Alina Kovaci. On Alastor's birthday, he received a poetic and enlightened text which labeled him a miscreant, a sinner, a horrid human being, a philanderer, an adulterer, and among other such noble titles, a disappointment.

Time finds a way to relay what is hidden beneath the torrents, below the reflections of the external world. By the time Katelyn and Camelia tried to make amends for their spiteful and rash words, Alastor was gone from the tower of forgiveness which oversees the past and the present. Eventually, they stopped trying. Graham needed Alastor to come to him, on Graham's own terms, as a dutiful younger brother should, but Alastor never acquiesced. Florin and Mădălina's efforts to facilitate a strong family core failed at that meeting of the minds. The sins of the parents would abide within the hearts and inclinations of their children.

7

The buzzing of six oscillating fans drowned out the honking cars on Wabash and lulled away Lennox's retention of the day. Everyone else had left. Lennox sat on the damp floor of Urban Whey with a Daisy Cutter perspiring in his left hand. He never held drinks in his right hand out of respect for a bet he lost in college. Cars blurred in and out of sight and the usual pungent smell of cheese was annihilated by a sharp chemical tinge. It was the aftermath of a day gone dreadfully wrong, but somehow Lennox could not find the motivation to get up and go home. The all-too-familiar lullaby of the fans elicited the conditioned response of closing his eyes and imagining a tiny dot somewhere far off in the distance.

"Hello! What the fuck does a man have to do to get a goddamn piece of cheese in this town? The Chicago rats don't even have to wait this long."

The loud banging paired with the hollering from outside the door startled Lennox awake. Even in a deep disoriented state, the voice was undeniably familiar.

"Are you kidding me, Alastor? What the hell are you doing here?"

"Well, I was in the mood for a piece of cheese, or was I in the mood for a piece of sleaze?"

"You know this part of town was converted from a red-light district a few years ago."

"Chicago is slipping."

"Yes, because lack of access to prostitutes is the first sign of a city gone wrong."

"I completely agree."

"Alastor, it's almost midnight; what are you doing here?"

"I saw you flash the Bat signal and I'm present and accounted for to save your damsel-ass."

"Awfully chivalrous of you."

"It's not awful at all. If anything, I should be commended. Perhaps with an escort, a piece of cheese, or something as simple as a gesture of decency. Are you going to make me wait out here with all the streetwalkers?"

During typical circumstances, Urban Whey was a quaint cheese shop with stocked shelves of domestic wines and international cheeses, pristine glass cases jam-packed with accoutrements and a designated area for purchasing freshly made sandwiches. Alastor did not get to see Urban Whey during typical conditions.

"You're doing a great job, Lennox. You've got a real back-alley, trash dump vibe going on here. Either that or you are setting up for a minimalist opera."

"I know."

"I can't believe they didn't promote you sooner."

"I can't believe you believed a streetwalker would be interested in going back home with you."

"Better chance of that happening than making sense of this shit-show."

"Do you want a beer?"

"Is the pope an atheist?"

"Let me get you one from the cooler."

"Just put it on my tab."

Alastor glanced over the cheese shop and designed several scenarios in his mind to explain the disarray and disorder.

"Why are you smiling like you just fulfilled the other half of your halfsie-conundrum?"

"You don't know, maybe I did."

"Wouldn't surprise me. Was it from the sharp cheddar in the corner?"

"There's a joke in there about dick cheese."

"I regret saying anything."

Lennox and Alastor plunked down on the tiled floor, spread out their legs, took note of the humdrum of the fans, and concurrently opened the new beers. Alastor wouldn't offer a direct answer as to why he made his way to the Loop, but Lennox was relieved he was there. It wasn't a miracle that Alastor showed up when he did. It just made sense to Lennox that he was there. Lennox's leg began to bounce up and down. His thoughts were whispering, urging Lennox to give them voice, but Alastor didn't notice.

"I hate the night. I didn't always, in fact, I used to thrive in it. I felt alive. Now I feel perhaps I'm too alive. I can hear everything, I can see everything, I can feel everything. It's too much, Lennox. It's like every ounce of me vibrates with dark energy after the sun goes down. I feel like I'm going to explode. It might be that I'm scared. Damn bed dwarves."

"Maybe you do need an escort."

"I don't conceal my true intentions."

"Are you going to Aunt Lena's funeral?"

"No, are you?"

"I haven't decided, but I bought a plane ticket."

"To everyone else in the world, to any normal person, that is the textbook definition of having made a decision."

"I pity them."

"The normal people?"

"The textbook people."

"Paper makes the world go 'round."

"So do carnival rides, external torque from the Sun's gravity, too much drinking..."

"I still owe you a toothbrush."

Time progressed slowly on the floor of Urban Whey. The beers were almost empty; the overwhelming chemical smell faded with each sip. Both brothers recognized they needed each other without having to say it aloud. They sat in silence as cars and wandering critters indistinctly rummaged about outside. Lennox took the can from Alastor's left hand, pulled himself up from the floor, and threw out both empties. Alastor proceeded to the door, waited for Lennox to set the alarm, glanced at his brother, and then made his way out the doors. Lennox turned left and Alastor turned right.

"Don't let the bed dwarves steal your treasure tonight."

"Why? That would be the only action I get."

"Goodnight, Alastor."

"Goodnight, Lennox."

It would have been too long a walk to the Blue Line for Lennox, and even if he arrived safely, he wasn't sure of the train schedule after midnight. He hailed a ride and sputtered out the Division street address to the driver. He regretted not telling Alastor the news. He relived the entire night over in his head, convincing himself there was no right time to divulge the information. Nonetheless, the pang of remorse moved up his body and evaporated his beer buzz.

Fifty-six steps up to the apartment. Fifty-six steps for Lennox to visualize his brother's pain. Fifty-six steps to bear the burden of not telling him. Fifty-six steps to open a door he would have to pry open. Fifty-six steps to finally laying down in bed.

"What happened, are you okay?"

"Just the worst day at work. Did you get my text?"

"Yes, I ate earlier. Lennox, what happened?"

"I don't think anyone would believe me if I said it out loud. It almost seems fabricated, even to me, except I was there and I'm quite certain I wasn't dreaming or hallucinating."

"Lennox..."

"I firmly buy into the theory that Urban Whey is cursed, or at a minimum, haunted. Tomorrow, first thing when Sean and I get into the shop, we're going to scour the entire building in search of a hidden voodoo doll, although I'm not discounting the possibility of ancient idols or black charms. There's probably a pile of them buried underneath the concrete, or a sacrificial altar where the cheese case is now. We might have to burn down the place to cleanse it. I mean, purify the son of a bitch with raging, engulfing flames. Let the ashes then be drowned in holy water."

"You're alive, so either you made a pact with the spirits, sparing your life and damning me to listen to your babble, or you need to sit down and explain why it's almost two in the morning, and all I received from you today was a text that said: EVERYTHING WENT WRONG. EAT DINNER WITHOUT ME. Right now, it's difficult to discern which is more probable."

"We were in the middle of our lunch rush, nothing out of the ordinary, just a line out the door. I went into the office to check the numbers for the first few hours so the dairy brothers could get their play-by-play for the day, when Sean comes in and tells me there's a leak in the roof. Now, as you know, it was sunny and eighty-five today with no mention of rain. So, I'm thinking Sean is delirious from hitting his head or hopefully buzzed from a beer he shot gunned in the walk-in. Well, he was neither. I go out onto the floor and sure enough, right above the newly displayed seasonal gin, there's a leak. Not just any leak. It was a constant stream of yellow-colored water, like there was a tiny pissing troll above the ceiling tiles. I swear I heard it laugh while it jumped up and down, pissing on us and cackling. We put down a bucket and asked the maintenance crew of the building why there was water oozing from the ceiling. They had no idea, so I went next door and told the guy at the front desk there was a leak. He said he would look into it. I went back into the shop, and wouldn't you know it, there were at least three new seepages. Water all over the floor, on the displays; it was raining piss-colored water inches away from the customers. Sean and a few others tried to mop it up as quickly as possible, but there was too much water.

The guy from next door comes in, utters 'oh shit' under his breath, then heads right back outside. By this point, customers are sidestepping puddles and cascades of what turned into sudsy water."

"Are you being serious right now? Wasn't there a possibility of the entire building going up in flames with an electrical short?"

"My thoughts exactly, so I call it. I shut down the store and ask the customers to please exit the building. Wait for it, this is golden. They actually complained, and refused to leave the store. They wouldn't leave without their sandwiches, cheese, or wine that they didn't even pay for yet. They didn't care about their safety, they needed to die with their gluttonous sausage fingers wrapped around their edibles. There were men and women in suits, eyes fixed, stewing in three inches of water, constantly moving to avoid the waterfalls, hands folded. They were unbending. There was a moment where I sincerely hated them. They were not only risking their own lives, but they also weren't permitting us to clean up. When workers asked them to move so mopping could commence, they resisted and responded, 'but I'm waiting in line.' I finally locked the doors, handed the stragglers their food and bid them good riddance."

"Just for a sandwich?"

"No, just for their privilege."

"So, you were all cleaning up until now?"

"I called off the closing shift because I knew we wouldn't be done in time to reopen for the evening hours. By five, it was me, Sean and a few others cleaning up and closing. Then it happened. The epitome of what the place really means. The dairy brothers came in after we called them earlier in the day. It took them five hours to come see what was going on. By the time they arrived we'd stripped the ceiling tiles to dry, used the wet-vac to eliminate all the standing water, and set up fans to add some circulation; the place looked half-way decent, which was the problem. They pulled me to the side and rebuked me for having closed the shop. They harangued us for having sent everyone home."

"Wait, what caused the flooding?"

"Remember the guy from the front desk who ran away when he saw the waterfalls? Well, he came back after we closed and told me the condo unit above the shop overfilled their washing machine, left it running while they were gone, and the machine overflowed into the cheese shop. That yellow water, if you're wondering, was all the delicious and appetizing filth the water picked up while it made its way down."

"I'm going to be sick."

"Oh, there's more. When I recommended we have someone come in and check for potential mold, they said, 'It will be fine. Leave the fans overnight, put the tiles back on, and open regular hours tomorrow.' They left and said nothing more. I'm sure there will be a follow up meeting with my boss and them very soon."

"I'm so sorry, Lennox."

"I'm sorry I missed Tuesday movie night."

"If only that were the worst thing that happened today."

"How was your doctor appointment?"

"It was really good. The doctor said everything was normal. Happy and healthy."

"Did you set up another appointment?"

"Yes, a month from today."

"Great, I'll put in the time off request tomorrow."

"You know, you don't really need to be there for now.

You can wait until I'm further along, when it gets more exciting."

"It's already very exciting."

"Have you told Alastor yet?"

"I will, I promise."

"Did you at least have something to eat today, I mean apart from the mouthful of laundry water you drank?"

"After the adjustment bureau duo left, Sean, the rest of the crew and I cracked open a beer and toasted the cursed place and its artillery of mischievous ghosts. We came to terms with it all. We now expect everything to go wrong, all the time. Since we made it through the deluge without being electrocuted or drafted into the Wabash legion of spirits, we can handle whatever comes next."

"Please put my mind at rest and assure me the persistent reference to a haunting is purely hyperbolic. Otherwise, I might consider having you committed along with the owners. I will of course insist the two of them be taken first."

"I think I'm exaggerating, but there is also a good chance I'm experiencing the initial stages of a renewed belief system. You should have seen it. It all looked staged—the downpouring of water, the slipping workers, the disgruntled owners, the insane customers, the sloshing of sopping mops. Staged by ghosts, or at least roguish imps."

"Then you are well on your way to sporting a new white wardrobe. I look forward to visiting you in your new digs with the barking people and the imaginary chess players."

"You know you're just proliferating stereotypes. I've known some insane individuals who drank tea with their pinky finger lifted, had impeccably combed hair, ironed jeans, said 'hello,' 'thank you,' and 'indubitably,' and when the sun went down and no one was around, they would sneak into their exes' house and sprinkle pubic hair on their pillows. Those are the truly insane because they work within the confines of normalcy and decorum within the public eye. They seem well-mannered and well-bred yet they're rotten inside and all types of miscreant. Talk about *Invasion of the Body Snatchers*. It's that lot of people I'm worried about. Not Communists or liberated crazies, although I do also worry about Communists."

"Lennox, I don't think anyone drinks tea with their pinky lifted or uses 'indubitably' anymore, except you when you get drunk or you're trying to be an ass. Also, people don't say hello anymore. It's very passé and too much of an effort. 'Thank you' is reserved for the rich who don't really mean it but have to say it so they seem grateful for something in this world."

"I'm so far behind in my understanding of what is acceptable anymore. What would I do without you?"

"Not much, that's for sure. Well, I waited up as long as I could and I'm glad you're okay. I've had a long day too. I'm going to bed. Come tuck me in?"

"Of course."

The nightly ritual of saying goodnight was exemplary of the habits of an anxiety and strife-ridden generation. It was an involved process of hugging and holding each other on the off chance that one, or both of them, would not make it to see morning. Fear of the unknown drove them to hold on tight to whatever they could. Their faith had waned with the deceptive pronouncements of the political, economic, and social harbingers of the era.

"Don't stay up too late, Lennox; you have an early day tomorrow. It's going to be a long day and you aren't so sprightly anymore, or young for that matter. All-nighters are a thing of the past."

After Lennox and Miriam said their goodnights to each other, Lennox pulled the door to the bedroom so the light from the living room wouldn't disturb Miriam. She would sleep through anything, but Lennox wanted to make sure. He took the red lighter outside with him, careful not to let the door slam or creak, sat down against the brick wall of the building and held his phone in his left hand. He assessed what he was going to say, how he was going to say it, anticipating how each word could be interpreted. He wanted to be sensitive to the situation, considerate of each person, understanding of every possible outcome. He stared at the darkened screen. He had put this off for months in the half-hope that a *deus ex machina* would resolve his quagmire, and another half-hope that magic was real. The delay was natural for him. The timing never seemed appropriate, perhaps it never would, but it needed to be done because he loved Miriam. He also deferred it because he loved his brother. Lennox didn't trust the sentiment or pretense that Alastor was okay. He knew his brother well enough, and he just knew he couldn't be okay.

Lennox placed the red lighter on the wooden planks underneath him. He turned on his phone and began texting the letters that became words, which then became a sentence. They were the words he had put off saying to Alastor.

: I WANTED YOU TO BE THE FIRST TO KNOW THAT MIRIAM IS PREGNANT.

PORTLAND

8

"I don't know why I'm doing this. Should I feel bad about taking another day off? It's very last minute and although I did get the time-off approved, I still feel like maybe this is a bad idea. Is this a bad idea? You would tell me if you don't think I should go, right? Are you sure you can't come with me? Do I have a good excuse not to go? People change their minds, things come up, agreeing to participate is not a contractual promise. They would understand. There are over a hundred cousins, who would even notice if I wasn't there?"

"What the hell, Lennox, I'm not even awake yet. Did you have your coffee yet? Don't tell me you stayed up all night, did you?"

"I may have slept a few minutes, on and off, throughout the night."

"Are you packed?"

"Packed? It's one day. What do I need to pack that won't fit in my duffle bag?"

"Did you bring your black suit?"

"Shit, no, I completely forgot."

"Well, you know, going to a Romanian funeral without

a black suit is fairly damning to your reputation as well as the future assurance of your soul. If you don't pay respect to the departed by draping yourself in black, how can god respect you in the future?"

"You may not be awake but your sense of humor seems to be bright-eyed and bushy-tailed."

"Are you calling me a furry?"

"Yes, exactly. My wife the furry. Thanks for reminding me about the suit. Is there anything else I'm forgetting? Maybe the reason why I'm going?"

"Lennox, you love your aunt. It's great you're doing this."

"She said she wanted us to remember each other as we were, back then, before the caskets and the lifeless corpse. Shouldn't I respect that wish of hers?"

"You respected her while she was alive. You loved her and brought her pride while she was breathing. You now have to go respect her loved ones. You said you would, and that should mean something. Do you know if Alastor is going?"

"He's not. He's reverting to his bad habit of digging trenches around him and expecting an onslaught of mustard gas."

"Did you tell Katelyn what time your flight gets in?"

"Even if I didn't, somehow she would find out. I bet my mom couldn't wait to tell her I was going to be in town for the funeral, even though she lives in Washington. Insisting I stay with her is a prison sentence."

"It's one day. Katelyn wants to see you. She made an effort and extended an olive branch. That's good news; that's a good sign."

"You're an optimist and I come at this as a cynic who

has reason and recourse for believing the worst of the situation."

"You mean believing the worst of your sister."

"You say potato, I say vodka."

"Lennox, promise me you'll try. Put forth an effort to make Florin and Mădălina proud. Consider the great relationship you and your sister had before it all went to shit. Please promise me you will stifle your spite, no matter whose fault it was or whose fault you believe it is. Promise me."

"I promise I will make an effort."

"Thank you. Do you have time for us to have a cup of coffee together?"

"I already have it brewing in the French Press."

A faint murmur vibrated underneath the city at three in the morning, bestowing the early risers with the feeling of a revving engine preparing for a long and arduous race. The air lacked the congestion and claustrophobic squeeze of daytime bustle. Lennox and Miriam took their coffee outside and momentarily rested on the slightly damp patio furniture. A view of the skyline not yet decided whether to glimmer in the waning moon or glint in the waxing sun slowly awoke on the horizon. It was the moment of repose, the last quick, stolen breath before the gentle humdrum became an overpowering inertia to the Adler's day.

"I love you very much, Lennox. I hope you have a great trip, even though it will be sad. Don't laugh at the funeral. Romanians don't like that. They don't see the humor like we do. Staunch people, the Romanians. Say hi to Katelyn, Brandon and the kids for me. I love you and I'll see you Thursday after work."

The Blue Line to O'Hare was sedated and without the

usual backpack face slams or briefcase shoves. Only the prophets of the subway laid prostrate on the benches, the smell of ritualistic elixirs emanating from the entirety of their holy corpses. Lennox wasn't unsettled because he was disrupting his work schedule or that he was spending time away from Miriam. He was going to a dwelling far apart from himself. He hadn't spoken to any of his Portland cousins since grad school. The once inseparable Prodan cousins were scattered throughout the country, falling out of communication with each other. Lennox's mother often mentioned one cousin or another having gotten married, or having begotten a small village of children, but other than the scant retellings, the extended Prodan family had become foreign to him.

Perhaps it was that Lennox felt some sense of obligation to his Aunt Lena. He had ignored any guilt or feeling of indebtedness towards his cousins over the years. The death of Aunt Lena forced the dam to buckle and Lennox now had to face them all at the funeral. She was beloved by everyone on the Prodan side of Lennox's extended family.

Of the sixteen Prodan children born in Romania, fourteen made it to the United States. Two children fell ill and died in Romania before receiving news of their eminent departure. By the time of Lena's death, there were ten Prodan children left; both parents died ten years after arriving in the United States with the memory of a squabbling and bickering family unfortunately seared into their minds. Together, the remaining Prodans amassed a number of offspring that numbered close to one hundred.

Lena Prodan was the second born and Mădălina Prodan was the third. The two sisters were the closest of all the siblings, and the only two of the Prodan children to keep communication alive. Lena's passing was a source of immense agony and dread for Mădălina.

After Mădălina met Florin Adler, the entire Prodan family was granted visas through a lottery system ironically sanctioned by the communist government. Most of them settled on the West Coast of the United States, eagerly nestling into their new home.

Lennox was on his way to unite with them in sorrow: nine aunts and uncles, and his hoard of cousins. During his commute to the airport, Lennox waded through a mental list of names which seemed never ending. He flipped through his codex of cousins', aunts' and uncles' names which he hadn't uttered in years. The refresher made him more anxious than put him at ease.

When he was last in Portland, he fielded questions about the true purpose of his visits with ease, but Aunt Lena always knew. She unerringly sensed why he was there, why his eyes glimmered when he arrived, and why he had lost a considerable amount of weight. It wasn't the grueling and cumbersome nature of his graduate course load as Lennox misleadingly endeavored to explain. The veritable impetus was the green blur across the room. He would have to revisit that place and try to come to terms with someone and something he'd tried to forget. He contemplated whether she was still there, if she would be at the funeral, if she failed to comprehend what happened between them as much as he did.

"Your shoes. Shoes have to come off and placed in a bin along with all other belongings. Read the sign, please. You're holding up the line. Step to the side and let others move their bins."

Lennox forgot to adhere to the safety protocols of the security check-in. He wasn't embarrassed for holding up the line as much as he was irritated he didn't know the answers to the questions he asked himself. He flung his shoes into the bin and walked through the detectors. Luckily, he didn't have very much time until his flight, so there wasn't much opportunity for him to torment over thoughts and remembrances that belonged buried alongside the Egyptian sarcophagi.

Lennox found an empty seat overlooking the tarmac. He put down his carry-on and his hanging suit bag on the seat next to him, glanced at his phone before turning it off, and stared outside as the sun began to reflect off the docked planes. He had been in a very similar situation before. The sun shone just as bright on his flight back from Portland to Oklahoma City a few years ago. One simple text altered the course of his mind and life. A meager and scant :GOODBYE did all of that.

"Now boarding flight 105 to Portland. Please have your boarding pass and ID ready."

There was no turning back. Lennox willingly decided to pay respect to Aunt Lena while, on some level, fearing he would have to pay respect to a past yet unresolved and still festering. Every step nearer to boarding the flight required a deeper breath.

By sheer luck, or the mercy of the seating gods, Lennox had a window seat, and due to the early hour of the flight, he had the entire row to himself. He placed his carry-ons above, rested his head on the backrest, closed his eyes and slowly allowed the recollections, sentiments, muscle-constricting reactions, and echoes to trickle into the forefront of his mind. It was a cacophony of ear-deafening engine feedback, angelic smiles, text alerts, air vents, lethargically circulating air, and then all at once, as though set on a timer, it all disappeared.

"I'm pretty sure I said I wanted to get married around 24/25, not 22/23. Either way, the numbers are not absolute. It would be ridiculous for me to have a deadline. Thankfully I don't expire after my 23rd birthday."

Lennox was all alone. It could have been a full flight with screaming children and wailing widows, and Lennox would still have been alone. Time became fluid and constantly moved as he felt himself drift without purpose. He was on his back, afloat on a stream, looking up at the sky. He was weightless and couldn't hear, his ears underneath water. Everything dulled as he was powerless to the current that was drifting him away, willing him away. He succumbed to the current.

Lennox was pulled into his seat, his head still leaning back, his mind far above the trajectory of the plane. The divinity of the green blur across the room stole him away like no god could ever do. With an intensity, greater than a multitude of smoldering chariots, he was pilfered away, dissected, and indiscriminately re-distributed to earth as moral fodder. Her emerald grace disfigured him. He slavishly peered into the greenness as its ethereal wafting delicately settled on his lips, flooded his lungs and sweetly suffocated him. He was imbued with her spirit—the augured ruin of his certainty. Within the shy warmness of her glow, hidden away, were Delilah, Sarah, Zipporah, and Salome, the greatest falls to the most primitive of men. Each one was camouflaged amongst endless curls of Elysian wheat, tightly wound and secured underneath a sheer head covering, like a beautiful Medusa with each head hissing in tongues learned from the great Sirens of old, waiting to discover who will be tantalized to drink from her fountain.

Drunk with enticement, the slow teetering of her body transformed into a dance to unveil and undress him. A pair of hands were raised in supplicant worship, but his eyes absorbed her devotion, taking the sacrifice which was meant for the altar. His pupils dilated; he inhaled her visage into the deep reservoirs of his consciousness. There she would rest, hidden, frozen in her moment of innocence, captured from the grasp of the sacred. She was the fruit that was untouched and untasted, prohibited even to the trying fires of life, more guarded than Brunhilde. If he could not steal her with his adolescent fervor, the gods would not gain another soul to add to their royal treasury. Just as Cain's offering was stopped before reaching high heaven, so too would she remain on this plane, in the hidden crevices of his heart where no deity dared enter, save for the day of reckoning where all that was hidden in his heart would erupt from the rock twice hit.

He felt every fetter cling to her corporeal form, yet she did little to notice the bondage of her fate. She did not feel the tightening of the shackles nor the weight of the bond which grounded her hands to her sides. Her voice, sincere in conveying a conditioned desire, was reduced to a whisper, the intensity of his gaze shrank her universe. He merely watched as his passion reduced her connection with the infinite cosmos to a confined coffin. It was the moment he fell in love and the moment she was destined to become a pillar of salt.

"Sir, would you like something to drink?"

"No, thank you, I'm fine."

The response was automatic. Lennox only had a cup of coffee the entire morning and desperately needed to drink some water. The flight attendant had surprised him, and he reacted impetuously by declining her offer. He urgently wanted water, but wasn't resolute enough to admit his initial response was uncalculated. He resigned in his chair, slouched down slightly, and hoped she would pass by again later in the flight.

The sky outside neared its full brightness and the clouds lingered below. Intermittently, the ground below was revealed through gaps in the fluff lining. Lennox was not taken aback in awe or easily impressed by sunsets, clouds, picturesque displays of sunshine, rainbows, or sunrises. Being miles up in the sky, above the human perspective of looking up at the celestial dome, he looked down at the wistfulness of the disintegrating clouds and the faded, naked blue hue of the sky across from him. The window was cold to the touch and smudged with all types of muck. When the sun was out of direct view, he saw his reflection in the small glass pane. It didn't look like him, or at least how he imagined he should look. His beard had grown considerably longer since the last time he was in Portland. The skin underneath his eyes puffed out just a bit more, his hair was considerably shorter, and he smiled less often. It wasn't that he was unhappy or even that he was happier then. Lennox agreed it was the overhyped process of adulthood, the metamorphosis which makes sages out of turds and turds out of sages. He conditioned himself to smile less because the world around him was skeptical and weary of smiling people.

When he smiled the last time in Portland, everyone

presumed he was hiding something, keeping inner machinations hidden from the arena of common knowledge. Family and strangers alike felt entitled to the goings on of his life, the obscure motivations of his plans, the elucidation of his dreams, even the words he furtively muttered to himself. They couldn't trust he was happy because no one was happy anymore, at least not authentically happy. Lennox ascertained there was no place to be happy in the world. Happiness comes later, in some distant land with gold placards and silver drinking water. You can smile when you are dead, when other humans have to manipulate your facial muscles into a grin even though your body gives into gravity and wants to plop to the ground.

Lennox amassed a great many things from his Romanian elders. They were simple and kindhearted immigrants, living in a realm and world unlike anyone else could envision. It was supposed to be the land of flowing milk and honey, interspersed with excruciating work that had a definitive end. Yet, the reality of their homecoming to the United States was a life preoccupied with toiling, perpetual working, agonizing, crying, striving yet not achieving, and countless nights praying to the god of the old country. It wasn't supposed to be that way. There was supposed to be an eventual end to it all.

Lennox became acquainted with the magnitude of sadness from them. It was a profound woe that numbed the part of the brain which controlled facial muscles. Sadness for them was not an expression feigned or manufactured by constricting or releasing the muscles around their eyes, mouth, or nose. Every facial contortion was allowed to succumb to the elements, to gravity and to the hardships of life. Each wrinkle was wrought over time, free to be defined not by the will of the man or woman which inhabited a particular body, but by the same forces which molded and shaped rock formations, sandy beaches, and glaciers. Sadness was etched onto their faces, and happiness became an uninhibited and unblemished expression of that sadness. Their true joy was the allowance to faithfully represent what divine forces revealed.

"Can I get you anything to drink?"

"Yes, water please."

9

"Ladies and gentlemen, we're preparing for our final descent into Portland. Please make sure your tray tables and seats are in the upright position."

After grad school, Lennox spent almost every day at Katelyn Treowe's West Loop condo. He loved his nephew and niece tremendously, and getting away from the peering eyes of his parents was an added bonus. Katelyn and Lennox were close from childhood and into their high school years. During Lennox's undergrad years, Katelyn helped him out financially whenever she could and never missed an opportunity to send him clothes. Arguably, Lennox and Katelyn knew each other the best of all the Adler siblings. They imparted their secrets and confided in one another. That was then. Lennox had no idea what his sister was up to. He would not have accepted the invite to stay with her had it not been for Mădălina's insistence on the matter. As intently as Lennox recalled the myriad of good experiences shared between them, it was impossible to forget the last meeting at the Adler kitchen table. He remembered walking to the United Center after the Blackhawks win, game nights with the siblings, sushi night, and *Homeland* marathons, all at the Treowe condo on Madison Street, yet the dam he'd built was too fortified.

As the wheels of the plane hit the runway, Lennox turned on his phone half expecting to see a dozen messages from either his mother or his sister. He was flabbergasted to find only one from Katelyn that read: HERE. Lennox grabbed his belongings and headed out of the plane into the small Portland airport. The drifting Portland air was familiar to him. It smelled like pine and fresh oxygen that was almost too concentrated for his system to handle. Lennox wandered outside, drew in a deep breath, coughed without cessation and saw Katelyn's black Buick crossover. Two separate years, two disparate SUVs, two distinctly different people, same Lennox.

"Hi, Katelyn, how are you?"

"I'm great. I'm really glad to see you. Here, let me pop the trunk so you can put your stuff in the back."

"It isn't that much. I can just hold onto it."

"Nonsense, what's the use of having such a big car if you can't use all the space?"

"Where are the kids?"

"They're on a playdate with some friends. I hosted last time, so I have some free time to spend with you today. We can drop by to say hello to them if you like."

"Whatever is good for you, I don't want to add to your stress."

"No stress whatsoever, I'm just really glad to see you. You know, you're the first person from the family to visit since we moved out here. We've invited everyone so many times, but what can you expect, people are busy and have their own lives to worry about. I bet this is a world apart from Chicago, huh? No traffic, no honking, clean air, trees, mountains. It's really a great place."

"It really is, although I never expected you and Brandon to move out of Chicago. I really thought that's where you guys were going to be for a while, possibly forever."

"Things change, people change."

"Isn't that the truth."

"Did you have breakfast? Are you hungry? If you are, we can stop anywhere you like."

"I can eat. What do you guys have here that I can't find in Chicago?"

"I don't know what's open at nine in the morning, but we have Kumamoto oysters at our house. I know how much you love oysters. I also think Brandon has some Marshal Zhukov from last year that he might be willing to part with, if you like. We also have buffalo milk camembert and fresh mackerel."

"Why Katelyn, have you purchased all of my favorite things in the attempt to keep me from ever going home again?"

"It crossed my mind once or twice."

"All that sounds great. To the Treowe household we go."

"Great. If you're too cold, too hot, let me know and I can adjust the temperature."

"Everything is just fine, just like I remembered it. What time is the funeral tonight?"

"I think it starts at seven. It's at Philadelphia, you know that right?"

"I heard rumblings. I haven't been inside that church in a while."

"Brandon and I don't go to services there. We go to an

American church nearer to our house. Philadelphia is like a thirty-minute drive from our place, so we can leave at 6:15."

"There's the Florin Adler sense of time. Better to be waiting in your seat in an empty church fifteen minutes early rather than one minute passed the start time."

"It's a habit I can't seem to shake. We were always the first ones anywhere. Can you imagine inviting a family over, giving them a specific time to be there, and they showed up earlier? We must've pissed off so many people, but no one said anything because who didn't respect the Adlers? Then again, I don't remember going over to people's houses very often. We went to Uncle Ionel's, but that's pretty much it. Brandon finds it unbearably annoying. He always reiterates that people set a start time for a reason. I agree in theory, but the river runs too deep."

"Should I even ask how long you've been waiting at the airport?"

"No, you probably shouldn't. I don't have the kids today so I had plenty of time to get here, and I honestly don't mind waiting. I'd rather take my time getting to a place than hurry and be stressed the whole time. The West Coast changed a few things for me, but the anxiety sticks to my bones."

"You West Coasters don't have a Zen technique or sushi to mend the affliction?"

"Still using clichés and stereotypes I see."

"Would it be me if I didn't use them?"

"Maybe you'd be a better you."

"Possible, but unlikely."

"I've missed you, Lennox. I've missed the whole family. I don't like being this far away from everyone."

"Is Brandon coming to the funeral tonight?"

"I think so. No one recognizes him at that church, so he feels comfortable being lost in the mass of people. He doesn't like to stand out amongst Romanians, but I told him there'll be quite an eclectic mix of people tonight. Plus, we haven't spoken to any of the relatives, so I doubt they'll even remember how we look."

"Mom probably sent them pictures. She wants to make sure we're noticed since she can't be here."

"How is she taking not being able to come?"

"I haven't talked to her about it, but I think a lot of it has to do with Dad. Mom really wants to be here, but it's only been two weeks since her surgery. Mix that cocktail up with a healthy dose of high blood pressure and her mourning, and you have a recipe for adding to the departed list."

"Have you talked to Alastor? Do you know if he's coming? I ask because he doesn't respond to my messages or calls."

"I told him about it. Alastor does what Alastor needs to do. I don't hold it against him either way. There's no requirement for him to show his face just so relatives can blather on about his personal life. So, no, I don't know if Alastor is coming tonight."

There was an uncomfortable and prolonged silence in the car on the I-5. It was not a Lennox and Alastor lull in conversation that was a build-up, a resting, before conversation would inevitably resume more vivacious than it had before. It was a Lennox and Katelyn lull in conversation which was teeming with awkwardness and no assurance of any further dialogue. It was getting cold in the car. The summer day in Portland was a far cry from the humidity and unbearable heat of the Midwest. Katelyn nonetheless cranked the AC even though it was a mere seventy degrees outside. As Lennox uneasily looked out among the landscape of the familiar city, he heard his hanging suit bag slide off the back seat and onto the trunk floor while his carry-on did the electric slide from one side of the car to the other.

"Fifteen minutes and we're already where we left off."

"I'm sorry, Katelyn. All I meant to say was I honestly don't know what Alastor has in that head of his, and I don't want this trip to be a rehashing."

"Do you remember when I asked you to sing at my wedding? Do you remember how Mom and Dad were so disappointed I was marrying a non-Romanian, how so many of our relatives bad-mouthed me because they thought I was damning my future? It should've been the happiest day of my life, but I cried instead? I cried the night before, I cried the day of, and I cried afterward. My bridesmaids were running out of tissues constantly having to touch up my make-up. Everything was so beautiful: the weather, the venue, the suits, the dresses, the heels, the food. We had mussels. You used to make the best mussels, that's why I wanted them. Then we had cupcakes, not elaborate Romanian pastries, but delicious, individual cupcakes because that's what Brandon and I wanted. It was never the same between me, Mom, and Dad again. For the longest time, I couldn't understand them. I couldn't grasp what was so dreadful that they couldn't simply see me as their daughter, their only daughter. I couldn't fathom how my happiness could've been such an incredible source of agony for them. So, I married an American, big deal. When they moved to this country, did they expect some ritualistic ceremony of keeping the blood lines pure, of keeping the tribe intact by ensuring intra-marriage? I was their daughter, first and foremost, not a propaganda tool in promoting some eugenic mindset. So, yes, I get I acted terribly with Alastor. Everyone, me, Mom, Dad, we all did because we judged we were doing the right thing."

"We don't need to talk about it, Katelyn."

"I'm sorry for what I said that night. I'm sorry for how I acted. The regret stays with me. I've tried so many times to convince Alastor, but he won't talk to me. He won't acknowledge I'm his sister, that I really want to be in his life, and that I want to help. I don't know if I can help, because I still can't understand it all. I know my limits. We were brought up in a vastly different way. I wasn't privy to his and Alina's marriage, and maybe that's a good thing. What I know is we were taught to make it work through whatever kind of hell or agony. We were instructed to always reconcile, and the promises we make should be sacred."

Even the briefest of silence between Lennox and Katelyn had the feeling of an unsettled boiling kettle. The slow release of air, the high-pitched noise, all of it would eventually erupt in a violent outburst of steam. Even a temporary abatement of the underlying burbling between them was illusory because discord had already been emblazoned on their hearts. Pacifying words and calming phrases reassured only the ears, but the heart heard beyond the fricatives and the labials.

"Oh no! I forgot to text Miriam I arrived safely."

"How are you two doing? Everything okay with you guys?"

"Katelyn, I just forgot to let her know I got here. There's nothing earth-shattering about that. Trust me, everything is great."

"Are you still living in the apartment in Humboldt?"

"Yup, two years now. We love that place."

"Any plans of moving to a house or maybe having a baby?"

"We've talked about both options, but we're still working out the timing. I was recently promoted, the job takes up entirely way too much time, and she is in line to be the head of daycare. I know busyness is not an excuse that is in vogue anymore because everyone is busy, but it is a deterrent."

"Are you guys at least trying?"

"Trying to what? Are we trying to look for a house? Trying to answer life's unanswerable questions? Trying to see whether we are dog or cat people? Trying to alleviate the weight of the world's problems?"

"Never mind I asked."

"Done."

"You know, Brandon and I have been trying for another baby."

"Does Brandon know you're broadcasting that information?"

"It's family, you're family. If I can't share the news with you, who am I supposed to share it with?"

"I hear the homeless are an extremely receptive lot. They're so often overlooked."

"And there's the ass attitude I know and love."

"I'm glad to hear you guys are trying. I know you wanted a lot of kids. Is that something Brandon wants too?"

"I think so. If not, the meandering idea of another kid will slowly make a home in his thoughts."

"Are you ushering them in or is he inviting them on his own?"

"Both?"

"How is he adjusting to life on the West Coast? I assumed Brandon was someone who bled Chicago. I never thought he would move out of that city."

"Actually, Brandon's parents live in Washington."

"What? How did I not know that? Did you ever tell me? I should've known."

"Brandon doesn't like to divulge much about himself or his family life to anyone. I'm still slowly waiting underneath the faucet of information, drip by drip. Both of them live in Cherry Grove."

"I've never heard of Cherry Grove. Does anyone actually live there? Also, I thought his parents were divorced."

"They are, but neither ever moved. Come to think of it, they haven't moved from the same houses they had after they divorced. They live ten minutes away from each other. Brandon was born in Cherry Grove but moved to Chicago to live with his grandparents."

"Okay, now you're just lying. So, Brandon has moved back home? All this time I incorrectly imagined he was born in the slums of Chicago."

"When we got married, he wanted to move back closer to family, but it merely seemed like a whim. I guess over time, the distance fostered a longing to return. He never explicitly said moving to Washington was the plan, but here we are, home sweet home."

"Jeez, is that your house or the neighborhood

community center?"

"It isn't that big, is it?"

"Do you remember the houses in Chicago? This is close to one of those McMonstrosities that pop up by Mom and Dad's. Wow, Katelyn, you guys are doing well."

"It isn't that big."

"Yeah, you're right. It only seems small compared to mansions, Victorian plantations, and skyscrapers. Other than that, it's tiny."

"Shut up and get inside."

"Lady of House Treowe doth commandeth."

"You can always sleep outside. It could be an adventure without food or water, heat or pillows. It could be a special adventure just for you if you don't quiet down."

The Treowe house was not as extravagantly large as Lennox originally surmised; however, it was elaborately lavish. It was pristine. Under normal circumstances, it would take a multitude of cleaners, maids, gardeners and full-time support staff to keep a house so tidy. That household needed only one Katelyn Treowe.

"You can either take your stuff upstairs to your room, or if you're really hungry, we can eat first. The food is ready; I just have to take it out of the fridge."

"I'm famished."

"Great. I'll get it ready."

The spread on the kitchen granite island was exactly what Lennox anticipated: an abundant tray of oysters, camembert cut into wedges, and the mackerel already fileted and garnished.

"So, Lennox, I have to come clean about something. I lied earlier when I said the kids were on a play date. The kids are with Brandon's mom. I wanted to have some time to talk and catch up, and she's always willing to watch them whenever we need a date night, or some time away from the yelling and the screaming. I don't know why I lied, it just somehow came out. I'm sorry."

"You don't have to come clean to me. It doesn't make a difference where the kids are. You could've told me they went to space camp and I still wouldn't have flinched."

"I know, I just thought you should know the truth."

"Okay."

"Go ahead and grab whatever you like. I looked for the Marshal Zhukov stout, but I couldn't find it in the fridge. Brandon must've hid it from me."

"That sounds sensible."

Eating gave rise to another elongated silence. Lennox sensed how Katelyn was formulating her thoughts, constantly second guessing the appropriate time to break the silence. Katelyn was a loud thinker. She didn't audibly make noises, but she emitted a sensation, a vibe of anxiety and unease. When her brain was working out problems or when her worry escalated, those around could sense she was actively thinking. Lennox wholeheartedly wanted to enjoy the fresh oysters, but he could feel the thick fog of anticipation rising from Katelyn's side of the kitchen.

"Aren't Miriam's parents divorced?"

"No, Katelyn. Miriam's mom died a few years ago, and her father left."

"Isn't that the same thing?"

"I don't think so, Katelyn. I think it's a different situation altogether."

"I know you say my name more often when you're being condescending."

"I'm not doing that. There is no need for us to sit here and pretend like there isn't something you want to say to me."

"Is it that obvious?"

"Nope, I'm just a superhero who can read minds."

"There are definitely better superpowers than reading minds."

"That's because you don't have the ability to read people's minds. If you did, you would see how it's the best superpower."

"I need to talk to someone. I don't have anyone here. I'm surrounded by Brandon's family. If there is anything we need, his family is here. When we're in trouble or having a spat, his family knows. He has someone to vent to, but I don't. Mom and Dad reiterate it was my decision to move here. Graham and I have never gotten along, let alone shared our troubles. I can barely ever get you on the phone, and when I do, you're somewhere else completely. My relationship with Alastor is already well-known by all."

"What about Camelia? I thought you two spoke often."

"We talk, but we don't have conversations about anything of substance. She tells me about Graham and his difficulties as though she's trying to mend a relationship between us that never existed."

"Well, I'm here now, so lay it on me."

"I have a therapist for that, Lennox, and that's not what I mean. I want someone to be here. I want my family to be here when I have some exciting news, or when I'm going through a rough patch, or when I just need the world to know I'm not insignificant. I have a husband and children, I'm happy, and I love them more than anything in this world, but I need to have a connection with the

Adlers. I'm so alone I can't breathe. We spent years with the same people, with consistently shared values and morals. I miss it more often than I don't. I can't express how wretched and secluded I feel when I can't go back there and resume everything, all the activities, all the beliefs, all the joys and sorrows, because Brandon doesn't get it. I don't expect him to get it, but I wish there was someone who could fully understand me. Everyone I know now, the people who I'm surrounded with, look at me with their heads tilted to one side when I share the stories of my upbringing. They pity me. I don't divulge to spit on or tarnish my upbringing. I want to share parts of me with people who understand me and can commiserate. I don't want pity, I want support."

Lennox was uneasy with crying, whether it was Katelyn tearing up, or his own surge of emotions which led to the same conclusion. He knew all too well he was looking at someone who was going to cry, someone who needed to cry. Katelyn's grief and feelings of loss could only be expressed by crying. She wasn't looking to unload, she was looking to share, and that required common ground. Lennox identified with the sentiments his sister was struggling to describe, although under the guise of a different issue altogether.

"What time is Brandon getting home?"

"An hour after I'll be done venting, and half an hour after I stop crying."

"Your timing is impeccable."

"It takes all possible effort to keep this face pretty and the passion alive."

"Gross."

"What do you think of the camembert? I found it at

this small cheese shop in downtown Seattle. It seems to travel just fine."

"It's great, it's all great, Katelyn. Thank you again for having me over."

"You didn't have much of a choice. If Mom hadn't convinced you to come, I would've just showed up at the airport and unwillingly whisked you away. It's nice to have you here, even though I can tell you're still making up your mind whether or not you should've come. I know you, Lennox. It's a good thing you came. Aunt Lena loved you and Alastor."

"Everyone keeps reminding me, yet I still fail to see how it's a bragging point. There must've been some dark stuff going on in that household for a mother to pledge her allegiance to me and Alastor more than to her own children."

"I think her kids needed to get away from her and the house they grew up in. They wanted to see the world outside the house windows and experience life for themselves."

"Do you mind if I head upstairs and take a little nap? I've been awake since yesterday, and I feel everything I say is just rambling nonsense."

"Sure, let me show you the way."

The upstairs bedroom door swung open to reveal a beautiful Victorian-styled abode. Lennox was not impressed with the polished décor, or the attention to every meticulous detail, as much as he was by the size of the room. His and Miriam's entire New York apartment, bathroom, kitchen, and living space could easily fit within the four walls of the upstairs Treowe guest bedroom.

The children's toys and playthings were organized

neatly onto shelves, fastidiously put away to give the allusion that the Treowe children were adult in their temperament and manners. The smell of pine and lemon pervaded throughout the house, a favorite scent of Lennox, and a deliberate attempt by Katelyn to make him feel at ease.

"Do you want me to wake you at any particular time, or are you going to set an alarm?"

"I thought I would let my natural circadian rhythms decide. Funeral be damned. You can't put a price on refreshing and rejuvenating rest. It's the currency of the rich and wise."

"And yet, Lennox, you're neither. Enjoy your nap."

Lennox abhorred sleeping anywhere other than his own bed. He had the disturbing habit of waking up in a disoriented panic in unfamiliar settings. He was worried he would wake up in a dizzying haze. He didn't want to add to Katelyn's responsibilities, having to worry about a panicking adult in the upstairs guest bedroom while also juggling the well-being of her own children. He convinced himself that the threat of an episode was not nearly as important as a fulfilled sleep. Lennox stared up at the white ceiling while feeling any prospect of sleep race away on the lines of the striped wallpaper.

"My questions arose because I don't want to become attached to something that may not be as real as I think it is. I think if we were to meet, I would have a better understanding of who you are. If one of us did decide they were no longer interested, I would rather find out sooner rather than later to avoid extended heartache."

Lennox awoke in a panic to the sound of a car door slamming. He quickly sat up in the full-sized bed, looked around, desperately attempted to acquaint himself with his surroundings, touched the wall, and reassured himself that the wall, not the dream, was real. He felt the room shrinking fast. He felt chaos seeping into his mind and squeezing out any last grasp he had on where he was, or who he was. He frantically recalled specific events, and listed names of people he knew aloud. He poked his face to associate the sensations to a physical reality. He searched for his thoughts on the stripes, hoping they were still there, racing, and hadn't exhausted and retired out of sight.

He was alone, he could sense it. There was no one there, no one left in the world. He kept his eyes wide open to take in as much light as possible. He took deeper breaths, exhaling slowly and imagined their elongated paths stretching before him. The room was steeped in a dull grayness that reached out to envelop him. He tried to remember colors as vividly as he could.

When all else failed, Lennox threw the covers to one side, got out of bed, and paced back and forth from one end of the room to the other. He reached into his pocket, hoping to find his red lighter, but he'd left it in Chicago.

"I'm Lennox. I'm married to Miriam. I live in Chicago. I'm visiting Portland for a funeral. My Aunt Lena is dead."

He repeated short statements to himself to formulate an acoustic cadence. Reciting the same sentences aloud usually lulled him, and put him into a semi-trance which sometimes ushered him back into a state of normalcy.

"I'm Lennox. I'm married to Miriam. I live in Chicago. I'm visiting Portland for a funeral. My Aunt Lena is dead."

He couldn't remain in the room any longer. He wildly forced on his shoes, swung open the door to the hallway, peered around, and allowed the new surroundings to shock his brain into curiosity rather than panic. He reexamined the details he observed upon entering. The hardwood floors smelled of pine and lemon, the toys were neatly arranged on the shelves, but he didn't hear anything. He cautiously made his way downstairs, hoping to find someone in the house, but even as he stumbled into the kitchen, he neither saw nor heard anyone. He glanced out the kitchen window overlooking the driveway and the black Buick crossover was gone.

"Well, at least she isn't seeing me like this."

Lennox was relieved Katelyn was not in the house to witness his bout of confusion. He dreaded the inevitability of others knowing about his episodes. He couldn't hide it from Miriam, but he made a great effort to keep it from everyone else.

Lennox scanned the kitchen and noted that Katelyn put away the spread from earlier, and she also sterilized every surface. The granite island glistened with the intermittent sunlight, and the floors squeaked loudly. He wasn't hungry, but chewing and digesting food was more favorable to forcibly watching the room spin. The cooled air of the refrigerator felt good, jarring and crisp on his face. He took out the camembert and mackerel that had already been placed in separate plastic containers, and was about to close the doors when he noticed a bottle of Marshal Zhukov imperial stout shoved in the back of the refrigerator. It wasn't out of place, and it didn't seem that any effort was made to hide the beer.

He rested on a bar stool, opened up the plastic containers, slowly ate a piece of cheese followed by a piece of fish, and stared at the stainless-steel refrigerator.

"Remember, we need to be quiet because Uncle Len is sleeping upstairs."

"No he's not. I hear he's running amok in his niece and nephew's rooms."

"Uncle Len, Uncle Len."

There were only two people in the entire world who Lennox allowed to shorten his name into the diminutive, Len. They were two tiny people, two beautiful human beings, and two innocent bystanders of a world gone awry.

"Oh, you know if you were anyone else, I would pop you one for calling me that. I'll give you both a forever pass to call me that. Your mother better not get any ideas though. I would make her pay dearly."

Charlotte and Andrew Treowe looked nothing like their parents. They were both shockingly blonde with eyes that were the envy of both Katelyn and Brandon. Charlotte had the deepest speckled hazel eyes that hid galaxies within them, and Andrew had crystal, light blue eyes that glistened with the color of the sky. Charlotte was six and Andrew was four.

"They kept bugging their grandmother that they wanted to see their uncle. They nearly drove her mad, so she called me and asked if it was okay for her to bring them over. I figured since you were asleep, I would quickly pick them up."

"You weren't even gone that long."

"She lives ten minutes from here."

"Yikes. Now I understand your quagmire."

"Yeah. Charlotte, Andrew say your hellos and goodbyes to your uncle because we have to go back to Grandma's soon. Remember the grown-ups have to go to a funeral tonight."

"Hey, Charlotte, you know what I found out? I found out it's now cool to call girls by boy's names. Your name, Charlotte, we can call you Charlie and that's supposed to be a good thing."

"Lennox, don't call her Charlie."

"Shouldn't she get to decide?"

"She's six, Lennox. On a good day, she can't even decide if she wants to make the effort of going to the toilet or soiling herself. You think she's ready to decide what to be called?"

"You never know until you give her a chance."

The deluge of incoherent and chaotic conversation that sputtered out of the Treowe children's mouths was enough to make Lennox forget all his nightmares. Charlotte and Andrew both spoke at once, crafting different stories, peculiar facts, all jammed into one loud narrative. At once, Lennox found out Brandon worked a lot, Charlotte likes to throw toys at Andrew, there was a spider upstairs, drugs were bad, and Katelyn cried yesterday. Lennox couldn't help but smile and remember holding both Charlotte and Andrew when they were just babies. He felt better.

"Okay, kids, time to say goodbye to your uncle."

"I could go with you to drop them off, if that's okay."

"Are you sure? It's literally a ten-minute drive, so I won't be gone very long. You're more than welcome to come along, I just don't want you to feel obligated."

"I don't get to see the kids often. I don't mind at all."

The non-stop chatter interspersed with bickering was soothing to Lennox. The drive was filled with aggrandized stories of banal and mundane things. Daily baths became something dangerous when the children were taught how easy it was to slip and fall. Rain caused mud, and their mother hated mess in the house. It was good to eat healthy because otherwise you die.

Lennox and Katelyn sat quietly in the car, allowing the children to unload their minds of all the things they deemed utterly paramount. They both listened and smiled.

10

"You said you no longer hold people to the ideals in your mind. Do you not have any sort of expectations? I have never viewed people or a person as perfect. I would rather set my expectations lower and then be thrilled when someone exceeds them than to have very high expectations and be disappointed all the time. This is not true in all cases. In some circumstances my expectations are nonnegotiable."

"Lennox, Lennox, wake up. Hey, it's okay. It's just a dream."

"Sorry. I didn't realize I fell asleep. How long was I out?"

"You dozed off for a few minutes, I swear I didn't think it was possible for someone to fall asleep and dream in such a short amount of time. What were you dreaming of?"

"I'm not sure if I was dreaming or not. I don't do well without sleep. This trip has thrown me for a loop."

"Do you need to talk about it?"

"Talk about what? I'm fine, Katelyn, I just need some sleep. I also need to get through this funeral without punching someone in the face, which let's be honest, is never out of the realm of possibilities. I'm already imagining my bed at home."

"You're fantasizing about your bed, Lennox. Don't you think your wife should factor into your fantasy?"

"Ah, sister mine, you don't know the love of a good mattress until you've had it. It asks nothing in return, it only seeks to grant you comfort. The perfect spouse. The perfect match."

"You need to get laid."

"Why Katelyn, I'm married. You know sex is forbidden in marriage."

"The phrase is, 'wait until marriage,' not 'give it up at marriage.'"

"I don't know what rulebook you're reading from, but mine clearly delineates the proper conduct for a married couple is abstinence."

"You're being offensive."

"I am not. We should all seek to live the life of an ascetic. Marriage is one thing, but the filth of sexual intercourse during marriage is dishonorable and incompatible with issues of the soul. To remain disconnected from earthly things and connected with the heavenly realms, how many ever there are, one must never pervert their temporal vessel with sexual relations."

"And children? How do they figure into your rulebook?"

"Immaculate conception."

"You're being really offensive. You should sleep before tonight. I don't want you to let loose among a congregation of conservatives when you're already saying things just to incite a reaction."

"I don't think I do it for a reaction. Is it possible somewhere deep down I actually believe what I'm mindlessly saying? What if I'm formulating a new belief system? What if I'm on the precipice of discovering the true meaning, the one true belief?"

"You're sure you don't want to talk about it?"

"Talk about what? I thought we were talking about it."

"Never mind."

"Do you believe in hauntings?"

"Is that a serious question?"

"I ask because of my involvement with what I'm starting to believe is a haunted place. I don't mean the childish notion of haunted houses, or white ghosts, or creepy Halloween ghouls, or TV shows that shake the camera to make you believe something otherworldly exists. I mean places that are marred, that are scarred somehow. Places whose fabric, and constitution of reality, were shredded or nicked by something sharp and extraordinary. Areas where something transpired, something tragic or dramatic, hints of the unseen that are seared within the collective consciousness. Do you ever walk somewhere and immediately have a reaction to it? You've never been there before, but it seems like you have because something happened. Not to you, but to someone; someone that's somehow reaching out to you, trying to let you know. It's almost as if they don't want to disappear; they want to remain physical, projected into the minds of their former species."

"Are you talking about Portland? Is this place haunted for you?"

"No, I'm talking about my work. Everyday something odd happens. A brand-new cooler breaks down, or there is random flooding from the ceiling, or lights erratically burn out, or the basement. The basement has red mold. Red mold!"

"You do realize, Lennox, all these things are explained as malfunctions, planned obsolescence, or simply poor maintenance, right?"

"Those are just byproducts. I wonder if the building was erected on an old burial ground. There are rumors it used to be a hospital."

"The Lennox I grew up with didn't believe in that nonsense."

"Perhaps I don't really believe the place is haunted, but I am certain some places are marked."

"Like Portland?"

Lennox sat silently as they pulled into the driveway of the Treowe's Bush Prairie residence. The house didn't seem as magnificent or immaculate as Lennox had first supposed. It was a good-sized house, but somehow it was smaller than before, less impressive.

"Do you want to go inside and maybe have a drink, or we can continue to sit quietly in a parked car, staring at a house you've already been inside of. No pressure; choice is yours."

The house was empty. There was no sound of excitable children and even the alluring scent of pine and lemon had faded. Visible spots on the hardwood floor and walls needed retouching. The wind picked up intensity outside, and the whistling of the burglarizing gusts echoed throughout the living room. The floors creaked as Katelyn made her way into the kitchen.

"Can I get you something to drink? Maybe a coffee or sparkling water? We just bought an espresso machine I've been meaning to use, but I never have the opportunity or interested company to use it on."

"I'd love an espresso, thank you."

Lennox dropped down onto the white suede sofa. It had recently been washed; the carpet cleaner smell was blatant. Travel magazines were distributed on the glass coffee table. White lace curtains were drawn in the windows of the living room. They gently billowed with errant gusts of wind that made their way through the spaces near the windows. It was drafty, almost cold, and the facade of the fireplace gave the impression it had been painstakingly cleaned but rarely used.

"Damned thing. I can't get the machine to work. Would you like a beer instead?"

"Beer sounds good."

Lennox hadn't taken off his shoes. Katelyn would not outright ask him to take them off, but she would silently lecture him in her mind. He wanted to spare her the internal dialogue, and himself the annoyance of knowing it bothered her, so he took off his shoes and placed them by the door. There was no designated area for shoes, no shelf or closet, but Lennox knew she discouraged wearing them in the house.

"Here you are. I hope this is okay. I swear, I'll ask Brandon about the Marshal Zhukov when he gets home. Lennox, you didn't have to take your shoes off."

"I didn't want to dirty the rug."

"That's okay. I'll put them in the hallway closet so they're not in the way."

The beer wasn't cold, which didn't surprise Lennox because Katelyn was not a drinker. Growing up, the Adlers never had alcohol in the house. It wasn't an automatic thought for Katelyn to supply her guests with alcohol because she herself wasn't completely sold on the moral viability of drinking. Graham absolutely prohibited alcohol in his household, Lennox had an entire cupboard devoted to the best liquors he could procure, and Alastor drank whatever Lennox endorsed him to buy. Brandon loved whiskey and beer, but would limit his drinking out of respect for Katelyn.

It didn't take long for Lennox to down half the beer; the occasion warranted a speedy consumption. Katelyn took tiny sips from the room temperature bottle, always fearful of getting drunk. She would stop once she felt the slightest buzz. Anything more would trigger the moral alarm in her head.

"Brandon will be leaving early from work today. He'll be here in a few hours. He wants to get home and mentally prepare for being surrounded by so many Romanians. I put some beers in the fridge since I know he likes them cold."

"I know how he feels."

"The last time you were in Portland, things didn't end well."

"Not an appropriate time, Katelyn. Not even an appropriate subject to discuss."

"But it's obvious you need to talk about it, Lennox. It's freaking you out and you started screaming in your sleep."

"What?"

"In the car, you were saying something in the car when you fell asleep."

"I don't talk in my sleep."

"Well, you did this time."

"I don't think it's something I want to discuss with you,

Katelyn."

"Who are you going to discuss it with? Does Miriam know? Did you tell her?"

"Of course I did. She knows. Even if we don't talk about it, she knows. She understands and she doesn't ask me to talk about it."

"I think we should talk about it."

"Of course you do. You've always insisted we chat and gab about my shit. You constantly poked and prodded. Isn't your mess enough? Don't you have enough to worry about?"

"You can get pissed all you want, but you came to me back then. I didn't pry, but you approached me when were you looking for someone to talk to. We may not be exactly as we were, but I know what you suffered through. I recall every word, and things like that don't go away. It may never go away, but you at least need to talk about it. Trust me, I know. If you let it linger, if you let it fester inside, eventually it will destroy you. Lennox, you need to talk about it."

"Having a heartfelt chat about it won't make it go away. Sitting in a sharing circle won't vaporize it all. It won't make this place less haunted. It won't dissipate the hatred, or the regret, or the confusion, or the straggling strings."

"Lennox, you knew her for a very long time. It only makes sense..."

"No, I never knew her. I may have known *of* her for a very long time, but I never authentically knew her."

"You're just angry. You two were connected since you were eighteen. I remember, you told me. You saw her across the sanctuary, I think you said she was wearing green, and her curly hair, you also mentioned that. She was wearing white heels with black scuff marks on the sides of them. You knew that because you only looked down when you finally did go talk to her."

"That wasn't her, Katelyn."

"Stop with your nonsense; that was her. It was also her that you texted and wrote letters to, what was it, for six years? When you broke up with Miriam you met her again. You're telling me that wasn't her, that wasn't the same person?"

"No. That individual was nothing like the girl I met when I was eighteen. I didn't know her to begin with. We only physically saw each other a few times over the span of a decade. Hoping someone accurately represented themselves through letters and words, expecting that the tone and inflection were pure and honest, that's not adequate. Getting to know a person is having the mutual trust to willingly open up and allow the physical and real them to be exposed. You know what it feels like to love a shadow? I fancied I loved someone, but it turns out I loved their reflection. It was a picture I projected. She wasn't real. Not one ounce of her was real, at least not until I met her again for the last time. Then she was real.

"She was it; she was the one I was prophesied to end up with. She was Romanian; she was the same as us.

"When she watched me, it was something otherworldly. I burned down altars for her, I set the universe spinning on a different axis, I unleashed chaos among the stars and planets, and I created an unsullied world. It was a place of pristine splendor. It was a sphere of perfect order, but of her designated perfect order, where holding hands was virginal and eyes had to be plucked to preserve integrity. It was the world of Samson and Delilah. Samson changed the entire realm for Delilah. He loved her completely."

"It's a little juvenile and cliché to be blaming all of misfortune on a Delilah."

"Blood runs deep, Katelyn. Blood doesn't change. When mixed, they attack each other. You need the same blood, an identical configuration, a matching lineage, a parallel place of origin."

"What are you saying, Lennox?"

"She was divined to be that. She should've been the answer to everything. She was quintessential to keep the hope of a promised land alive. She was ideal to keep it all pure, to keep it authentic, to keep it consecrated and holy."

"Holy? We're talking about a person; we aren't talking about some idealistic mechanism or transcendent word. She is a real human being, not a heavenly host."

"Ezra."

"What?"

"When the Jewish people came back from exile in Babylon, Ezra, the holy man, the enlightened man, the godly man, the connection between this world and the others, came to the holy congregation and berated them for having married wives from Babylon. I actually think he tore his hair out, or maybe he tore his clothes off. Prophets back then were always so eager to rip off their clothes. It must've been because it reminded them of physical things, of earthly things, of the things that kept them disconnected from a closer relationship with god. It reminded them if they approached too close to the altar, to the holiest of holies, they would be burned alive. Their clothes would catch fire and set their skin ablaze. So, they ripped everything off, at least that's my take on it."

"What the hell does Ezra have anything to do with what we're talking about, Lennox?"

"Ezra suppliantly came before the holy congregation after he found some book which denounced them as bad people. How he made the correlation between being bad people and having married foreign wives I will never understand, but he convinced the majority of them to divorce their wives. Divorce! Can you imagine? Here we are condemning divorce while Ezra gave it as an ultimatum to the Jewish people. There were those, of course, who inevitably loved their wives, even if they were foreign and labeled miscreants by the holiest of men. Those must have been some families, huh? Leaving your people, leaving your loved ones, leaving the promised land, giving up on heavenly assurances, giving up your blood for love. Yet, those Jews were stricken; they were never to be mentioned again. They went back to Babylon, back to a foreign land, with their foreign children and foreign wives, never to be heard from again. They had no home. They chose love and gave up their blood and native land. It was their promised home, too."

"Lennox, do you need to rest? Do you need to lay down?"

"Time and again, I think about Ezra. I muse about those men who divorced their foreign wives and remained with the chosen people. They rebuilt their domiciles, a city that had waited for them for so long. It was a land which received them only because it was pledged. Those men were all alone, sword in one hand to defend against the onslaught of enemies and piling bricks with the other. It would always be that, their own. They shunned their wives and kids back to Babylon to fend for themselves. Everything they erected, they rebuilt for something which wasn't human. It's as though they proliferated it for a god, but I ask, what the hell did god have to do with a human city? He didn't give a shit about their vowed dwelling, or wayfaring, or standing up to the infidels, demolishing the enemy, liberating the world from evil, as much as he questioned why the fuck they'd sent their wives and children packing back to Babylon. Alone, nonetheless!"

"Lennox, please, you're getting too worked up. You're using God and swear words in the same context. Anyway, they didn't all divorce their wives."

"Of course not. The wives deemed acceptable by blood standards were graciously permitted to remain married."

"I still don't understand what you're trying to say."

"They turned their back on their families, their loved ones, the people they promised to take care of, all for pure blood. The holy congregation was of infinite value, more so than love. It wasn't the sentiments which kept a family together, it wasn't the vows they took, or dowry they gave or received, it was their own blood that was worth more to them than anything on this Earth. She was Ezra."

"Ezra was a man."

"In the story, yes, Ezra was a man, but in real life she was Ezra. She found a book and deemed me unholy and unworthy."

"Do you mean the Bible?"

"No, she found an old journal she had written in until she turned fifteen or something. In that tome of childlike ramblings were written all the qualities she required of a husband. I don't mean suggestions; I mean uncompromising requirements. The exact physical description, his precise occupation, and specific signs."

"Signs?"

"Yeah. For example, her determined spouse would have to, without being prompted, readjust her purse back onto her shoulder after it accidentally slid off."

"That's a joke, right?"

"No, and the irony of it all was it did happen. We were hiking Multnomah Falls, and it happened just like she scribbled in her journal."

"Are you making this up, or are you being serious?"

"I'm being completely serious. I bought into it. I accepted she was the one, the predetermined one, the destined one, the conflated one. So, I went along with it. She was adamant, so unflinching about what was written in her book that I couldn't help but be sucked into the maelstrom."

"She broke your heart, I get it."

"No, it wasn't my heart she broke. She fractured my world. She swayed me to burn my world to the ground, a scorch-earth policy to ensure suffering for any potential future other. She became the architect of the worldview I adopted."

"That's placing too much control in one person's hands, and I've never known you to be the type of person who allowed that."

"Exactly, I wasn't the type of person. But, love is stupid."

"It's not stupid. I love Brandon completely, and I don't think it's stupid. It's just love."

Silence slowly set into the living room. Lennox had long since finished his beer, placing it on a coaster atop the coffee table while Katelyn held onto her still full beer. She had begun peeling the sticker off the bottle at the corners, but left it attached so as not to make a mess.

"Would you like another beer, Lennox?"

"I'd love one, thanks."

It was calming for Lennox to be alone, even if only for a fleeting instant. He exhaled heavily, trying to expel the nagging uneasiness and elevated emotions that choked his lungs. The once pestering and robust drafts from outside withered into too insubstantial a gust to properly circulate the air within the tiny and cramped room. He felt like he barely had enough room to stretch out his feet.

"I'm sorry, Lennox, but I still don't understand what exactly happened."

"Is that a bottle of Marshal Zhukov?"

"Yes. I found it in the refrigerator. Brandon must've figured I wouldn't find it in there. Do you not want it? I can get you another kind."

"This will be great. Do you want some?"

"No thank you."

"Not even a little taste?"

"No, I'm good with what I have. I don't like beer."

It had been three years since Lennox tasted the Cigar City imperial stout. It was his absolute favorite beer when he worked at a small cheese shop in Astoria. After moving to Chicago, he was never able to find it stocked in any bodega, liquor superstore, or supermarket. Memories of blistering summer days in a cramped apartment, garbage flooding the sidewalks, deafening screeches of the N line at the Ditmars Boulevard stop, backed up sewage, Artichoke Pizza, power outages counteracted with candles, screaming Greek landladies, OK Café, New Orleans Cold Brew, Magic Eight Balls, beautiful Belizean baristas,

Astoria Park, and boundless ramen all rushed back to him with the first mouthful. It was perfect. Impeccable for recollecting, for making his experience in New York rosy and idyllic, and for adding cover-up to an experience which, for the most part, thwarted him. New York seemed so much more beautiful with Marshal Zhukov.

Katelyn discerned the change in Lennox's demeanor and general disposition after giving him the second beer. She watched as he absorbedly stared out the window at a changed scenery: rain with a healthy sprinkling of rain. Lennox's expression remained unchanged but his collective awareness wandered. He didn't have an unfriendly look on his face, more of a vacant guise, as though he didn't have a deliberate destination. Katelyn absorbed Lennox's suffering. She had only ever seen Lennox cry once in his adult life, and that was the year he and Miriam broke up. He confided all his misgivings, mistakes, aspirations for life just as they had done in their childhood. She was made aware of the Portland incident a few weeks after it happened. She wasn't surprised when he told her everything. It seemed inevitable to Katelyn.

"Lennox, do you remember the last time you were at our condo in Chicago? You said something that has been plaguing my memory. It hasn't left me since."

"I've said a great many things in the span of my lifetime."

"You said, 'she found my sin and created a devil of me.' Do you remember saying that?"

"I don't remember uttering those exact words, but it sounds like something I would say."

"What did you mean?"

Lennox felt the bricks tumbling down. He held on for

as long as he could to what he considered his dignity: the manufactured devil within. Beyond the stories, the twists and turns, and the contrived phrases and derivations, Katelyn expected Lennox to arrive where he needed to be, to the final altar in the high places, hidden away from prying eyes and caring ears.

"She picked me up from the airport, and the first hug, the first time I hugged her in eight years, it was long and amazing. It was the longest hug I shared with anyone. If you can fit eight years of absence into one action, one gesture, that hug would've been its poster child. She smelled amazing. From the time I wrote her the first email, she was finally palpable to me, she was tangible, she was there, hugging me back. I wanted to stay there. I didn't want to separate because shit always happen when you let go, critters have space to come between, bodies and hearts grow colder. Hephaestus' net didn't seem constraining in that moment. I had a glimpse of love. Emotions were definitely heightened, I mean, we hadn't seen each other in eight years.

"All those damned cousins kept prying, but I didn't want to tell them a goddamn thing. They were like Alberich obsessed with stealing the Rhinegold; they transformed into tiny, wrinkly, greedy, stingy and foul looking beings. I hated them for asking, for trying to ruin it.

"I couldn't be away from her. I skipped so much school to see her. I lied and said it was all okay, but it wasn't. I was so behind in my coursework. I eventually caught up, but only after she disappeared. I was a grad student; I literally had no money, but I nonetheless spent money I didn't have to see her. I flew out three times in a few months. The last flight, the last attempt, the last time I ever made an effort for her, I had a layover in Vegas. I hate Vegas. There is so much sand. I was finding sand on my clothes for weeks. I had two hours to decide whether or not to make the final, sweeping gesture. I sat in the airport, looking out at the tarmac, my phone opened to the last text she sent. I yearned to go to her even though she told me goodbye, even though she meant goodbye, and even though I was certain she wanted goodbye. I was in the airport for two hours. I weighed the nasty things I said to her against the vitriol that radiated from her, and all the while I referenced my phone. I turned back around, finished grad school, and came home. I never spoke to her again."

"Vitriol, Lennox? That's kind of harsh, don't you think?"

"I'm sure I've exaggerated her offences. I've made her parents out to be crueler than they actually were, and I'm sure I've made her out to be more callous than she was. I turned against my own people, against my own blood to forget her, to erase the castles she built in the sky.

"She was Ezra, proclaiming to the people that Babylon had invaded my heart, and the defilement of a doomed civilization cloaked my being. I became a wolf, a hooded scoundrel in the night. She, as Ezra, used the very god she worshipped to denounce me as blasphemer and pagan. She condemned me back to Babylon, back to the foreign city, back to a place that wasn't home, a land that wasn't promised, unsanctified, and outside the walls she built. She facilitated my separation from home, from the people I recognized, from the god I thought I knew."

"From the God you knew? Lennox, there is only..."

"She presented me with morality, her god, a god that fit neatly and easily into her pocket. It was a pocket-sized god whose strength and insight were only as big as the pouch it occupied. Hers happened to be small and dainty, so morality and ethics were compactly squeezed.

"I worked it out later. I stepped back and it all fit together. She was a representative of what my people, our people, had become. Our people never left Romania. They remained there with their hearts and minds, weighed down by memories of repression and a government that force-fed fear as an everyday ration. Eventually, they shrank. They shrank from view, shrank with gravity, they avoided the sun and inhabited the darkened crevices of the Earth. They needed a god that could accompany them to the depths of the Earth, to the depths of despair. That god became justification for them, for their actions, for their hatred, for their judgments, for the darkening of their hearts instead of something bigger, something that elevated them. They chose the earth, they chose to turn their gazes downward, they chose to keep their god small.

"There she was, an Ezra among her people, proclaiming separation from the others. Ezra decreed purity, but not blood purity. This Ezra proclaimed ethereal purity, an indefinable, a *je ne sais quoi* attribute that was left up to each spiritually-driven individual to employ. Morality morphed into personal preference, forgiveness became a withheld currency for the spiritually rich, justice was distorted, love developed into the enemy of a logic, plain-evidence faith."

"She was only one person, Lennox. She didn't speak for everyone. She didn't speak for God. I've seen it happen before to Romanian kids we grew up with. They think God is there to listen to every demand. They consider God their butler or servant, there to serve a slew of personal desires on a gold-plated tray. They anticipate their prayers to be answered in the strict way they ask. When it doesn't happen, they lash out and make sinners and villains of everyone around them. That's why I left the community. I couldn't stand how they looked at the world, at people, at human beings. The world, to them, needed to be pitied, and no one, no matter the amount of good within, could ever be as holy because no one else was as chosen. Their blood wasn't the same as ours."

Brandon walked through the front door, drenched by the rain, and taken aback to see Katelyn and Lennox sitting together on the sofa.

"Hey guys, how's everything? I hope I didn't interrupt anything."

"No, Lennox and I were just talking, and wow, I didn't realize what time it is. I put some beers in the fridge for you, in case you wanted one right away. We can order dinner tonight since we don't have any food in the house."

"Give me a chance to get into the house and catch my breath. It's really coming down out there. There's not a dry spot on me. Wait, what do you mean order dinner tonight? I thought we were going to your aunt's funeral."

"We should stay at home. I don't want you to feel obligated to go. You didn't know her and I didn't spend much time with her while she was alive. No need to expose ourselves to a trove of people that don't know us anyway."

"This is sudden, but what about Lennox?"

"Lennox could make his own decision about going."

"I meant about the car. We were going to be his ride

tonight."

"Lennox, do you feel comfortable driving my car? It's only about half an hour away, maybe forty-five minutes."

"As long as I have the address. Are you sure you're okay with me taking your car? What if you guys need it?"

"We have the sedan in the garage in case of emergency."

"Don't get me wrong, Katelyn, I don't mind not going. I've been dreading having the conversations about who I am and how I'm related to your aunt, but you said you were looking forward to seeing all of them again."

"No. I've realized my people are here, in this house, you and the kids. Speaking of which, they're at your Mom's for the night."

"Your people? What is that supposed to mean?"

"Nothing, Brandon, just something Lennox and I were chatting about. It's not a big deal. It will be nice for us to have the rest of the night together."

Katelyn and Lennox's conversation lingered as an intensity in the air. The momentum of the emotions rang like a buzzing noise throughout the living room, and was noticeable to everyone. Brandon continued to stand in the entryway, unsure of what transpired, or of the reasoning behind the change of plans. His enormous relief eclipsed the need for resolve.

Katelyn and Brandon both made their way into the kitchen, leaving Lennox alone on the sofa with two empty beer bottles assigned to their respective coasters. Lennox leaned his head back for just a minute and stared at the lights from the ceiling fan. They were energy-saver bulbs, coiled and extremely white. He looked directly into the lights until the rest of the room was bleached with the same brightness.

"*What do you mean when you say people have become demystified? You also said you are not piecing me together anymore. What do you mean? What are you doing then?*"

"Hey man, I wanted to make sure you're okay. You started convulsing there for a little bit."

"Sorry. I haven't had much sleep. I really don't do well without sleep. Honestly, I just close my eyes for a second and I knock out. Where's Katelyn?"

"She saw you dozed off, so she went to grab a few things from the store. Do you know if something is wrong with her? Did you two have an argument because she seemed kind of pissed?"

"We were talking about our childhood, which is always hit or miss with her. I don't know if you noticed."

"Yeah, I've heard enough stories to expect her to get stressed about seeing Romanians. I was surprised she wanted to go to the funeral. She told me your aunt was close to you and Alastor, but beyond that I have no idea why she insisted we go. She gets very worked up about being around those people."

"She seems to be calmer and more at home with you and the kids though."

"No problems there. I see you found the Marshal Zhukov. What did you think?"

"It's my favorite beer. It brings back a lot of good memories."

"Katelyn mentioned that. I'm glad I still had a bottle for you to try."

"What do you mean?"

"I bought ten of them last year. After having about three of them, I kind of got sick of it. Don't get me wrong, it's a fantastic beer, but ten was definitely too ambitious. I'm surprised I even had a bottle left. I'm not sure if I drank the rest or gave them to friends, but luckily Katelyn remembered I had one left and insisted she put it in the fridge for you."

11

The church parking lot was empty when Lennox pulled up in the black Buick. Lennox parked closest to the exit, well-knowing and fully expecting a packed house. He turned off the engine and grabbed the steering wheel with both hands. He dreaded that place. It was a disquietude directly associated with the people he knew were going to be inside.

When he was there last, she was standing before him: green dress, hair curled, peach heels, purse in hand. They'd stood at the entrance to the church and Lennox could feel her parents' eyes denouncing the union from the comfort of their car.

She was beyond beautiful. It was the first time she flirted with him. She innocuously inched closer, the click of her heels as she etched nearer sent his heart racing, getting close enough for him to see her dilated pupils. Everything was subtle. She gently stirred, moving in infinitesimal increments, stopping just as her hand grazed his. He didn't know what to do. He wanted her parents to like him, he sought to maintain a sense of decorum for onlookers, he intended to be decent, but she kept edging closer to him, and he needed to hold her, to be ensnared within Hephaestus' greatest work with her. Her smile was inscribed into his memory. She tilted her head to the left, the field of Elysian curls dangling behind her, and her cheeks hid her eyes as she radiated her smile at him. He was smitten. He couldn't recall everything she said to him. The only vestige of unearthed conversation was the debate on whether or not sarcasm should be considered a form of lying; she loved to be sarcastic. Lennox decided to extend his visit to Portland; it was her birthday.

Three days later, one of her aunts phoned her and cautioned that god declared the man she was seeing as a wolf in sheep's clothing. Rumors started to swirl, and gradually Lennox's character was called into question.

It was in the same parking lot that Lennox sat frozen. He clutched the steering wheel and gawked at the well-illuminated building. It took a Herculean-effort to brighten up that edifice.

Other cars began to trickle into the parking spaces around Lennox, with the same idea of a quick and unspoiled exit. It was as good a time as any to get out of the car and make his way into the assemblage. It was the Adler curse: always early to a function.

Lennox closed the car door behind him, locked it, snorted a breath, and quickly stepped closer to the flickering flame. He avoided the main path to the front doors, and instead went the long way around.

"Bine ați venit."

"Sorry, I don't speak Romanian. Is it okay if I just go up to the balcony?"

The greeters at the door were fairly easy to manipulate. Lennox was familiar with how uncomfortable most of them were with strangers, especially foreigners who didn't speak their language. They both nodded their head in acquiescence while Lennox took a pamphlet, and then scurried towards the balcony stairs. He didn't feel decent about starting his homecoming with a lie. Lennox spoke fluent Romanian, his parents saw to that, and had an affinity for the language. He found an unoccupied aisle seat in the last row of the balcony; his disheveled beard would scare off anyone wanting to engage.

The choir loft behind the pulpit was empty, but the flower arrangements and wreaths hid the desert of red, empty congregation seats. One by one, the color black replaced the color red, and Lennox watched as a slow, belabored sea of mourners flooded the empty sanctuary. The sound of voices reverberated off the hallowed walls, head-coverings and handkerchiefs obscured identities, the pings of a tuning guitar and a piano buzzed in the background, commotion began to overtake solemnity, and wailing onlookers made their rounds to the coffin.

The lower section of the sanctuary filled quickly with mourners, but no one besides Lennox and the sound crew sat in the balcony. Lennox looked around, but didn't recognize anyone. Their features were skewed. Kindness and understanding faded from the etched wrinkles on their faces and new, unfamiliar contours were carved. The pastor made his way among the family seated in the front rows. He was a man who clutched the Bible with his left hand and had it perpetually pressed to his left pectoral. He had aged since the last time. His eyes sagged and he was slightly hunched. Lennox's heart tightened; he remembered the man's shadow. That man had a crooked smile. Lennox knew nothing of what was within that man, but he knew what poured out from inside him.

Lennox reiterated to himself he was there for Aunt Lena's memory. The lights in the sanctuary were abruptly turned to maximum brilliance. Lennox's pupils contracted. He couldn't distinctly see Aunt Lena, but that was his goal. He sought to keep her animated like the last time. That is what Aunt Lena wanted.

The music-making clumsily commenced and the faces molded with an affected expression of sorrow. A young gentleman from the sound crew nervously walked over to Lennox and offered him a headset. "If you like, you can use this for the service. We have someone who will translate from Romanian to English." Lennox took the headset and thanked the young man in Romanian.

Communal prayers were uttered aloud. The congregation was beckoned to stand, bow their heads, close their eyes, reveal their innermost worries aloud to the heavens, and to the prying ears of their neighbors.

"You know god doesn't like when you sit so far away from the pulpit. It takes longer for grace to reach you, and that requires too much effort, you sinner"

"Alastor, what the hell are you doing here?"

"You must mean what the heaven am I doing here. Let's not show our hand to the masses so soon. We have a whole service to get through. No use expending all our profanities in the first few minutes."

"I should've known you would wait until the service started to slither your way in."

"I left the apple in the car."

"It's a shame, I'm famished."

"You were always so easily tempted."

"Luckily I don't like lentil stew."

"Your birthright is assured."

"Seriously Alastor, you said you weren't coming. When did you get in? Where are you staying?"

"Not at Katelyn's house, that's for sure. Yeah, Mom told me."

"So, Mom knew you were coming?"

"Not for sure. She had an inkling; you're familiar with that mother instinct she brags about. I'm surprised she didn't share her suspicions with sister dearest. Is that where you're staying?"

"A dutiful brother indeed."

"Is it as terrible as we've always imagined?"

"No, it's colder."

"Where can I get one of those neat Walkmans? I don't speak Romanian either. What does a man have to do to get some service around here?"

"Ask god."

"Nah, we're too far from the pulpit. Do you think people mind that we aren't making an effort to whisper? Could you imagine seeing us? Two hoodlums shucking and jiving in the rafters of a sanctified building. It would bring such dishonor to our family. Weren't Katelyn and Brandon supposed to be here with you?"

"What *didn't* Mom tell you? And yes, they were supposed to, but Katelyn changed her mind at the last minute. Can you blame her?"

"Yes, yes I can. I've earned the right."

"Communal prayers are a lot louder than I remember."

"They must've accrued more sins to atone for since you were last ostracized, or maybe they're all getting old and can't hear anymore."

"Or the person standing next to them. Do they really have so much to say to god? My legs are getting tired, and I've barely slept in two days."

"You shall rise only after the third day."

"Then why am I standing now? Screw this, I'm sitting down."

"Get up, you lazy bum. Be a part of the community. Besides, you would draw too much attention to us. You couldn't have trimmed up that beard, huh? That would've saved you from a few disapproving snarls, and me the effort of pretending I'm not with a homeless man. You know they'll just want to pity you with that beard, and then we'll have to show them we don't deserve pity. We'll be tarred and feathered."

"Just think, Alastor, this could've been all ours for the low, low price of submission, self-flagellation, donation of a firstborn, blood-letting, more self-flagellation, a lot of bowing, sacrifice of two knees, denial of self, denial of others, denial of reality."

"I do, Lennox. I miss it sometimes."

"Yeah, me too."

"How's Aunt Lena looking?"

"She's seen better days."

"How can you tell? You can't see anything from here. Could you have picked a further view from the casket? It's like we're seeing things from god's point of view."

"How did you even know I would be here?"

"Please, the balcony was a given. Only the hoodlum, riff raff and English speakers sit in the balcony. I bet you even pretended you didn't speak Romanian. I hope you freaked out the greeters. Then I thought, 'Lennox wouldn't want to see Aunt Lena dead' so I figured you would choose the absolute last row of the balcony."

"I didn't freak out the greeters. They weren't phased at all, almost like they expected it. I think the young ones are imitating our methods."

"I hope they're at least giving us credit."

"Finally, we get to sit. I hope that was the last prayer because I'm not getting up again."

"Seriously, I want a headset."

"Have mine, I'm not using it."

"No, that's not the point. If they don't give me one it means they think I look Romanian, and I run the risk of being unmasked and my plan foiled. I can't risk it. I need a headset. We both need a headset so no one will bother us."

Alastor bent over in his seat and stared down the audio and visual crew. He imagined he was speaking to them, communicating through the vibrations of his angst, until, at last, a young girl turned around and saw Alastor gesturing to his ears. She was accustomed to the particular gesture. She immediately picked up an extra headset and practically ran it over to him. Alastor thanked her in German.

"Was that really necessary?"

"Which part? The urgent pointing to my ears, the communicating via telepathy, the awkward yet sincere smile, the fake tremor in my hand, the face twitching, the stuttering, or was it the German? I bet it was the German. That just threw it way over the top. I should ask her to come back so I can apologize and maybe ask if we can try it all over again. I think I can do better."

"You know, Alastor, god's watching."

"Yeah, but you know what? No one else is. No one is

going to bother the crazies anymore. We have half of the balcony all to ourselves."

The two brothers inserted the buds of the headset into their ears without turning on the device. Every few minutes, they would simultaneously nod as to suggest they were listening and participating.

The service lingered on with more songs in minor keys, exasperated preachers denouncing earthly woe and exalting heavenly freedom, interjections of crying and sobbing, out of tune solos, mechanically performed poems with simple rhyme patterns and predictable meter, and, most notably, an impenetrable mist of longing.

While the stage uncluttered and the senior pastor presented his thoughts on the insignificance of mourning and the exaltation of biting the dust, both Alastor and Lennox had exhausted their fixed reserve of patience.

"You know, I met god on a Tuesday. I could just have easily met him at a picnic in the park or fishing first thing in the morning, but I happened to meet him at church surrounded by an older generation of Romanian immigrants. I say *him* because I didn't ask whether or not the pronoun matched the corresponding anatomical fixture, or what he identified as, or what his gender preference was, or whether or not he even bought into the social construct of gender. He didn't say much. Come to think of it, I was the one picking up the slack most of the time and making sure there's never a lull in our conversations, if they can even be called that. We didn't meet under an enormous spotlight or on the sandy shore of some crystalline beach. We met somewhere in between a throng of asylum seekers and a horde of religiously persecuted zealots. I say "we," but most of the time I feel like it's "me" and "god"—consistently separated by a conjunction. "We" implies some form of cooperation or aggregation, but honestly, it's a lot of me way over here and him, it, whatever, way over there. To this day, I'm still not sure if we were supposed to meet on that Tuesday or whether he had a standing appointment with someone else. There are a lot of good people. By "good" I mean holy, sanctified, cleansed, spiritual, chosen. I'll let you pick the adjectives best suited to your appetite. It just worked out that, tangentially or intentionally, god and I happened to have a pow wow on a Tuesday. I'm sure it was a Tuesday because it was trash day. Every Tuesday at 4:30 in the morning, the garbage truck drove through the alley, banging and slamming every trash can as loud as possible. I hate trash day.

"Anyway, I asked god for a few things, here and there, to get me through the day. Nothing too big, definitely nothing expensive. For a while, it was really good between me and god. I didn't necessarily get anything I asked for, but I figured that's why I had earthly parents. What did I need another parent for anyway? Two were enough. So, one night I'm sleeping, right, and I have this wicked dream. I mean vivid, lucid, real, as though it was my reality. In the dream, I'm the captain of a submarine, at least that's what was conveyed to me. It didn't look like a submarine at all. It looked like a plain ol' room with steps everywhere. There was this officer, a first officer or someone of reputable rank, who decided to abandon my submarine. It wasn't mutiny or anything, but the bugger clearly wanted off the sub. So, I moved on to the next part of the dream. What's the use of waiting around for someone who wants to leave anyway, am I right? In the next part of the dream, there are these beautiful ladies trying to force feed me pills, small white pills. I decline and move along until this huge hand, not an arm, I mean just a palm and fingers, shoves an enormous, over-sized white pill down my throat. I nearly choke, but somehow manage to keep it down long enough to see the other officers on the sub taking the same gigantic white pill. I stand and watch as their faces melt. The pill disfigured them badly, every single one of them, except me. I was fine. Then, they looked at me like I had a secret because the pill didn't mangle or mar me like it did them. That same hand, the floating palm and fingers, opens this steel door to a hallway and tells me to walk through. What was I supposed to do when there were a bunch of face-melted officers chasing me? As soon as I stepped into the entry, the door slams shut. I look down the hallway, and I realize I'm all alone. It's a cramped corridor, fit for one, and no one was there to keep me company as I stared down the never-ending hallway."

"Was the first captain supposed to be your Green Lantern?"

"What?"

"The one who wanted off the sub, was that supposed to represent her?"

"The Green Lantern is a dude."

"Not exclusively. Uh, hello, Jade, also known as Jennifer-Lynn Hayden. She was a Green Lantern."

"Why do you know that?"

"Our last conversation piqued my interest."

"Were you just waiting for the right moment to shift the conversation in that direction by interjecting with your newly acquired knowledge of Green Lanterns?"

"I can't tell for certain. It could've been done subconsciously. I don't control it. Ironically though, I have discovered an interesting little parallel in my acquisition of DC knowledge. The Star Sapphires, ever heard of them? They were an organization of women who weren't heroes or villains, and, get this, there is a character named Miri Riam. What are the chances? She fights for love or something like that, but Miri Riam, you can't make that stuff up."

"I didn't know you were into comic books."

"I'm not, but I like to know things. What, are comic books too low brow for you, Lennox?"

"Not at all, I just didn't realize you knew much about them."

"There's a lot of vacant space in my brain now that this whole scene has faded out of existence for me. I need my fix of the supernatural. You can't quit that cold turkey, or you lose grip of the reality you've built. Yes, oddly enough, the supernatural is beyond this reality, but it becomes like a duality, exclusively dependent on this reality. You can't have one without the other. Take *Lord of the Rings,* or anything scribbled down by C.S. Lewis. Everyone here eats that literature up like it's divinely inspired. Why? Because they've lost their faith in the supernatural and they have to replace it with something. They'll be the first to correct you and say they are merely *supplementing* their faith, but when you step back and analyze it, I mean scrutinize it, you see they've all lost faith in the supernatural. They don't believe in miracles anymore, or that love supersedes all things, or that forgiveness is a superhuman act. They've lost faith in all of it, in the parables they memorized as kids, in the teachings of a man who has increasingly become more historical than divine. So, then they look to something else to latch onto. They make themselves feel better by saying those writers were of the same belief system, or the same inescapable faith, or structured dogma, but really they're just trying to keep up appearances for everyone else: everyone outside these four walls."

"I'm actually surprised they aren't shushing us, or at least shooting us dirty looks."

"Nah, they're too scared. We're fairly invisible, I made sure of it earlier. So, was it?"

"Was what, what?

"Was she supposed to be the first mate who wanted off the sub?"

"I really don't know. I'm no Joseph in my interpretive skills."

"If you were to take a guess, or better yet, if you were filling out a Mad Lib story, would you input her name in the blank space that reads, "The one who wanted off the sub"?"

"That would be a terrible Mad Lib."

"Well, it's a terrible dream if I don't know who's supposed to be who. What's with all the standing? Was there this much standing when we were here? I mean, I think he's still in the middle of his sermon, why did he ask us to stand?"

"I think he wants to pray."

"Pray? For what? Isn't he supposed to be talking about Lena Prodan? Isn't he supposed to be paying homage to a life well-lived, and a compassion well-exemplified? Shouldn't he be extolling the congregation to live a life like she lived?"

"Alastor, I think he wants us to pray for the people who are still alive; you know, the ones who are still here, crying and moping about."

"What do they need prayers for?"

"Consolation seems to be highly coveted at these functions. Comfort comes in a close second, and I think fulfillment of their own needs rounds out the top three."

"She was great, wasn't she? What did she used to call us?"

"Brothers of thunder."

"That's right, brothers of thunder. That woman sure did believe in destiny, more so than any other person I know, except for maybe Mom."

"I received a letter from her when Miriam and I were still living in New York. She knew how to lift someone up. She asked to be remembered in the context of the last time we saw each other. She wouldn't want us to be sitting any closer to the casket than we are right now."

"She wrote me a letter."

"She did, when?"

"It was a few years ago, probably the same time she wrote you. I mean, the woman was pragmatic. If she was going to sit down and write a letter to one of the brothers of thunder, why not just go ahead and write to the other one? Same pen and paper; efficiency, duh. She knew quite a bit without being told. I mean, Mom and Dad didn't even know the extent of it all, but somehow, Aunt Lena knew. She didn't flat out say anything about it in the letter, at least not intentionally. She said she missed our conversations. She was being nice of course. I've said some things to that woman that should've shocked her into an earlier death. She was intent on listening to what I had to say, and then she would come to terms with it in her own way and time. She desperately tried to connect, on a human level, with me. I miss her. I wish they would learn from her."

"That man sure has a lot to say. Is he even reading off of anything? I see the tablet there, but he hasn't swiped it in thirty minutes."

"Someone should swipe it from him."

"It still wouldn't phase him. He would continue, uninterrupted, with what he desires to say."

"What exactly is he saying?"

"I think I heard him mention something about sleep earlier. I nearly salivated at the thought."

"Hey, Len, what do you say we ditch this ceremony early, Adler style, out the back with no one noticing?"

"I don't know, Al, it sounds *Al*right with me if it's *Al*right with you."

"Point taken. Your delivery lacked elegance and not an ounce of subtlety throughout. I expect better, even given the circumstances. Never sell yourself short, Champ."

The two brothers got up from their seats, and ducked down to not draw unwanted attention. They made their way to the top of the stairs which led downward to the main floor, and Alastor whizzed around in the direction of the sound crew.

"Pssssst. Hey, yeah, hello, remember me? You gave me the headset. We're done with them. I'll leave them right here. Merci."

"That was definitely uncalled for. I thought you wanted to leave incognito."

"They needed something more substantial to remember us by."

"They'll never forget us, that's for sure. Years from

now, when they're grown and have children of their own, after life's toils and troubles have infested their lives, they'll still remember our faces. Way to go. Mission accomplished, Alastor. You just couldn't leave quietly, could you?"

"Quiet, Lennox, you're making too much noise. We're trying to leave under the cover of darkness. What part of "Adler style" don't you get? Hey, not too fast, I have to pee. They better have a bathroom here. I hope they aren't the type of people who think suffering with a full bladder is good for the soul."

"You know there's a bathroom; you've been here hundreds of times. Can't you hold it until we're outside? There's a forest in the back."

"I want this to be a blessed pee, Lennox."

There was no one outside the sanctuary, not even the door greeters. An unobstructed path to the men's bathroom gave the Adler brothers renewed optimism in not being noticed. They hoped for the best and walked as fast as they could without transitioning into a full-fledged sprint.

The bathroom was entirely draped in white tiles. There were two urinals and two stalls. The smell of urinal cakes and bleach filled their lungs.

"I feel like we should whisper in here too."

"Because god is here? We're even further away from the pulpit."

"No, because it echoes. Who lines an entire bathroom with tile, white tile nonetheless?"

"Does white tile resonate better? Does it amplify sound more than, say, black tile, speckled tile, polka dot tile?"

"Yes, Alastor, it reaches to the ends of the universe."

"Do you think the Temple at Jerusalem was bedazzled with white tile? Do you think they had a bathroom in the Temple, or were *they* the people who believed that suffering with a full bladder was in a sick, sadistic way, enlightening?"

"You said you had to pee."

"Not with you watching me. No, don't use the urinal next to me, that's weird. Use the stall."

"I'm not going to use the stall when I only have to pee; that's what urinals are for."

"I don't care. If there are ever two urinals in a bathroom, it is implied only ONE be used at a time. It was written on the tablets, man."

"You're being blasphemous in a church."

"No, I'm being relevant. Anyway, we're practically a mile away from the pulpit."

"I'll use the stall."

"Also, don't talk to me while you're in there. That's weird too."

"You should write all these rules down for me."

"You should've paid more attention in Sunday School."

It was deafeningly silent. Neither of the brothers wanted to be the first to start, somehow each imagining the other waiting in anticipation to ridicule the flowing sound. The door to the bathroom creaked and swung open to reveal a short, stout man. The top of his head was completely bald, and the sides of his hair were painted with the color of age. He wore dark green khakis, and a checkered long sleeve shirt underneath a black wool sweater vest. There was no tie around his neck, but the top button of his shirt was nonetheless buttoned. A pacifying energy preceded his steps, a lightness, an ethereal quality, that made it seem he was floating. He paid no heed to Alastor's established urinal etiquette, and proceeded to join Alastor on the same wall. Lennox immediately gathered what had just happened. If the door to the other stall did not open, whomever walked in was peeing next to Alastor, and his brother would instantly pretend like he finished. He couldn't leave his compatriot alone with a stranger, especially one who didn't follow the rules of urinal engagement. Almost synchronously, Alastor zipped up his pants and Lennox exited the stall. The brothers met at the sink, and proceeded to wash their hands.

"*Pace.*"

The man from the urinal spoke to the two brothers while mid-stream.

"*Pace,*" the brothers responded in a tone which slightly suggested they were asking a question. They were caught off-guard. They quickened the process of washing their hands, but the soap kept uncontrollably sudsing. They panicked. The man at the urinal began to whistle.

Alastor and Lennox anxiously made their way to the paper towels, their pace slowed and their curiosity piqued. The man finished at the urinal and started to wash his hands. They saw the old man, and recognized him, but before they had enough time to register the connection, the old man looked at them with his blue eyes and adorned face.

"Frații Ardelescu."

There were few people who continued to call the family by the original, unabridged surname, and all of them frequented the old church. Everyone there knew them as Ardelescu and not Adler.

"Fratele Pavel."

"How is you boys?"

The man spoke with incredibly broken English, but always made the attempt to converse in their adopted tongue. They referred to him as brother Paul in Romanian, but whenever they strained to brush up their Romanian in conversations with him, he would revert to a simplistic, and basic version of the English language.

"We're good, thank you. How are you?"

"Good, won't complain. How is your families, good?"

"Yes, good."

"Good. We miss you both. Come home soon. We wait."

The old man floated out of the bathroom. The two brothers continued to dry their hands, even though they used an excessive amount of paper towels to make it appear they were doing something during the exchange.

"Always fond of that man."

"Yeah, me too."

"I wish they could all be like that, or at least learn something from him."

"What is the probability of that?"

"Abysmally low."

"Is that a probability? Is that a proper response to the question? I never know."

"I don't know either. Let's get out of here."

"Why do you think Pavel was here? I didn't think he knew Aunt Lena."

"I don't know, Alastor, but the quicker we get out of here the less significant those questions will be. Hurry up."

The pastor's voice was easily discernible through the speakers. The sound of crinkling programs and the scent of stale oxygen seeped from underneath the doors of the sanctuary. Lennox and Alastor hastened their pace until they were outside, at the back entrance of the church. They pinpointed the small forest behind the ecclesiastical lot, and with a blatant disregard for their clothes or what others would think, each picked a spot a considerable distance from each other, unzipped their pants, and finished what they didn't have a chance to do in the white-tiled church bathroom.

"Too bad this pee isn't sanctified. Here we are, peeing, what, one-hundred feet from the church, our backs turned to god, and our manhood fully exposed. It's a slippery slope, Lennox."

"It's going to be even slipperier when we're through."

When the brothers were finished vacating their bladders, they turned and regarded the towering building in its full illumination.

"Where are you parked?"

"The closest spot to the exit."

"I should've known."

Alastor started walking towards the far side of the parking lot, furthest away from the front entrance to the church.

"I think I felt some raindrops. Let's get to the car before it starts to downpour."

"Wait, where's your car, Alastor?"

"I was dropped off. Do you mind giving me a ride?"

"Not at all, where are you staying?"

"Nowhere. Would you be willing to drive me to the airport? My flight leaves in an hour."

"That worked out perfectly for you, didn't it?"

"What can I say, I'm a lucky man. By the way, did you see her?"

"No, she isn't here."

12

"You're back early. I didn't expect you back until ten or so. Let me guess, you left as soon as you heard the 'amen,' maybe even a little before."

"You know me too well, Katelyn."

"So, how was it? Did you see anyone we know? Did you talk to any of the cousins? Were there a lot of people?"

"You wouldn't have so many questions if you were there. You missed out on quenching your curiosity. Besides, I'm exhausted. I feel like I've been rambling on for days without sleep."

"You sat quietly through a funeral service for two hours. How could have been rambling? Talking to yourself doesn't count. Besides, who knows when I'll get to see you again, and we both know you never pick up the phone when I call. This might be the last time we talk in a long time, who knows, maybe for years."

"Katelyn, if you're going to guilt me, let it be known I won't be held accountable for anything I say. I am partaking in this late hour discussion against my will, and against my better judgment. I've been up for almost two days, and I don't think my filters work anymore. We should call it a night and forego any possibility of either of us offending each other."

"Come on Lennox, let's talk like we used to."

"You've been forewarned."

"Do you want me to make you an espresso so you can be alert?"

"No, besides, you don't know how to work the machine."

"I'm sure I could figure it out. Was Alastor there? Did you see him?"

"I sat up in the balcony. I highly doubt he would've made the trip just for a funeral."

"That's too bad. I'm curious what he would've thought about it, you know, seeing all those people. It probably would've dug up his past. That's why he didn't show. That's why I didn't go. I'm perfectly content with my life now, my family, and what I have going for me. How did Aunt Lena look?"

"Like she was dead."

"Lennox, you know what I mean. Did it look like her? No one looks like themselves when they're dead in a coffin. They look so flat, kind of like their skin is being pulled taut."

"She didn't look like Aunt Lena."

"Were there a lot of people? Did you recognize a lot of them? I bet they all look different now. I doubt I would even remember any of them. I don't think they would recognize me. I've been told I've changed a lot."

"It was a full house. Everyone loved Aunt Lena."

"Did her kids sit on the front bench?"

"You know they did, Katelyn."

"How am I supposed to know? I wasn't there."

"You know that's how it's traditionally done."

"Yeah, that's also partly why I didn't want to take Brandon. It was for the best we didn't go."

"Where is Brandon?"

"He went to sleep. He has a big day at work tomorrow, and he wanted to make sure he was prepared for it."

"Brandon sure strives to be prepared for things."

"What do you mean?"

"Well, he came home early to prepare for the funeral, and now he is going to bed early to prepare for tomorrow. Seems he spends a lot of time preparing for what's next."

"He doesn't like to be surprised. He needs to be mentally prepared for whatever comes."

"He can't possibly gird up his loins for every pesky nuisance. Things happen, unexpected things. What does he do when the unknown creeps in, cowl in the corner?"

"We're getting way off-topic; we were talking about the funeral."

"You were the one who wanted to talk."

"Yeah, about the funeral, not about my husband's habits."

"I thought we were talking like we used to."

"If we were talking like we used to, you would recognize I still want to chat about the funeral even though I didn't attend. I ask for the details to discuss what I missed. Yes, I know, I decided not to go, and I don't regret the decision, but it doesn't mean I'm not curious. If we were talking like we used to, you would see that."

"I do see that, Katelyn, but you stepped away from it all. You backed out, no one chased after you with a walking stick. Mom and Dad didn't excommunicate you, the church never forbade you from getting married, your brothers by no means shunned you for the sake of family honor. You created assassins out of us. You convinced Brandon we were terrible human beings who lacked decency, who acted atrociously towards you, and who never considered him part of the family. The man doesn't feel at ease spending time with us, even talking to us, because he deems it a betrayal. All those devised stories have turned you and him against us. Now, you sit here trying to manipulate me into divulging every detail of a ceremony you didn't want to attend, and frankly, I don't think you understand anymore. If you miss it, if you miss us, then prove it. If you need to know about the funeral so feverishly, if you pine to see all those people again, if you crave to be part of it all, you should've gone with me."

"You're an asshole!"

"You've always known that about me. It shouldn't come as a surprise to you now."

"Your stuff is already upstairs and your bed is made. I'm going to bed. Goodnight."

Katelyn cautiously made her way up the stairs and vanished without much of a sound. She'd learned how to leave behind a lingering scent of disapproval and disappointment. Lennox sat alone on the sofa, head rested back, wondering why he hadn't ignored Katelyn's request to talk.

"What if your perfect girl does, in fact, exist? You can't be sure she doesn't just because you haven't met her yet."

"I don't think you would hate me if you met me...well I hope not. I was exaggerating, but I am very aware our communication only allows us to know what we want the other person to know. I do not expect to ever fully know who you are. I do not even want to get to know everything

about a person in three days. That isn't a miracle to me. It is miraculous when I see a couple grow in their love with each passing day. A relationship takes time and I want to continue to learn about the other person for as long as I live."

"Lennox, hey, it's past midnight."

"Ugh, not again. I fell asleep on the couch, didn't I?"

"Yeah, and now you only have four hours before you need to get up again."

"Why does this keep happening to me? I guess four hours is still better than none at all."

"Lennox, do you mind waiting for just a little longer? Please. I really need to talk to someone."

"Sure, Katelyn, what's on your mind?"

"I haven't expressed this to anyone. Not because I don't have the opportunity, but because I don't know how. It's something I've tried to twist and formulate as inoffensive in my head so I could talk about it without feeling guilty, or dirty. It never worked out though. I could never find the right words, or the right phrasing to make me comfortable sharing it with anyone else. I don't have anyone I can talk to about this."

"You don't have to sugar coat anything for me, Katelyn."

"I don't know why it still bothers me, but every so often, it bubbles up and I lash out. I know it's the reason for several outbursts, but I can't help it."

"What is it, Katelyn?"

"There was a time, a brief period of time, when I broke up with Brandon. It was before we were engaged. We'd been seeing each other for a year, and I really started falling for him. Somewhere deep down, I started loving him. I was willing to give it all up for him. I'm not stupid and I'm not rebellious, you know that about me. I loved him so much I was prepared to relinquish everything and anyone for him. I knew I found the person to spend the rest of my life with. He was the one I wanted to make a home with.

"One night, we decided to do laundry together, nothing happened, but we started talking about our past relationships. I can't remember how, or why we started, but I'm almost positive I brought it up. I found out he had sex with other girls before we met. I was angry and relieved all at once. I was so mad at him because I'd waited. I saved myself for marriage and I fell in love with someone who didn't care enough for me to wait. I felt betrayed. I felt cheated and tricked. He let me fall in love with him. I put my guard down for him and he betrayed me."

"Katelyn, he didn't have the same upbringing as we did. There was no betrayal. He just didn't necessarily ascribe to the same things we were taught as children."

"So, I broke up with him. I never wanted to see him again. He cheated on me and I'm glad I found out before it was too late. I blamed him and I was certain he had purposefully tried to deceive me. I deserved better, I merited someone who was like me, someone who waited just like I did. I dated other guys who shared my values. A few were decent, but it was too late, Lennox, I'd completely fallen in love with him. I couldn't forget him. I couldn't forgive him, but I couldn't let him go either. I went crazy. I waited all that time for someone. Brandon was the complete opposite of what I expected, but he was exactly who I needed. I didn't know instantaneously, but when I realized it, I felt terrible."

"And you're happy now?"

"Of course, but it still tears me up inside. Our upbringing clashes with the person I am, the person I want to be, and the person I have to be to keep my home and family. I love Mom and Dad, you guys, and the people I grew up with. I'm simply trying to find a way to fit them all together, under one roof, in one brain, and in one body. I need to find reconciliation between who I was raised to be, who I am, and who I eventually want to become. Every choice I make, even the ones that seem ridiculous to you, is for that purpose. That's why I didn't go to the funeral tonight, not because I'm a backseat driver."

"You asked me about my sin earlier."

"Your sin? When did we talk about that?"

"The reason she said goodbye was because I wasn't a virgin."

"Oh."

"I was at the airport, leaving Portland, and she called me. I was unthinkingly focused on the windows overlooking the tarmac. She had a question she had been meaning to ask me for years. She'd never found the right time, so she waited until I was at the airport, the day after her birthday, to ask me for the truth. The truth, as though that feigned theory absolutely defined me as a human being. As though that fragment of information should decide the fate of love between two people. The detail became god to her; it was to judge the future.

"She said she needed some time to think it over. I didn't hear back from her for six days. When I finally gave in and called, she said she needed more time to mull it over. I invariably got angry. How could the decisions I made for myself, in my own life, have such an impact on whether or not we, me and someone who wasn't a physical presence in my life for eight years, *should* be together? I became evil in her eyes. All the signs that proved I was right for her were in some way deceptions. She accused me of finagling the universe into tricking her. She thanked her god for having saved her from such a reprobate, citing grace when she should've cited self-doubt. She said goodbye. I never heard from her again."

"I didn't know that, Lennox."

"I've never told anyone."

"I'm going to head off to bed now. I'll let you rest."

"Okay."

"Oh, I just remembered why I came down here in the first place. I have to pick up the kids tomorrow morning, so I won't be able to drive you to the airport. I'll order you a cab, though."

"Thanks."

RETURN TO CHICAGO

13

The black Buick was in the driveway. The sun was nowhere to be seen and it smelled like rain, even in the house. Lennox held back the lace curtains with his right hand, his bags resting against his left leg as he peered out onto a vista of groaning crickets and plopping dew. There was no emotion left. He had gone through the entire gamut in one day. Lennox didn't sleep after Katelyn went back upstairs. He didn't want to risk waking up late and having to see either Brandon or Katelyn in the morning. The nightmares he could handle, his sister he could not. He didn't move from the couch since he'd arrived after the funeral, so fluffing out the indent in the cushions would be the first task of the day for Katelyn. Lennox imagined her smiling and whistling while expunging any evidence of his presence in the Treowe household.

There was no exact time at which he expected the cab, but he had faith that Katelyn had ordered it. Katelyn was calculated in her actions. He looked at his phone to check the time and noticed he had an unread message.

:BY THE WAY, CONGRATULATIONS.

Lennox stared at the message on his phone until the

display light faded and the room went dark again.

The taxi honked outside, and he took one last look around, picked up his bag from the living room and cautiously exited the Treowe house.

"PDX, please."

"I was told to drive you to the airport."

"Yeah, to the airport, please."

"I can take you wherever you want, but I was told I was picking someone up for the airport."

"That's me. I'm going to the airport."

"It's just you said something different, and I didn't know if you changed your mind or wanted to go somewhere else."

"I haven't changed my mind. The airport is where I want to go."

"Alright, to the airport."

"I had a dream with you a few days ago. I don't know if I should share it...I will.

Okay, so I was a bride in my dream and I was marrying some guy. I remember having the most horrible feeling about getting married and I remember the whole time I couldn't do it because I still knew you existed. I don't know what happened in the end, but I do know I didn't end up getting married to that guy.

...the reason I don't like to share some of my dreams is because first of all you might think I'm crazy (which I very well may be), and secondly I don't want them to sway your thinking."

"Are you okay, buddy?"

"What? Yeah, I'm fine."

"Are you sure?"

"Of course, why?"

"Well, we were in the middle of talking, you went quiet for a little but, then you started muttering to yourself."

"We were talking?"

"You don't remember?"

"Sorry, I haven't slept these last few days. I must've fallen asleep. Don't take it personally, I just really need to get some sleep before nothing makes sense. What were we talking about?"

"I just finished telling you my opinions on religion. I guess it wasn't interesting for you."

"I asked you about god?"

"Yeah."

"That was very intrusive of me."

"I wouldn't have answered if I thought it was intrusive. Then again, I already said all of this after you asked."

"How long was I out?"

"I don't know. I assumed you were awake the whole time. I didn't even realize I was talking to you while you were asleep. I would've let you sleep had I known."

"Do you like opera?"

"Like soap operas?"

"No, like singing opera."

"I can't say that I do."

"Sometimes I get the convincing impression that I'm Rigoletto. I feel I'm used as a means to show people the true face of what we humans deem as illogical. Maybe I'm the poster child for chaos and illogical thought processes. Maybe god wants us humans to go back to the mysticism mindset and abandon the scientific revolution way of thinking all together. If god cares, boy does he have a weird way of showing it. If god is Verdi, or maybe the Duke of Mantua, then I'm here to be a source of entertainment."

"Are you sure you're okay? I don't understand what you said, but you've got quite a bit on your mind."

"He was a hunchbacked jester."

"Who?"

"Rigoletto. He was kept around as a source of entertainment for the royals. The Duke in the story fell in love with his daughter, and after having sex with her, he just left. He discarded her like his countless other conquests."

"That sounds terrible."

"Ironic thing is the jester's daughter actually fell in love with the Duke, at least that's what she kept repeating to herself. The audience assumes she was a virgin, so she could've merely convinced herself she was in love with the Duke."

"What an odd transition from talking about God to falling in love."

"You're telling me."

"You sure you're okay?"

"I just need sleep."

Lennox stared at his hands instead of looking outside the window. He watched his fingers as he continually moved each one to give himself something other than sleep to focus on and repel the urge to close his eyes. He couldn't trust himself while he was asleep.

"It's too bad it's dark outside. You're missing the beauty of Portland."

"I've seen it too many times. The luster fades with each visit."

"You visit Portland a lot?"

"Not anymore, but I used to vacation here every summer with my family."

"So, you have some good memories here?"

"Some good, some not so good."

"What are some of the noteworthy ones? It's a beautiful city."

"It is a beautiful city. We used to have a summer house in Clackamas. Every fifth of July, we raced over to the park and surveyed the playground for fireworks that didn't explode. The lawns were littered with them. It smelled like gunpowder and fire. We had some family who lived in Gresham."

"Will you ever come back to Portland?"

"I can no longer return and recognize the green glint of evergreen trees as something awe-inspiring. I climbed all the way to the top of the Multnomah Falls twice; once when I was a kid and once when I wished I was still a kid."

"Don't take this the wrong way, but I agree you need some sleep. I don't understand anything you're saying."

"Yeah. I guess hiding behind words can obfuscate a fairly simple reality."

"Do you still have the summer house?"

"No, we sold it to some relatives who converted it into a nursing home."

"That's a shame. Sounds like you had some memorable times. You said the American terminal, right?"

"Yeah. You can drop me off right here."

"I hope you have a good flight. Don't give up on Portland just yet."

"I'll keep that in mind, thanks."

Lennox heard the eagerness to make a quick escape in the driver's voice. He smiled considering he had done his part in keeping the weirdness alive in Portland, even if only in keeping a cab driver on edge during a twenty-minute ride to the airport.

"Before you speed off, do you by any chance remember what I was muttering to myself while I was asleep?"

"I have no idea."

"Thanks anyway, you've been so wonderfully obstinate and easy to get to know."

There was no need to belabor getting out of the cab, or to stand watch as the car sped away after Lennox planted both feet on the pavement.

If Lennox was to survive the day, he could ill afford spending energy on inane cab drivers, overbearing sisters, or disorderly remembrances of a ghoul that haunted an inordinate amount of his dreams. There was no room for error and no time to dawdle on anything but his meeting with the owners of Urban Whey. He had been granted the time off request for his aunt's funeral, but the owners were unwilling to forego the necessary meeting to discuss the outcomes and failures of Tuesday's haunting. Every second had to be devoted to spreadsheets, profit/loss analyses, impact evaluations, reasoned assessments, and most of all, sewing together strings of words and sentences to appease two owners who would rather ransom off their employees' well-being rather than close the doors to potential profit. It wouldn't be enough for Lennox to merely describe the hazardous circumstances from Tuesday. He would have to craft an argument so disconnected and disinterested, that weighing the financial impact and needs of a non-existent entity over the flesh and blood of the employees seemed absolute. Lennox knew the egregious act of closing early, regardless of context, could potentially cost him his job.

The metal detector beeped because Lennox forgot to

take off his belt.

"Sir, the sign clearly states belts must be taken off before getting in line for the metal detector. Please remove your belt. It belongs in the plastic bins. You're holding up the line. It helps to read the signs before inconveniencing everyone else who took the time to read. Do you have anything else in your pockets? Anything else? Please make sure and remove everything from your pockets while you are also taking off your belt."

Lennox stared straight ahead while the security guards asked him to step to the side for a pat-down. He must have sneered too visibly for it to have gone unnoticed. His mind was fixated on his meeting and what he needed to say even as his inner thigh and armpits were poked and prodded. Lennox couldn't remember if he had put on deodorant before he left Katelyn's.

He had little time from when his flight arrived at O'Hare and his meeting with the dairy brothers. Every second needed to be utilized to appease the fury and twisted understanding of two men injected with the virus-like delirium of profit mongering. Lennox would have to adopt their patois and ingest the same craven bile to come across as believable and convince them of his devotion to their cause.

Lennox had met with the two owners of Urban Whey three times. The first was his interview for Operations Manager, the second a follow-up meeting for the same opening, and the third a quarterly review one month after his hire date. In all their meetings, Lennox surmised they were looking for a yes-man: an attribute Lennox could eloquently feign in appearance only. Hal and Ian O'Brien never completely trusted Lennox to fulfill the obligations of the position as they had envisioned. The two were desperate in filling the vacancy, placing an emphasis on the appearance of competency rather than actual competency. They expected a dolt who followed directions, much like a kindergartener. They gave Lennox *carte blanche* to make his line of business more profitable, but Lennox made the mistake of attempting to also make the Urban Whey a hospitable place to work.

He sat down, facing the windows which overlooked the runway, and rehearsed every crafted line. Dread inched up his fingertips, over his shoulders, and down his back, leaving contorted muscles in its wake. He could visualize their disinterested faces and hear the even-keel of their voices as they reprimanded him with words cloaked with the nuance of a technical vocabulary, like hurling jagged rocks draped in velvet.

Lennox distractedly thought back to the string of malice he texted her. He was cruel in his disappointment and fervent rage. He antagonized her, called her out for being weak and susceptible to the whims and persuasions of those whom she surrounded herself with. He scared her. She begged him never to contact her again. He could hear how terrified she was of him, of who he could be, of his weakened humanity. He could make out her crying and see her hiding behind her veil of confidence. She said she was glad she saw his inner monstrosity because she was reaffirmed he wasn't the one. In all the time Lennox spent with her, he was afraid to let her see how mean he could be, how much he had to struggle to subvert his brashness, and the lashes he administered whenever he failed. He was broken and put back together every day. As much as he tried to reconfigure himself, the aligned pieces were destined to cling to their sharp edges and hair-line fractures. He strained to mend the pieces with a mixture of gold and adhesive, exasperatingly struggling to add a glint of beauty to a binary of feverish zeal and a gloomy disposition. There was no beauty in the Frankenstein attempt. To her, he remained a monster.

Lennox was stuck in the seat, understanding the importance of his meeting with his bosses yet unable to forget the green blur from across the room. He was terrified he would be stuck in that seat, in that airport, staring out the same window for all of his life. He didn't want to be there; he didn't want to struggle anymore. He didn't want to be in that city, and he didn't want to be trapped. Though the rest of his life moved on, though his body walked ahead of his mind, the green blur remained. It never came into focus to reveal a beautiful being, neither did it fade into oblivion. Even in his dreams, he never saw her. He was destined to arrive just seconds too late in a place where she had already left.

The unstable physical stratum, the collection of evergreens, Mt. Hood, Multnomah Falls, PDX during the day, Canon Beach, the oozing innards of blackberries on the sides of hills, the sharpened edge of uncontaminated oxygen, were all scarred and torn in places where no one but Lennox could see. It was a collection of dismay and melancholy only felt but not explained. The throbbing of the wounds rippled and disrupted Lennox's mind. They slashed the delicate fabric and marred the silken veil; he had to face her haunting alone. He was confined in that seat at the airport with the haunting of the green blur on his right and the haunting of Wabash Street on his left.

He resolved to exorcise the Wabash haunting; he could

not bear to relinquish the green blur.

His focus austerely returned to creating a strategy to maintain his job and to pacify the unquenchable sirens who demanded their dues. Lennox closed his eyes and harkened back to last year's statements as they were projected onto a white wall in a small, coffee-scented office. He summoned every nuance of that meeting as he lived with those numbers for ten to twelve hours a day. He studied the language of the black and red print.

"At this time, we would like to invite all passengers of flight 102 to Chicago, O'Hare airport, to please line up."

The fog of early morning was held at bay by only a few inches of glass and plastic. It was hard to discern any forms outside the brightly lit airport terminal. The numbers continued to play in front of Lennox's mind as though displayed on his fourth-grade diorama movie-projector he made with pencils, a shoebox, glue, markers, and colored construction paper. He took out his phone, glanced at the smudged screen, and sighed. There were two missed calls from Graham. Lennox turned off his phone.

* * *

"Didn't you hear me calling you from downstairs? You know I can't yell; the kids are asleep."

Camelia Adler huffed up the stairs, tactfully subduing her burbling impatience and frustration with Graham. She leered over him as he obsessively stared at his phone.

"I was trying to call Lennox. I figured I would catch him early in the morning."

"You should put your energy into something more

useful like answering me when I call you from the basement. I wouldn't have to come upstairs if you had just come down to see what I needed."

"I didn't hear you, Camelia."

"I need you to look at me, right now."

"I'm trying to reach my brother."

With one quick, fell swipe, Camelia knocked the phone out of Graham's hands, and tightly gripped his right thigh with her hand. Her freshly manicured nails dug into his exposed skin.

"I'm at my wit's end. Put your fucking phone away for just a second and give me your attention. It's first thing in the morning and I demand we start it off correctly. Look at me. I'm done with this shit. I'm done with your constantly disappointing behavior. Let's make breakfast together and show our children how two parents work together."

"Nice language, Camelia, real nice. You should've said it louder so the kids could hear what two parents are really like."

"Just get up and start making the pancake batter."

Camelia and Graham adorned themselves with the tattered attire of feigned cooperation. The tasks were divided equally between them; Graham made the pancakes, Camelia made the eggs and bacon. Physical separation between them was a prerequisite for a simulated ceasefire to the ever-present murmuring of battle. They made no eye contact. The drifting smell of breakfast, the clatter of pans, and the thumping of the refrigerator door awakened the sleeping brood. With the arrival of the children, Camelia abruptly and perfunctorily put her hand around Graham and smiled.

"Good morning, my loves. Daddy and I made breakfast for you so you can all grow up big and strong."

The children made their way to the dining room table, still in their pajamas, while Camelia kissed Graham on the cheek, watching each child take their seat. Graham pulled away from her clutch, walked over to the sofa, and picked up his phone. Camelia turned back to the stovetop, banged down the frying pan, and held in a scream.

* * *

"I'm sorry sir, we have to ask you to make your way off the plane."

"What did I do? I just sat down."

"Sir, we've arrived in Chicago."

"Arrived? How can that be?"

"You must have fallen asleep on the flight."

"No, I can assure you I haven't slept; at least, I don't feel like I've slept at all. You know the aching feeling you get, like you have the flu? There's no way I could have slept, or else I would've had some relief from my body being torn to bits."

"I don't know anything about that sir, but I can assure you we are in Chicago, and you have to make your way off the plane."

"You're sure we're in Chicago? Well of course you're sure, silly of me to ask again. Sorry."

"It's okay, have a great stay in Chicago."

"Do you like opera?"

"Excuse me?"

"Well, it's a long walk to the front of the airplane and I was just curious if you like opera?"

"Do you mean soap operas?"

"*Don Giovanni* is the story of Casanova, the embodiment of a womanizing ideal. Apart from being sent to hell at the end of the opera, he lived a fairly plush and carefree life. The audience is convinced Don Giovanni snuck into Donna Anna's room and took advantage of her. She runs after him, hell-bent on taking his life for what he did to her. Ends up Don Giovanni also killed her father on the way out, who, coincidentally, is the one who takes him down to hell in the finale. Donna Anna never gets her vengeance. Mozart writes all this beautiful music for her and her betrothed, whatever the hell that means nowadays, maybe like her main squeeze or her beau. Anyway, Donna Anna and Don Ottavio were supposed to get married before Don Giovanni defiled her. She spends the entire opera reliving the horror of the event and the death of her father, while Don Ottavio follows her around lamenting about what they once shared and insisting on a reinstatement of the wedding. She pleads for time to figure it all out, on her own terms, alone. She was destined to relive that night for the rest of her life. Mozart buries the anguish underneath lyrical melodies and consonant harmonies, almost like he meant for misery to be a daily component for every character in the opera. Nonetheless, Mozart gives the audience a beautiful show."

"That sounds absolutely terrible. I can't believe it's a story that's performed."

"It's opera. Come to think of it, on a smaller stage with a smaller audience, it's everyday life."

"I don't think that's life at all."

"Are we talking about soap operas?"

"You're right, this is a long walk to the front of the

plane, sir."

"All good things must come to an end. Thank you for alerting me to our arrival. If you ever get a chance, you should really go see an opera performed live. It's a grand spectacle. Goodbye."

"Thank you for choosing to fly with us. Have a great stay in Chicago, sir."

"Who was that?"

"Some guy who really needed to get some sleep. He was spouting some nonsense about rape in opera and killing. Sounded like a weirdo to me. Who talks about those things with complete strangers, and especially women? You just don't do that."

"Did he make you feel unsafe?"

"No, but him just bringing them up, especially to *me*, it just feels wrong. I don't know why he did that."

"What a pig. Should I alert security?"

"No, I just can't believe he would bring it up."

14

Lennox had ninety minutes until his meeting. A car was waiting for him as he exited the airport, which streamlined the process and allowed for some minor relief. Morning commutes into the city were torturous at best and traumatic at worst.

Traffic was light and the driver was uncharacteristically apprehensive to incite conversation. Lennox exuded a furrowed visage to guarantee limited interaction, but the driver innately appreciated tranquility anyway. Lennox was ensconced in his ritual to exorcise the Wabash haunting.

"Is the corner a good place to drop you off?"

"That'll be fine. Actually, I'm kind of early. Would you mind driving just one block further; I think there is a coffee shop on the right side?"

"No problem at all."

There was no coffee place on the next block. Lennox wouldn't admit to a stranger he planned to walk around aimlessly before his meeting. Coffee seemed like a logical excuse considering Lennox's exhausted and tattered appearance.

"I guess I was wrong. Just as well, the corner is fine. Thanks again for the ride."

Lennox lingered at the stoplight and questioned why he added 'again' when he only thanked the driver once. Blankly staring at the orange, androgynous figure in the small black box, he ruminated over his habit of uncensored blurting during his bouts of sleeplessness.

The meeting was scheduled at the Lakeview branch, taking Lennox outside the ghoulish frenzy of the Loop and dropping him in the land of an unnerving lullaby. Lakeview had a superficial lull which left Lennox just enough at ease to half-believe he was out of the Loop. It was an eerie rocking back and forth which eventually nauseated him. He was used to the bustle of Wabash Avenue with its expected patterns of behavior and clearly delineated social strata. Lakeview, however, confused him and convinced him to look over his shoulder when he walked down the street.

"Lennox, right on time, punctual as usual. I'm glad we can depend on you."

"Thanks again for coming, we know you've made a great effort to sit down with us today."

"Let's not detract too much from our goal; I don't want this to linger on for more than it should. Hopefully, we can get through this and you can maybe take some time to get some rest."

"Rick couldn't make it today. We like our Senior Operations Manager to be present at these meetings since he has a better insight into the day-to-day operations and interactions with the managers at the store level. However, we'll have to make due and rely on you to really fill us in on the details. We want to put together a composite of all the available information for the sake of transparency and also for insurance purposes."

"Insurance purposes? I'm sorry, I don't understand."

"Let's sit down first, Lennox. No need to jump into things before you're even settled."

"Are you sure you're well enough to be here, Lennox? You've been through quite an ordeal this week. Rick assured us you were prepared for this meeting, but I just want to make sure you have enough time to grieve."

"Thanks, Ian. I really appreciate it, but I think I'm good to continue."

"Good. Like Ian said, we're here for you if you need anything. Now, let's talk about the exact details of the occurrences of this Tuesday. We're writing up a report for the insurance company, and we want to make sure it's thorough and accurate."

"Insurance? I was under the impression after our walk-through on Tuesday night, our initial assessment found no damage to the building or storefront."

"That's correct. The claim is for lost income."

"So, when you talked to me on Tuesday night about my decision to close the store and the financial implications of such a decision, you were asking for the insurance?"

"Well, no, we wanted to understand your reasoning for closing the store before our evening rush. Our insurance will cover our income based on historical figures, but we potentially lost clients."

"Sorry for interrupting Hal. Again, I want to make sure you're okay for this meeting, Lennox. We can always have a meeting later on this week or even early next week."

"Since we're here we might as well talk about it. I

mean, he said he's fine to continue, Ian."

"I know what he said, but Lennox, you don't look well."

"Ian, we need to get this squared away to make sure we followed protocol and that every decision was properly calculated, and no unnecessary risks were taken."

"You mean the decisions I made?"

"Lennox, we've all had a very eventful week. Let's take some time, put our thoughts on paper, and have an insightful sit-down next week."

"Speaking of which, you don't seem to have any documentation with you here, Lennox. Rick assured us you were ready, but it doesn't seem to be the case today."

"I just got back from the airport less than two hours ago."

"I understand you've been through some stuff, but you agreed to this meeting and guaranteed you would be ready for us."

"Rick assured you, not me. Rick said there was a meeting on Thursday. That was the extent of any conversation we had about the situation. Actually, that's the extent of mine and Rick's interactions over the past two weeks."

"Hal, Lennox, let's stop right here. Lennox, thanks for coming in, but let's postpone this meeting until Monday. Get some rest and take care of yourself."

Lennox, fixed on Ian O'Brien's eyes, understood the undertones of the message; he needed to leave immediately. Lennox heard Ian and Hal bicker as to who was in charge of the meeting, their responsibility to every line of business, and the need for their managers to be held accountable for the decisions they make.

"You always do this; you always try to undermine me."

"I'm not undermining you. I'm preventing you from making an ass of yourself in front of our employee. You can't take your personal shit out on them. You can't be a prick to them and then surprised when they leave the company two months after starting their jobs."

"That's turnover; it's the nature of the business, of the industry."

"No, that's you being an asshole."

Lennox couldn't stomach the idea of taking the subway—the simmer of heated body odor choked him—so he used the company expense account to order a car. He would cite his failing health when asked to justify the incurred expense.

Numbers mixed with colors in his brain. The crisp jaggedness of numerals and summations mated with the curves and ambiguity of hue. Eights became blue, fives grey, sixes were red, and orange shared fours and elevens. He could still hear Ian and Hal bickering in Humboldt Park and the area around his healing tattoo began to throb. Lennox stumbled out of the car and used the walls to climb the fifty-six steps to the apartment. Portland became Chicago, and Chicago became nowhere. He kept imagining he was still on the flight back to Chicago, flight 102. The stewardess had lied to him; he was still asleep. It didn't make sense why the flight was so short; it should have felt longer. The yellow walls in the hallway curved and bumped him from side to side. It became narrow, just like when the picture frames littered the textured, vibrant yellow walls. He started to panic. Why couldn't he wake up? Why was this dream so real? He needed to open the apartment door and go to the only place that could wake him up. He needed to fall asleep to wake up; he needed to lie down.

Lennox faltered to the bedroom, forgetting to lock the door and running into a side table. Halfway to the edge of the bed, the dread of an unlocked door tormented him more than the need to stop moving. Fighting himself, yearning to take just two more steps to fall onto the bed, his body betrayed him and hypnotized him back to lock the door. Lennox ran into the side table for the second time on his way back to the room. There would be no more delay. Lennox fell onto the bed, face first, and felt the throbbing of his tattooed pec align with the gradual darkening of his eyes.

"Lennox, I've been trying to get a hold of you all day. Get up, come on, they're going to be here in an hour."

"Why does everything hurt?"

"Lennox, seriously, get up. I tried reaching you throughout the day, but I just assumed your meeting went long. What time did you get home?"

"I honestly couldn't tell you. I went straight there after my flight landed."

"I had to stay later because some parents were late picking their kids up from the daycare, and now the apartment isn't tidy."

"Who's going to be here?"

"Lennox, I know you haven't forgotten."

"I haven't, it's just momentarily escaped my memory."

"You look terrible. Did you sleep at all in Portland? Please answer while you get up from the bed."

"I slept a little. How long is this tattoo supposed to hurt? Is it infected?"

"No, you just need to sleep so it can heal properly. Now, quit whining and help me clean up. Throw the pile of clothes in the closet."

"Again, who's coming over?"

"Rich and Tereza."

"Today is Thursday, and Rich and Tereza are coming over after a concert. Yes, that's it."

"I really wish you would've answered your phone so we wouldn't be in this predicament."

"You're upset because I didn't answer my phone which led to me not having cleaned up the apartment?"

"Could you please just make the bed and then tidy up your books in the living room?"

"At once, right away."

"You know, you were talking in your sleep again. I heard you from the hallway."

"It didn't feel like sleep."

Both Miriam and Lennox preferred an uncluttered apartment, but neither of them made sure it was. A schedule was drawn up for the separation of duties: Lennox, the garbage, dishes, kitchen, bathroom, and Miriam, the bedroom, living room, and dusting. No matter how they decided to divide the household tasks, equality was never reached. Lennox never took out the trash in a timely enough manner for Miriam's taste, Miriam left the bedroom in disarray until an untenable living situation arose, so both surrendered and left the chores to the cleaning staff they always imagined but never hired. When the two had visitors, it was silently agreed the bulk of the cleaning would be relegated to whosever's guests were in attendance, while the other would assist in the smaller and more menial tasks. With Lennox being away and Miriam being caught up with extended hours at the daycare, the apartment was a battleground of neglect. Laundry had not been done for three weeks, the dishes were piled in the kitchen sink, Lennox's books were heaped around the apartment, and Miriam's yoga equipment was strewn about. Their strategy to give the appearance of calm and cleanliness had been battle-tested through countless similar encounters. Dirty clothes were flung in closets, dirty dishes were half-cleaned, blankets were utilized to cover eye sores, and diffusing essential oil was used as a refreshing calming agent. Separately, both Lennox and Miriam were obsessively tidy.

"Do we have anything to eat?"

"We have a full bottle of tequila. I say that only because I know you mentioned they were coming from a concert. There's nothing like riding an alcohol wave all the way to bedtime."

"Have you eaten today?"

"I think so."

"Should I even ask why you don't know for sure?"

"You're being somewhat contentious. Did you have a bad day or are you just stressing about them coming over?"

"I haven't seen Tereza for a while, so it's a little unnerving. It's a general feeling of being overwhelmed. You really don't look good. Are you sure you aren't getting sick? Did you pick up some bug in Portland?"

"I'm fine. Do I have time to take a shower before they get here?"

"Yeah, the apartment looks sufficiently nice and spiffy. I already set up the extra bed in the other room for tonight, so we won't have to do it later. She said she'll let me know when they're on their way."

The stentorian hum of the bathroom fan drowned out

the entirety of the past few days. The water was set hot enough to sear Lennox's skin.

He lingered in the shower, hoping he had more time than he felt he had. The faucet eventually squeaked off and he applied ointment to his wound and replaced the bandages. He wiped the accumulated steam from the surface of the mirror and noticed his distorted reflection. He sat down on the toilet seat and enjoyed the distinct feel of the cold surface on his scalded body. When there was no longer any further reason for delay, Lennox wrapped his lower half with a grey towel, opened the door, and turned off the light and fan.

"I know, we had so much fun."

"We really did."

The interplay between the two voices came from the living room. Lennox began to question whether or not he was in the bathroom so long that Rich and Tereza had already arrived, and were now making conversation with Miriam. He didn't hear anyone knock. Even if Miriam tried to alert him of their arrival, the fan would have drowned out any warning signal.

"Lennox, Tereza and Rich are here. Don't worry, we won't look while you go into the room and put on your clothes."

"I might."

"Tereza! Go ahead, Lennox; Rich went to bed already. He had an eventful night."

Lennox scurried into the room and closed the door behind him. He could hear Miriam and Tereza continuing to engage in energetic conversation, although he couldn't decipher the muffled exchanges through the closed door. Lennox opened the bedroom door, sheepishly entered the living room, and noted the bottle of Blanco tequila he mentioned earlier to Miriam. It had been opened and generously consumed.

"You two have already gotten a head start."

"Not Miriam, just me."

Lennox turned to his left and saw Tereza sitting on the sofa. Her eyes were impeccably large, enough to notice, but symmetrical to her other features to convey a profound sense of beauty. She sat with an unencumbered demeanor, pent up and excessively unsubdued. She drew the room into her with the hidden energy and compaction of a black hole. She did not try to draw attention with over articulated gestures or sultry words.

"Lennox, you remember Tereza."

"Glad to finally meet you. Miriam speaks very highly of you and your time together in Iowa."

"Thank you, and I'm glad to have met you *again* with what can only be described as an impeccable taste in tequila."

"Tereza and I were reminiscing about Iowa. Are you going to stand the whole night, Lennox? You can sit down on the sofa, it's okay."

"Why wouldn't it be okay? I don't bite."

"You said Rich has already gone to bed. Maybe I'll see him in the morning."

"I doubt it. He went a little too hard at the bar and will be regretting everything tomorrow. I guess Indiana living hasn't agreed too well with him. All that desolation needs to be supplanted with alcohol and loud bars. Maybe Indiana living doesn't agree with either of us. I shouldn't be the only one drinking. Lennox, you have some catching up to do. Miriam explained to me the week you've been having, so let's empty the bottle."

"Alright."

"Do you remember when we would walk through the ped mall in Iowa City? I loved that place so much. It was the energy there. No one really cared about anything because their brains were fried from studying and practicing. It was such a sexy place. There is no other place like it on Earth. I really loved it there. Lennox, you should take another."

"I remember having to leave my car at the bars all the time after our nights out together. I racked up so many parking tickets. At the end of the two years, I paid enough in fines to have warranted a dedicated placard, right outside Joe's Place that would read: *Miriam, patron of the drunkards.*"

"Only if it could have a picture of you in the short black dress you used to wear. I used to grab your ass so much when you would wear it. It drove all the guys out of their minds. Lennox, you're falling behind, please take another shot. You have a way to go before you can even begin to comprehend the depths of my drunkenness."

"You did used to grab my ass a lot in that dress. By the end of grad school, it was completely faded and worn in the back. Lennox doesn't know that about us, but I'm sure he's glad to have learned it."

"Miriam, not all guys fantasize about two women. They might be gay, but again, not all guys have that persistent earworm. Lennox, another one is in order."

"I will politely decline the last invite. I need to maintain my wits, not the least the contents of my stomach."

Lennox ungracefully slumped back into the sofa cushions. Miriam and Tereza laughed at his lack of worry at coming across as abrupt and crude, and his disregard for what was tenderly beginning to unfurl around him. He didn't need tequila to dizzy his mind or unencumbered conversation to propel him into a spiraling rabbit hole. He imagined trying to put together a one thousand piece puzzle of a complete blue sky, and only the sky. The entirety of the puzzle was made from a sheet of magnet, and the individual pieces were oppositely charged. Any small cluster of the puzzle he tried to imaginatively put together, it would burst apart and repel in every direction.

"I think he's assessing the complex construction of pine cones."

"I think he's trying to calculate the forces required to make airplane propellers work."

"Is this a full-audience participation event, or am I excluded because I already know the answer?"

"You don't get to answer because you've left us all alone. You don't want to drink with me, and you'd rather slouch back on the sofa and distance yourself with such alacrity. Not alacrity, melancholy."

"I've had, what seems to me, a year's worth of activity compressed into a few short days."

"I've had, what seems to me, a few short days' worth of activity stretched over the course of a year."

"Tereza, you really don't like Indiana? I thought you were starting to feel at home there."

"I can't find my bearings. Rich goes off to work and I'm ravenously trying to find any performance opportunities. I'd even settle for teaching voice lessons, but it's Indiana. I don't need anyone or anything to make me feel like me. I know what I want, I know what I expect from this life, I know what I've given up in order to receive what I want.

I've worked too hard to be stranded somewhere in the middle of a plot of land that feels more like a Salem witch trial haunting ground than it does a place of the living. Shit, I've blurted out more than I wanted. Lennox, for the love of god, please take another shot of tequila and join me."

"If only to allay the menace behind your blurting, I will happily do so."

"Finally, a willing participant. Did you know, Lennox, I genuinely loved Miriam when we were in grad school?"

"You don't anymore?"

"You know what I mean, Miriam. Of course I still love you, but back then, Lennox, I loved her with the intensity of a cult follower. I could still sense the feeling I would get when I was with her. That part of life, leaving home, finding yourself in a new place with few things to do other than study; it leaves you lonely, or at least alone. She would walk into a room, a class, a party, and she would suck me in. She's amazing now too, but back then she was a force. I wanted to grab onto her every chance I could get. If she exploded with the brilliant energy that was inside of her, I wanted to benefit from it and live like she did. I wanted to see life like she did, I wanted to be blindingly aware like she was, I wanted to fuck like she did; ugh, I just wanted to be inside Miriam. She warped every room she ever walked into. I swear, I would see the paint peel off the walls when she walked by. I'm so glad I met her, but now I can never go back to how I was before her. No place can hold you once Miriam gets a hold of you."

"Tereza, you're making it sound like I was the leader of some fanatical group, and I required the blood of their firstborn as the price of admiration."

"I can't have kids, so I can't afford the entrance fee."

"Tereza..."

"I'm fine with it; actually, I'm kind of glad. Rich is taking it hard though. He doesn't look at me the same way anymore. He used to make me feel an ounce of what you made me feel, but even an ounce is better than none at all. He loves me, of course, but I don't know if I love myself with him. When someone feels about me the same way I've felt about you, then realizes he can't look at me anymore because his tears are blurring his sight of you; it kind of repulsed me. I don't want to see myself differently because he thinks of me differently. I am myself regardless of who I am with him. I don't want to be any different. Shit, I think I blurted out again."

"Lennox, I think you should drink another one for Tereza."

"Why do I suddenly feel like a piñata?"

"Come on Lennox, one more and then I'll tell you a story about Miriam."

"I already have a lot of those stored up."

"Yeah, but not like this. Drink."

Lennox picked up the tequila bottle and nearly emptied the rest of it into his shot glass. The thud of the glass bottle returning atop the wooden coffee table made him seem more aggressive than he intended. Miriam was sitting across the room on the yellow arm chair, intently watching both him and Tereza on the sofa.

"I love the way she looks at you. She makes it seem like she wants to devour you. As promised, here is my story. Miriam, as she mentioned, loved Joe's Place in Iowa city. She loved to drink gin and tonics there. A friend of ours was the most skilled person I have ever met at drinking

Irish Car Bombs. His record was 1.6 seconds. I digress. It was the night after midterms and we decided to go out and celebrate, even though we technically still had one exam left. It was an aural skills test, so we had a few days to procrastinate. She was kind of off that day, but I thought it was the letdown after the intensity of our studying frenzy. When the assistant stage director of the opera showed up, I saw a distinct change in her. She had a thing for him. After a few rounds of drinking, more accurately several, Miriam wanted to leave with the director but she asked if I could go with her. She didn't say she felt unsafe with him or that he was sketchy, she just wanted us all to walk back to campus. Afterward, I assumed, we would go our separate ways: Miriam and the director together, and me alone. At first, I thought she wanted to make sure I got home safe, but she took us down a side road that didn't lead to either campus or anywhere near where any of us lived. She held my hand the entire time. In front of this random apartment building that was very secluded and very dark, she let go of my hand and started making out with the guy right in front of me. She didn't utter a word to me, and she sure as hell didn't give him a chance to say anything, or do anything for that matter. She threw him down on the lawn, bent down on top of him as he was helpless on the ground, undid his pants, pulled his boxers halfway down to his knees, stood up, faced me, hiked up that black dress of hers and fucked him right there in front of me. She watched me the entire time and I was frozen in front of her. I didn't look away, I didn't move, I just watched her beautiful body move up and down on this irrelevant person lying on the lawn in a dark corner, in a lost part of Iowa City. I couldn't stop watching her; I didn't want to stop.

"She made me feel unbelievably alive. I could see the whites of her eyes glaring at me. I didn't hear him finish when she got up, but she pulled down her dress, walked over to me, took my hand, and we both walked back to campus through the ped mall. We never even looked back to see the guy's reaction. We left him there, his pants around his knees, laying on his back on someone else's lawn."

Tereza's account of the past sucked both Lennox and Miriam into her sphere of influence. Lennox had completely turned to face her while she divulged the details, and Miriam slightly hunched over the yellow arm chair, smiling and watching Tereza's lips as she spoke. It was as though the story became Tereza's—the way she told it, the means by which she crafted each cadence, changed her timbre for emphasis, sculpted an event which could not have existed without her.

"It was well worth the one drink minimum to hear that."

"Lennox."

"Yeah?"

"Kiss her."

"What?"

"Kiss Tereza."

"Miriam, I don't think you know what you're saying. Let's be real here, I'm not going to kiss Tereza."

"Why not?" Tereza interjected.

"Because, Tereza, I'm married and my wife is right there, sitting not five feet away from us."

"So, I'm married and my husband is passed out in your guestroom, not twenty feet away."

"Lennox, it's okay. Kiss her. I want you to. Please."

"Miriam, I don't understand. I haven't slept in almost two days, I've had a shitty day at work, and I've had enough tequila to know there's a chance this is only happening in my head. I don't want to wake up tomorrow and realize I've made some stupid mistake."

"Lennox, just kiss her. Kiss her for real. Kiss her like you always meant it to be. Kiss her like you always imagined it would be. Kiss her without regret. Kiss her like she's here."

He looked at Miriam. He tried to uncover why. He tried to piece together why she was gently smiling, why she seemed so at ease, why she looked at him so intently. She wasn't ashamed, at least there were no tells. She was on the edge of the yellow cushion. She looked at Lennox, but didn't say anything. Her hands were folded, elbows resting on her knees, and her body leaned further towards them. She kept looking at Lennox; she never broke eye contact.

The tingling of unease slowly crept up his back and extended to the nape of his neck. His mouth opened slightly and his brow furled. He took a breath. Miriam refused to look away. Lennox felt a hand gently touch his left thigh and a sudden surge of warmth drawing near. Tereza had moved directly next to him. She moved her hand up his back until he felt the skin from her bare hand meet his exposed neck. Lennox's eyes were locked with Miriam's. Tereza tenderly turned Lennox's head away from Miriam's gaze. The contour of the yellow armchair blurred and swished away.

Lennox's head swiveled on his obdurate body until he was looking into Tereza's eyes. She effortlessly got up, and using his shoulders to maneuver his body, guided him so his back was against the inside arm of the sofa; his legs extended the length of the couch. She kept looking into his eyes and grinning. Lennox looked into her darkest of brown eyes as she climbed on top of him and straddled his legs. There was nowhere, and no way, he could escape. Lennox touched her for the first time. He moved his hands up her thighs, feeling every turn and detour of her lower body. The feel of her was new, unknown, and mysterious. She felt thrilling and different. The pulsation of her excitement was unchartered and dangerous. Lennox's hands were steady, as though they were sending out sonar waves to compile the layout of a newly discovered land. He could hear Tereza's shallow breaths; he could feel her rising body temperature.

The air became thin and the room went silent.

Tereza placed both of her warm hands on Lennox's face and intently moved her face closer to his. He moved his hands up her back and felt every muscle in her back tighten. Her lips instantaneously emitted every color imaginable when they met Lennox's lips. He pulled her closer into his body, and absorbed every emission. He could hear her desperately trying to transport enough air for both lungs through her nostrils, enough air to feed her bursting frenzy. They moved in tandem on the couch, never opening their eyes, losing themselves in the room, in that space, and in that time. They synchronized their bodies to each other. They kissed each other with increasing fury and passion, melding into each other's needs.

Lennox wildly and passionately moved his hands over Tereza's body. He felt every dimple, every groove, every inch of exposed skin. He took it all in. He zealously kissed her. He wanted her to feel everything he felt. He wanted to convey it all to her, to expose everything he spent so much energy and time burying. He wanted her to burn with the flames that were devouring his insides.

Tereza kissed him back with a reciprocated, unbridled ferocity. She touched him and felt what it meant to live something, even if for a fleeting moment, that was different. His lips excited her, changed her, introduced her to a world apart from the one she had adopted as her own.

The couch scraped and squeaked with each fervid motion.

Lennox's heart slowed. He remembered the swing set in Norman on a lightning filled night, and what it felt like to sit next to someone who was never fully there. Flashes of cold water at Canon beach, a retracting delicate hand, and the isolation of all those moments were relived on the couch. Tereza's lips slowed. Lennox opened his eyes. Her dark hair, beautifully disheveled, covered the sides of her face. Lennox looked into a tunnel. Her enticing, dimmed eyes did not glint or glimmer with any other hue. They were Tereza's brown eyes, and he felt alone. She smiled at him, satisfied the excursion lasted as long as it did. Lennox brushed the hair from both sides of her face behind her ears and tenderly kissed her lips one more time. They both whispered goodnight to one another. Tereza got up from the sofa, walked over to Miriam's yellow arm chair, kissed her, then said goodnight.

Lennox turned and focused on Miriam. She walked over, and sat down on the opposite side of the sofa while Lennox laid down. He placed his head on her lap, and peered up into her eyes. She gently brushed her fingers across the left side of his chest, well-knowing the area was still sensitive.

They both fell asleep on the couch, laying side by side, with the lights still on. Lennox slept for the first time in a very long time.

15

"Oh, come on! You put the chain on the door?"

"Who's there?"

"It's a burglar in the night. Who else? Now open the door, Alastor."

"What the fuck, is that you Alina? Have you lost your mind? It's midnight and you're asking me to let you into an apartment that is no longer yours? Were you trying to get in without me knowing?"

"I want to say hello to Arthur and Edna."

"You were planning on innocently sneaking into the apartment, while I was asleep, to say hello to the cats? You were just going to break into my place, silently stay downstairs while I slept upstairs, and unassumingly leave after you fulfilled your need to see them?"

"That's the gist of it; now, can you please take the chain off the door?"

"You've officially lost your mind. I can't believe you were going to break in."

"It's not breaking in. I still have a key."

"You mean the copy of the key you swore you no longer had?"

"It might be a distant cousin to that particular key. I didn't lie. I made a copy of the copy before we went to court. Technically, I did give the initial copy back to you, but I wasn't asked whether I made another one. It's cold out, let me in."

"It's seventy degrees outside. It's colder in here than it is out there."

"Fine, I'm just going to leave the door ajar until the cats come to me."

"I'll come take the chain off."

"I knew you could be sensible."

"You have to remove your arm so I can take the chain off. I need to close the door before I can let you in."

"Yeah right, so you can shut the door and leave me outside."

"Alina, the cats are in the upstairs bedroom with the door closed. They aren't coming down and there's no way in hell I'm letting you in. I'm not sure if you're drunk or high, or just plain insane, but you have to go before you wake the neighbors and they call the police."

"You're not man enough to call them yourself? I can see your habit of hiding behind other people so they can do what's necessary while you sleep soundly hasn't changed."

"We've been through this before. We agreed you could take the cats to your place once a month, with the emphasis on the *we*. Remember when the cats were at your apartment the last time? You left them alone for three days without food or water. If it weren't for whichever one of your idiot friend's drunk call when you were out, they would've died in that shithole. By the way, thanks for trashing it before you left. You call me a coward, but you sure as hell weren't facing any consequences when you absconded from the apartment and left it in utter disarray. Little did you care it was my name on the lease, my deposit, and my credit that would take a hit. It was awfully valiant of you."

"That was before. I'm a new man. After all, we had an agreement."

"An arrangement we haven't upheld. Are you lucid enough to realize you haven't been here, visited the cats, or given a sign of life for over a year? We're divorced, Alina, and you're losing your grip on reality. I've tried all I can."

"I don't care about your trying, I'm here to see my cats."

"They aren't your cats, now leave."

"You know, a lot can be said about *here* and *now*. I get all confused and start garbling my words and mixing up my thoughts into a hodgepodge of brain clutter. I don't have a neat way to eloquently express my standing between two infinities, one hurdling back towards my days in the womb and the other lunging forward to my days underground. When I try to describe the narrow platform labeled 'here and now,' I simply can't stay long enough on it. Within every passing transitional moment, half of myself is ripped in one direction and the other half is catapulted into another. I stutter when I try to express to anyone I'm not a whole person, I'm a little more than that. I have to be. There is more to me than an equal fifty-fifty split. I'm obligated to have a minute piece of me standing still while this platform constantly totters between the two eternities. Maybe it's the part of me that mixes up my thoughts and makes me seem crazier than other people. But it's also the little fragment that helps me stay in the *here* and *now*."

"It's after midnight and you want to start discussing the here and now? Fine. You're here, now leave."

"You may believe I'm the insane one, which I don't disagree with, but know you are far from being considered blameless. The signs, Alastor, the signs. You were there with me, you heard them too. A mighty voice awakened from an eternal slumber to focus their entire attention and care on two plebeians, oh, that's me and you in case I wasn't clear. The story revolves around us. The story of everything, of divinity, of deities, of whispers and providential plans begin and end with us. Didn't you know?"

"I've gathered enough from experience to let you talk it out. You'll eventually recognize it. What signs are you talking about?"

"I must admit, I never liked the narrative of Israel's return to Jerusalem."

"Which one?"

"Take your pick; you have plenty to choose from. I couldn't quite wrap my head around the whole deity-telling-men-to-leave-a-plush-ass-situation-in-a-foreign-country thing. They learned so much, had a merry ole time, and then travelled back to a place that was a wreck. Not only that, but oh, wait, they were shamed into divorcing their foreign wives. I mean, seriously, sending off your family because some guy said so. That takes some balls. Is that why you divorced me, because you needed to fulfill your yearly sacrifice offering? Was I a stain on your garment? Was I a foreign wife?"

"Alina, I've asked you to get help."

"There are other times I think Zerubbabel, Ezra, and Nehemiah were women. The prophets were undeniably women. The narratives were flipped for the sake of a coherent chronicle; you can't change the essence of the perspective. It's essentially feminine. You think men can take that kind of abuse and still remain a person? Not like a woman can. You think men are able to see things clearly? Not like a woman can. Ezra, now she recognized the insanity of traversing a desert only to find an inhospitable land, deserted and cursed, far away from the comfort of Babylon. Men had lost their minds, so why not allow women to make their own decisions and get the hell out of Dodge? Divorce was the answer to everyone's problems. Men could go on with their holy war against everything, I mean everything: the physical world, the spiritual world, the material world, the social world, the plant world, the animal world, the atmosphere, outer space, the list goes on. Women though, they just wanted to go back home. Jerusalem wasn't their home and Israel weren't their people. They yearned for Babylon, their own people, their own customs, and their homes. Look at it now, you can keep searching for your myths and legends and I can go on telling the world what's really what."

"Are you still getting headaches? Are you making sure it's being taken care of, properly, by a doctor?"

"I pop a few Tramadol and hope for the best. I barricade myself in a soundless, odorless, and lightless bathroom rocking myself back and forth hoping and pleading for it to stop. The Tramadol masks the pain, puts a cone of silence around the horror they call migraines. It's always there though. I can almost see it out of the corner of my temporarily relieved eye, patiently waiting for the dose to wear off and create more agony than I ever thought possible. The hurt always wins. It always gets its way. Each time a new narrative. Each time no real remedy."

Gradually, the arm between the door and the frame, wedged in-between the space between the golden door chain, slid down to the white-tiled floor. Alina Kovaci sat on the welcome mat outside of Alastor's apartment. Alastor positioned himself opposite the opening of the door, away from view but still within distance to close the door when Alina would surrender. It was a common exchange, like a tractable soil that remembers the weight and direction of the plow. Sleep during their marriage was a negotiable currency, exchanged only when it served the purpose of both parties. Alastor had grown fond of sleep since the divorce, going so far as to completely silence everything around him and paint the entire apartment black to strangle any errant light. All the lights in the apartment were off; Alastor knew the drill once he heard her voice. There was no need to turn them on and alarm the neighbors, or even to scare off the lingering drawstring of sleep which kept dangling before his eyes.

"I was listening to the radio the other day, some NPR shit. This brain doctor with a suave voice was trying to convince the air waves that cigars are dicks, or some fluff like that. I mean, I flip the radio on, still don't know who turned it to that station, and some phony is telling me if I smoke cigars, I want dick or something. As though putting together an IKEA shelf isn't really that. It's a 'process of projection,' kind of like reading tea leaves if you ask me. He says, if a shelf is lopsided, or if you put it together all wrong and don't fix it, you're the shelf. I once put together a shelf and that Swedish piece of shit broke. Yeah, I assembled it wrong, but that's because an illiterate Dane was writing the instructions in English. I mean, what the hell were they thinking? I just slapped some C-clamps on there, and that was that. This voodoo master tried to convince me I don't take care of or maintain my friendships properly because Sweden wants me to be an engineer. I've got two friends in this life, my right hand and my dick. We all get along just fine and I make sure to maintain that relationship."

"Are you still going to Xavier? Are you studying philosophy? Are you living in the dorms, or do you live off-campus? You don't have to answer, but I mean, you did barge into my apartment at midnight."

"I *attempted* to barge into your apartment at midnight. That's an important distinction. I'm pretty sure it's the difference between getting arrested and getting ticketed."

"You're making that up, aren't you?"

"How should I know? It could be a thing."

"Have you talked to your family at all?"

The AC kicked on and whooshed throughout the apartment. Alastor was sitting on top of a vent, and the cold air was a welcomed relief to the muggy, sopping wet, outside air. The light-cancelling curtains clicked against the wall as the bursts of cooled air shot up to the ceiling. Alina didn't respond. Her finger nails were painted solid aubergine, but the color distorted as she gently tapped them against the white tiles.

Alina felt out of place with the people she was closest to. She loved being an American, she loved what it meant, and she loved how it felt. She despised her heritage; she abhorred the languages she knew. She felt sullied whenever someone she knew identified her, or when someone remembered her from school, or from growing up alongside her. She couldn't create enough distance between her inheritance and the life she was promised, or rather, the life she was convinced she was entitled to in the United States of America. The surname Kovaci was a modification of the Hungarian form Kovács. Alina's parents changed the surname to preemptively forego the healthy dose of Magyar discrimination and hatred that ran through Romanian's veins, even in the United States. Overnight, they abandoned a country and an identity that was left tattered and abandoned on some dusty unpaved road from Hungary to Romania, for the United States.

Alina knew her family's history; she knew the stories. She'd sat through countless retellings of the Tisza family on her mom's side and the Kovács on her father's. Drawn-out narratives of Matyas and Rozsa Tisza giving birth to Veronika, Alina's mother, Mozes, Hanna, Oliver, and Zsofe, and how they illegally immigrated to Romania after the family had lost everything to a corrupt government that seized the people's wealth and consolidated power. There was no excuse in her mind for someone to illegally enter a country; it infuriated her. She rolled her eyes when she heard about how a small Tisza farm was purchased near the city of Covăsânț, Romania. Farming dirt land, cleaning up after barn animals, wearing scarves and skirts every day, not having enough food, not being educated because it was a duty to support the family, it all depressed her, and more so, enraged her. Alina felt like the tattered reputation of her family left her unclad and naked. They should have been better, should have been regal, should have been powerful by birthright.

Alina's father was an only child. László didn't speak

about his family, his upbringing, or his life before the move to the United States. On some level, Alina was convinced he hated the bloodline as much as she did. The poverty, the disgrace, the begging, the depending on others, embarrassed her.

Alina ignored her family. She was the eldest of six children, but when questioned about siblings, she would readily reply she was an only child. In her mind, her father and mother, an only child and the eldest of five siblings, should have known better than to allow procreation six times. Before Alina was married, she refused the implied obligations and responsibilities of being the eldest sibling. She fundamentally opposed using her given birth name, Anka Kovács. It sounded too Hungarian and foreign to her, more so than Alina Kovaci did. She envied the rest of her siblings because their names had softer consonants. Emilia and Lavinia had lulling l's, Emma and Milo had murmuring m's (Milo had the added benefit of both), and Samuel was the youngest and had curly hair and blue eyes. There was no competing with Samuel.

Alastor and Alina grew up attending the same church. It was the ecclesiastics who sponsored the Kovaci family to emigrate to the United States. The congregation vouched for them, taking the asylum seekers under their care and responsibility, and the U.S. government took them at their word. The Kovaci clan was the charge of a sponsoring church, and Alina regretted the fact. She could not stand to be indebted to someone, or to admit to have taken charity from any person, whether family, friend, or foe. The resentment ran deep, erupting and spewing out onto everyone and everything at the dissolution of her marriage.

"I've always had a bone to pick with this life. From the get go, my imagination served as a better rendition of reality than what actually is. It isn't my fault colors in life aren't bright enough, relationships aren't emotional enough, cars aren't fast enough, success isn't fulfilling enough, sex doesn't satisfy enough. Life should be willing to compromise and at least hear my suggestions for improving. Would it be too much to expect life to mimic more of my imaginative scenarios that I compose hourly than the half-assed schemes it takes years to develop? Colors aren't bright enough. I wonder if life is holding open mic suggestion nights so I can add my two cents for improving this shit show excuse for existence. Someone really dropped the ball on this one.

"Then those goddamn shrinks try to convince us we aren't living life to the fullest, or not appreciating what life has to offer. No shit! There isn't much to living this life. What, get a good job, fuck a decent blonde, hold off on knocking her up until she starts getting grey hairs, buy a house in the burbs, and eventually find a younger version of what you really wanted? It rings true to me, but I mean, it seems there's a conspiracy. Life whispers these shit notions into those smart-ass snowflakes; they hypnotize us into thinking we are pieces of stale shit, then dope us up to see prettier colors. Why the fuck wouldn't life just listen to me and spruce up this breathing room a little bit? I don't need pills to tell me there isn't much to living this life. Shit, I figured that out for myself real quick. No sooner than you figure out the circus behind the curtains is staged, bop, some smart-ass is feeding you words like "dissociative," "defense mechanism," "disconnected." They tell you you're not seeing straight or pissing right.

I've learned my lesson. If I have shit to resolve with life, its half-ass attempt at making this experience livable, I just shut my mouth. No one is listening. Life is out there fucking some better version of what it wanted, and everyone else is enjoying its sloppy seconds. Fuck this life."

"Alina, it's getting late and I have neighbors. I don't know why you came back; you hated it here. You're repulsed by me; you even detest the cats. I find it hard to come to terms with your reason for coming here was to see the cats. Why are you here, Alina?"

"Is this the point where I go into a soliloquy?"

"No. I don't get it. I don't have to, I realize that, but I wasn't the one who showed up somewhere unannounced. I'm not the one refusing to leave. It isn't me hanging on someone's doorway. Alina, I come from a family of secrets, half-truths, and omissions; I can relate."

"I think it's *in* someone's doorway. Big difference. A painting with someone hanging *on* someone's doorway is a stark difference to a painting with someone *in* a doorway, you know, with their arm flailing about like this."

"Maybe you're right, maybe I've been searching for a place that doesn't exist. Maybe there's a desert with my name on it, or a corner of the universe with a welcome mat that doesn't have a half-passed out person on it."

"Three-quarters at most."

"I think you should go."

"I will. I'm on a journey to an anti-home, the space in between where I came from and Jericho, a destination that can never be reached. The anti-home is the journey, the distance of space which is in between. I'm travelling to the heights and depths of humanity, searching for the one immutable, minute, and indistinguishable part that is authentically me."

Alina's hand dragged and squeaked across the tiles which had accumulated moisture from the mixing of the humid outside air and the cooling silence of the inside apartment. Fading aubergine fingernails, clanking no more, cleared the door's threshold and Alastor softly kicked the door closed. After re-engaging all the locks, he dragged the sofa against the door, blocking any potential path into the apartment. Sitting on the floor of the living room, Alastor opened up his laptop that had been packed away, turned on the power, and began composing an email:

Dear Elevated Space Realty Management,

Due to dire personal circumstances, I am writing to ascertain the feasibility of an earlier move into the unit this weekend. I hope we can come to an agreement as the situation has become untenable in my current living space. Please let me know as soon as possible. Thank you.

Alastor Adler

Arthur and Edna had been meowing the entire time Alina was at the door, but Alastor didn't move a muscle in the hopes Alina wouldn't hear them. He made his way up the stairs, eyes constantly darting back to the door with the expectation she would open it again and try harder to get inside. Halfway up, stopped on the landing, Alastor turned around and sat next to his laptop again. He would have to endure the gut-wrenching calls of the confused pair of felines, scratching at the door and calling out in uncertainty. Soon enough they would succumb to the quiet and fall back asleep, even though their master was downstairs. It was for their own protection; sacrifices needed to be made.

1:08 am—

Alastor sat upright against the living room wall, his eyes glazed over as he inattentively stared at the screen. A feeling of discomfort rose up his body as the wall and the floor became progressively uncomfortable.

"She will be like a millstone around your neck..."

Alastor surveyed the first floor of his apartment: stacks of boxes strewn across the floor, the discarded pile of unnecessary accumulations, furniture stacked on top of other furniture. Relief seeped out of his body, punctured by the midnight encounter with Alina, and dampened the carpet. He wished to maintain the liberation he painstakingly accumulated over the course of a year, but it was the apartment that would claim ownership. Balance needed to be restored. For every kilogram of worry, panic, regret, and darkness churned out, vows required a replenishment, a balancing and equalizing payment. As the warm comfort of Alastor's residual relief dripped outward, it undulated and disturbed the artificiality of a superficial placidness. He could no longer suppress it all. Countless ripples took life around him and projected themselves against the black painted walls. The release poured out of him like an unrestrained hive of angry wasps.

Fear of another knock prohibited sentiments of pity or disappointment; he needed to protect what was his.

There was no other alternative than to watch the years play forward and backward in his mind. Each blink from his eyes resurrected a memory, a sensation, an extended string into lightly-trodden potentialities. The apartment was nearly vacant. Arthur faintly meowed upstairs and Alastor looked at the clock in the bottom right corner of the screen.

2:13am—

Sounds, that during the day were logical consequences of established laws of physics, morphed into wandering phantasms and restless spirits during the two o'clock hour. Alastor had overheard his mother mentioning that evil lurked openly at two in the morning. In her natal village, commoners, flourishing primitives, would sometimes fast and pray during that time in the attempt to forever expel the much-feared apparitions. Alastor wasn't sure whether his mother believed the lore, or whether she was using it as a demonstrative tool.

With the constant threat of the front door being forced open, the battleground had been ceded. Miniscule, hidden doubts masqueraded as behemoth truths. Seeds of doubt, guilt, toil, and pessimism sprouted like beanstalks. Beanstalks that grow sideways, defying gravity, extending to expansiveness and yet confining to infinitesimal compaction.

The keepers of the underworld were silent upstairs; they had fallen asleep and allowed the gates of the buried to swing open within the mind of Alastor Adler. Light now soothed him, and fed him a morsel of comfort every few minutes. The clock progressed.

3:17am—

Numbness slowly crept up through Alastor's thighs and hinder parts. Poking needles kept him alert enough to respond in case the doorknob turned. He was near enough to the sofa that an immediate push would deter hope of entry. Images of Alina sleeping outside, or stealthily waiting for an opportune moment to make her second effort began to fade; the farce was becoming apparent. Whistling throngs of demons and scurrying patter of disfigured spirits politely exited the apartment, leaving as inconspicuously as they entered through the fissure in Alastor's logic which gave them naissance.

He pondered the journey. Questions abounded and ricocheted in every direction. It was the road to anywhere that was dangerous. Peril struck on the way to a destination, seldom at home or upon arrival someplace.

Destinations are the comfort, goals need to make sense, places should fortify and surround, chaos is outside on the side of the road like a wild lion awaiting the traveler who fails to heed warnings. The rise of cities assured protection for the traveler from the perilous road. There is no need to leave a city—the amenities, the comfort, the riches, the safety, people, society, logic, frills. Inhabitants of metropolises and societies were weary of the traveler for they could not be trusted; they were chaos incarnate. To survive and even excel on the journey was deserving of suspicion. Divergence of thoughts branching wildly onto intractable paths. There was a click at the door and Alastor's heart broke outside his body. Silently, in complete tension, both Alastor and his heart stared at the door, not breathing and not beating. Out of the corner of his eye, Alastor saw the bottom corner of the lit screen.

4:01am—

The final ghost dissipated, disintegrating into the faintest, dark glow of sunlight waking from its nocturnal grave. Outside light tremendously comforted Alastor. Shadows disappeared, warmth reemerged, particles vibrated, sanity was temporarily restored.

Unlike Alina, Alastor held onto the stories of his ancestors with reverence. They had left their home out of necessity, bracing the journey, the anti-home, building homes and a life in the wilderness where the vistas were vast but incomprehensible to their conditioned logic. Their lives made no sense to them in a place that was supposed to be home. Their inheritance was worthless in the new land, their customs deemed backwards, their language foreign, their physical attributes unsavory, their children bastards, their thinking dangerous. Yet, they accommodated their names and offered their children as sacrifices to a land with foreign gods and barbaric rituals.

What was their inheritance? If the wealth of their forefathers was worthless in this new land, what have the children inherited? Who are the children of the wilderness? Where do they belong? To whom do they pledge their allegiance? What is their aim? Who is their god? Whom do they worship?

Babylon wishes to see them back within her arms so she may comfort them and nurse them with milk and honey.

With the same veneration he apportioned to his parent's history, Alastor erected a reserved place for the inherited narrative of the Kovaci family. The two storylines mixed and intertwined, swirled and capitulated into a synthesized chronicle. If Alina would not carry the weight of the stories, Alastor would make room in his satchel.

Alastor's eyes drooped. His peripherals fuzzed out of focus and he did not trust his dwindling determination to defend the apartment.

5:07am—

Alastor imagined himself loading a burlap sack full of fourteen large boulders gathered from all over the world to serve as remembrance stones. He intended to lay them at the foundation of his home in which he would settle, and rest in peace. As he carried the sack of stones from place to place, the boulders bruised his body and grotesquely callused his back. Even when he put the weight down to rest, the unending ache endured. Within the sack were mementos of wonderful places, of miraculous views, of interesting people; all things he could never relinquish. When he envisioned himself putting down the heft from his back, there was a pang that pinged from ear-to-ear.

The inheritance of the wilderness was the wilderness. The children of the wilderness carried the image of a place, the hopes of a people, the creation of a humanity that is lost and wandering. There is no anchor, no port, no tower of Babel that can collect them all together again. They are far when they are near, scattered when they are together, and forever alone because they belong to the wasteland, to the maelstrom within the infinite pool of potential. The journey is their home.

Alastor pulled his laptop near to him and informed his work he was taking a personal day. He buttressed his legs up against the sofa, laid on his back, and fell asleep.

7:38am—

Dear Alastor,

Since the unit you will be occupying is currently vacant, there is no issue with you moving up your move-in date. We will have an associate waiting in the front lobby on the day of your choosing, and at the most convenient time for you.

Thank you,

Elevated Space Realty Management

16

"Lennox never answers his phone. I've called him at least three times this week. How is it possible he's busy every minute of every day, unable to even look at his phone and make a mental note his oldest brother is trying to reach him? What if it was an emergency? What if Mom or Dad was in the hospital, or if one of the kids was hurt? He would feel terrible he didn't answer his phone."

"Graham, you can't begin to understand what's in that brain of his; there's no use even trying."

"Is he screening my calls? Does he see I'm calling but doesn't want to talk to me?"

"I've given up wasting my energy on why Lennox does the things he does."

"All I wanted was to tell him about Aunt Lena's funeral. I wanted to relay all the good-wishes from our cousins and family. I don't care why he wasn't there, although I still believe he should've been. It was the right thing to do. I made time, even Uncle Ionel was there and he's not related to her, not directly at least."

"That was so kind and generous of him. Did he really offer to pay for a dinner in her honor?"

"He did. After the service was over, he expressed his condolences and extended his generosity to them. We all understood it was a stressful time for them, for all of us really, and they needed some time alone with immediate family, but the sentiment was beyond kind."

"Typical Lennox. He probably had something urgent and important to do like make sure his imaginary kids were safe, or clean his apartment, or drink himself into oblivion. It frustrates me that so many people made an effort to commemorate the life of your aunt, and for him not to even show up. He better have been taking care of some life-ending situation, otherwise I just can't rationalize what else could've been so important."

...

Miriam gently shook Lennox awake, knelt beside the couch and leaned her forehead against his. Lennox sensed the sun was breaking through the windows; the brightness of its beams colored the backs of his eyelids a deep orange. He pulled Miriam on top of him and buried his face into her shoulder. Opening his eyes would be a disappointment to the created comfort in his imagination and mind.

"Your phone has been going off all morning. It would seem Graham desperately needs to get a hold of you because I think there are five missed calls."

"Bury the phone deep in some desert so only the mummies can hear it."

"They're dead, so they wouldn't hear it."

"Then throw it away so the rats can have a sound system."

"I think they would rather have something useful."

"Well then tell Graham to bother someone else."

"I'll answer and tell him exactly that."

"Good."

"Tereza and Rich left about an hour ago. They understood why you weren't able to say goodbye."

Lennox didn't know how to respond. His mind was wide awake recalling the events of the night, but the words required for a complete thought were tangled in a pile of crossed wires, elephants, and tequila.

"Do you want some coffee?"

"Yes."

"You mean, yes please."

"I mean yes, please."

Miriam kissed him on the forehead and reintroduced the sunlight into his surrounding space. Lennox quickly brought his forearm across his eyes to block the advancing photons, but the damage had already been done. As a venom surged through the body with every pump of the heart, so too did the reminder of the now empty tequila bottle throb from head to toenail.

...

"It's like I don't have any brothers. Have they both died and I was never told? Did they both move to outer space, or maybe the Caribbean, or maybe they're partying together and didn't invite me. I call Lennox, he doesn't respond; I call Alastor, he doesn't respond. Maybe they never existed. All this time, I imagined I had brothers. Some people have make-believe friends; I have make-believe brothers."

"I've tried to reach out to Alastor, too. He ignored every single one of my texts. I've given up trying to be the better person. I don't see the use in putting forth the effort with people who don't reciprocate. I'm going to live my life, and not worry about other people's mistakes or bad decisions. I'm going to focus on my family and my kids, and that's all I can do; that's all I'm now willing to do. They pushed me to be this way. I tried to help."

"Haven't I reiterated I'm here as their older brother? Haven't I offered advice whenever they needed it? I've been nothing but available to them, and now for them to treat me this way is unbelievable."

"You can't change people, Graham."

"I know they'd like to hear about the funeral. They have so much family out there, so many cousins, aunts and uncles who would like to know what they're doing. Why do they insist on isolating themselves and alienating everyone they've ever known? They're just making themselves look bad. They're ruining our reputation."

"I doubt they consider that. Your parents have worked so hard to form good relationships with everyone in the community and now it's all going to waste. Everyone I ever talk to knows the Adler name. It brings so much pride to know there are still people out there who care about the importance of a reputation, a good reputation. I get so frustrated when I witness the ignorance. We just need to focus on our children and family and make sure we don't repeat the same mistakes and foolishness. That's all we can do."

"I'm still going to call them, Camelia."

"I'm not saying you should or shouldn't, but you need to be realistic. They haven't answered your calls up until now. There's no reason for anything to drastically change overnight, maybe ever. Some people don't change no matter how much help they have available, or how much kindness is provided."

...

Arthur and Edna were scratching at the upstairs door; It was time for them to eat. Alastor had been conditioned by his love for his cats to wake up at the slightest indication of their distress or discomfort. Knowing he had left them upstairs, all night, locked up without access to the entire apartment filled him with remorse and anxiety. The front door remained closed all night. Alastor checked the unread email in his mailbox, closed the laptop, and made his way up the stairs to set the preaching felines free.

"Three missed calls from Graham, what the hell? Doesn't he have work, or literally anything else he could be doing? Wasting his damn time."

As though imprisoned for years in the savage jungles of Borneo, the two American shorthaired cats bolted from the confines of their detention and darted downstairs to their feeding bowls. They petulantly waited for their sluggish Dayak convert to feed them. The downpour of manna into the cat's bowls satisfactorily occupied their attention while Alastor stole away his focus to prepare for the change in his living arrangement.

...

"Damn it, Graham, don't you have work today? Don't you have anything to do other than torture me with your incessant, half-hearted attempts at contact?"

"Just turn off your phone; not that complicated. Here's some coffee."

"Oh, actually it's Alastor. He texted me if I can help him move this weekend. Did I know he was moving?"

"That's news to me. That's not something you would forget. You forget a lot of things, but I feel your brother moving is something you would've remembered."

"Do I just respond with an: OK? Do I ask him every question tallying up in my head? Do I shoot a quick: WTF? Do I call, do I answer cryptically, not at all, a delayed response?"

"Why don't you stop making this so complicated. You know you're going to say yes."

"I think brevity is paramount in my current condition."

"Did you like kissing Tereza last night?"

"Do you purposefully wait until you catch me off-guard, or do I just perceive you as more maniacal than you actually are?"

"I know you did, and Tereza was smiling the entire morning. Either Rich was ignoring it, or he knew something happened considering she was happy."

"I'm going with the: OK, response to Alastor. I think I'm decided on that. Yeah, that's a definite, hard yes."

Miriam grabbed Lennox's face with both her hands, coffee still in his left hand, and passionately kissed him. Lennox's focus had to be divided between not spilling hot coffee on himself, and relinquishing trepidation and experiencing the transfer of love and ardor from his wife's lips onto his own.

"What was that for?"

"For answering my question."

"I didn't answer your question."

"You couldn't hide it."

...

Graham Adler sat irascibly at the kitchen table, twirling his phone in his right hand as his left leg raced up and down in obvious discontent. Camelia got up from her seat and went to dress the kids. In an attempt to offset the dejection of the children's third hand experience with death, Graham and Camelia, as a parental unit, decided their family should take a trip to the Field Museum. Chicago's heat had temporarily subsided for the day, and a Friday morning visit to an educational attraction was the agreed upon destination.

"It could've been nice if we all met up downtown. The kids want to see them."

"Did you say something, Graham?"

"No. Are the kids ready yet?"

"Yes, they're putting on their shoes."

Graham stabilized his phone in the palm of his hand; his leg momentarily ceased its agitated bouncing as he glanced down at the darkened screen. Denouncing everything and everyone around him, he stood up and peevishly dropped his phone into his cargo short's pocket.

"I'll go start the van and put on the AC."

"Did you say something?"

"No."

…

Once the expectation of an intruder was ensconced into Alastor's memory, every knock, any unexpected sound triggered a visceral response. He anticipated the doorbell to sound. He prepared himself by reiterating food was on its way; he repeated it like a calming 'ohm' to his agitated senses. The sounding doorbell scared the cats back into the upstairs room. Dragging the couch away from the door proved more difficult than Alastor anticipated. Fear was a tremendous motivator and strengthener in the initial barricading, but the depletion of adrenaline and lack of sleep transformed the couch into an Atlas stone.

Drooping eyebrows and a stoic face greeted Alastor at the door. Alastor answered with the lower half of his body hiding behind the door.

"You order food?"

"Yes, thank you."

Both the driver and Alastor retreated before the order transferred possession. The displeased driver turned away to leave, and Alastor, clothed only in his underwear, began to close the door before grabbing the bag. The brown sack of sustenance was in a free-fall. Alastor swung the door open and clutched the bag centimeters before it crashed onto the welcome mat.

Alastor was bent over the threshold of his apartment door, a bag of food in one hand, and an exposed lower-half in full view of the world. He fought the urge to check the bushes to see if Alina was hiding and instead backed into the apartment with a brown bag as a makeshift set of shorts.

...

"Did everyone in Illinois decide to take the day off from work and go downtown? It's bumper-to-bumper as far as I can see."

"We're doing this for the kids, Graham."

"Of course, but if I would've known traffic was so bad, I would've suggested something closer for us to enjoy as a family activity. We could've had an entire day instead of spending half the day sitting in a car staring at rear bumpers."

"Maybe you could be more patient and set a good example for the kids. If they were ever in a similar situation, we would want them to react differently than with anger, right?"

"No, I think the situation calls for anger."

"He doesn't mean that kids. Graham, darling, just because you're disappointed with other individuals doesn't warrant such an egregious reaction to an everyday circumstance, wouldn't you agree?"

"Kids, your dad is angry with your uncle Lennox and Alastor. Be better brothers and sisters to each other."

A 1996, aqua-colored Dodge Neon cut off the Adler van in an attempt to avoid hitting an entering truck from the on-ramp. Graham held down the horn in a fit of rage well after the incident had cleared. His wide, crazed eyes darted back and forth from the semi-truck to the Neon as his hand firmly held down the horn. Only after traffic sluggishly began to move did Graham release has palm from the deafening admonition. He reestablished his ten and two position on the steering wheel, took a deep breath, and gently released the brake.

...

"Exactly what I knew was going to happen. I text Alastor: OK, and he didn't respond, goofy bastard. He doesn't tell me when, or where we're meeting. Typical Adler ad-libbing. We should've started a family improv group."

"That would've been terrible."

"Are you saying we're not a funny family?"

"For sure you're a funny family."

"I meant humorous."

"Then, no, you are not a humorous bunch. I remember when Katelyn and Brandon suggested we do a zombie escape room together. I laughed out loud, literally laughed out loud and everyone was insulted. To this day, I still maintain they were joking because there is no way any of us would've come out of the room alive. That's a little harsh; some of us would've come out alive because some, like me for example, would've sat in a corner and watched as you all murdered each other, blaming this person or that for not being quick enough, or expressing incredulity at not knowing the answer, or breathing wrong. The zombie in the room would've feared for their life. Even if it was a real zombie, an undead, a walker, it would've feared for the little morsel of existence it had left."

"So, are we not funny or are we a danger to one another?"

"I think the two are synonymous for the Adlers."

"I don't know when it happened. We were a very close-knit bunch of weirdos. It was us versus the world, but then it was us versus each other. Maybe I'm imagining it, but it feels real."

"When the world isn't your enemy anymore; no one is your friend, or in this case, family. Or maybe it's everyone is your friend so family becomes your enemy?"

...

Crab Rangoon was cold, General Tso's Chicken had too much sauce, a Pepsi was mistakenly included instead of Dr. Pepper, and the fortune cookie read, "Now wood be a god thyme to take up a sport."

Sleep deprivation and elevated levels of Cortisol seasoned the food with a blandness that tasted authentic to Alastor.

He gave up trying to reset the couch to its original position. It rested halfway on the tiled entrance, and half on the carpeted floor. Arthur and Edna disdainfully watched Alastor poke at the Chinese food. They stared at him with no reason or motivation beyond their propensity to do so.

...

"Lennox, invite him to do something today. You have the day off, I have the day off, seems like he has the day off, why don't we go do something downtown? We can steer clear of Wabash."

"I'll be surprised if he responds."

...

Alastor half expected the alerting sound on his phone to be a notification that something terrible had happened, and the other half leaped in fury at the thought of another Graham communication attempt.

: "WANT TO HANG OUT WITH ME AND MIRIAM DOWNTOWN TODAY? TAKE THE TRAIN IN?"

It didn't take Alastor long to pounce upstairs and put on a pair of shorts. The maddening aura of the apartment was depleting him millimeter by millimeter, chipping away and haphazardly gluing the pieces back asymmetrically. No remaining part of him agonized over the state of the apartment, the well-being of the cats, the uncovered Chinese food on the couch, whether or not all his belongings were packed, or whether a blazing fire would decimate his apprehension along with the apartment.

Arthur and Edna continued to stare at the spot where Alastor had been sitting. Without any curiosity of how human food tasted, they intermittently blinked until they fell asleep on the carpet.

...

"We haven't moved in half an hour! I'm considering turning around and taking the kids to my parents' house, or maybe the park. I can't take another minute of this traffic."

"We promised them we would go to the Field Museum and we should keep our promises and fulfill their expectations. It's important for us to keep true to our promises so they can learn to do the same. I'm sure it will pick up any minute."

"There is absolutely no way that's happening. I'm getting off at the next exit."

"No, you're not. If I have to drive this car all the way into downtown, I will. If I'm the one who needs to show our kids the meaning of patience and keeping to one's promises, then I will, but don't you dare get off this highway. There's one thing I won't stand for, and that's..."

"Be my guest."

Graham unbuckled his seatbelt, opened the driver door, walked around the front of the min-van, and waited as Camelia did the same. No one spoke. The children glanced up from their activities, but were unperturbed by the exchange of drivers. Traffic continued to be at a standstill.

"Your shorts are dirty. You wiped them on the outside of the mini-van."

...

The Metra station was slightly damp, and the seats were uncomfortable. The weather didn't know what it wanted, leaving the maintenance workers with the impossible task of regulating the internal temperature to accommodate any change in humidity or uptick in heat. Summer's continuous heat roasted the brick and mortar, and even with a slight decline in temperature, the building's exterior retained the sun's residual intensity. ¬he air was like a glop of semi-heated honey: sticky and sweet.

Alastor chose the furthest seat from the walls, and slouched back with his legs fully extended. He felt something wet on the chair, but exhaustion overtook him and he forget about the mugginess, the inevitable stain on his shorts, the apartment, the cats, the train, the day, the plan, and everything else that could have possibly been. The passing horn of the Chicago-bound train sounded like a lullaby.

...

"I don't feel well, Miriam. I thought I could muscle through, but I don't think I can make it out the door."

"You play, you pay. Are you going to text Alastor you can't make it? You better do it quick. He might already be on the train."

"Yeah."

"What's on your pants? Is that coffee?"

"I must have spilled some when you ferociously attacked me earlier, you minx."

"Does that make you a Mensch?"

"I suppose it would, Miriam, I suppose it would."

...

There was no end in sight to the stagnant stream of cars on Northbound I-55. It was added salt to the wound to see the empty Southbound side. Every Chicago driver teetered on the edge of jumping the median and driving the wrong way as long as the inhumane torture of traffic would subside. There would be no ticket price too high for the relief of getting out of that congestion.

Camelia gripped the wheel with a hidden vigor and concealed disdain. Not one car moved, yet she held onto the steering wheel as though she were at the starting line of the Indy 500. Peripherally she noted Graham staring at his phone, and the black stain on his cargo shorts infuriated her. She turned her head to the passenger side-view mirror, jerked the steering wheel in one aggressive swoop, drove a few hundred meters on the right shoulder lane, and took the first available exit off the interstate. The children mustered enough energy to divert their attention from their electronics for a fleeting millisecond, but Graham never once took his eyes off his phone.

17

"Some psychologist, or psychiatrist, or psychopath, I always get them mixed up, thinks men are innately heroes. The historical narrative of our civilization, of our simian nature, takes into account some triangle, or rectangle, or rectum, or nonagon, of dominance hierarchy, which is a way of saying all the pretty pictures and cute words are for the boys. Well, are *about* the boys, but it's all semantics. You think you're a hero, sitting here with your whiskey, wait is that whiskey or Chicago tap water?"

"It's whiskey, well, technically bourbon."

"That's real masculine, real hero-like, very butch, swallowing down what no other human would want to swallow, like cum. Don't you think woman are the real heroes for ingesting man's infested guck? Everything you heroes eat or drink, smoke, snort, lick, all that shit ends up down women's throats. Sounds like a harrowing, heroic journey to me."

"What are you on about? Would you like me to call you a cab?"

"Does it look like I'm the type of hero who needs a cab? I need another drink, something a great big, walloping hero would drink. Barkeep, a shot of whiskey, sorry, bourbon for me and my sidekick here."

"Are you sure you don't..."

"What is that you're wearing? Is it a scarf, or a cowl, or a shawl perhaps? Looks like it's hand-knitted. You have a sidekick at home making you that shit? She sitting in the corner, headphones on, knitting your socks and cowls? You bring home the bacon for her, into her, on her, wherever? Wait, I apologize, I misspoke. Perhaps it is a *he* who is the object of your projectile, or maybe a zee, a meep, a boop, a kitkat, or even a whatsit, a whosit perhaps, a Dinglehopper, or a thingamabob. A great many dead guys, sorry, dead heroes, believe Disney ruined this country. Remember the scene where Ariel is in her special little undersea cave? Stupid girl, or fish, or zer, or der, or hebejebee, or doodat, whatever she goes for. She has all this shit, a great pile of waste, not unlike the real floating island of garbage. She's like a damn child using gibberish to identify mystical and unknown objects. Hot enough to give a priest a boner, sorry, allegedly give a priest a boner, but dumb as the damn coral undersea creatures shit on. Useless objects held up to unfathomable esteem, fathoms beneath the ocean surface, and they're presented as invaluable. Cutsie, futsie, shit that Disney. Completely fucked up our heads. Redheads thinking underwater forks are different than forks used on the surface; might as well call a spade an aardvark."

"There was a boner in the Little Mermaid?"

"Nice cowl, dipshit."

The screech of the moving barstool echoed in the nearly empty bar room of Friar Tuck. Regulars wouldn't begin to show up until three in the afternoon, two at the earliest on Fridays, but few mavericks dared to transgress social norms and begin their drinking before two. Pariahs and hipsters tended to disbelieve in stigmatized milieus.

Alina Kovaci sat alone at the bar; her companion left her stranded. The shots arrived, filled to the brim, and both comped by the bartender. Alina expected nothing less. The popcorn machine was at too great a distance to be worth the effort for her to traverse the sea of sticky stains and chipped laminate tile. Somebody would come, someone always did, and she would convince them to get her popcorn.

"Hello, gorgeous. I'm glad I decided to stop in here. I've heard only great things, and here I stand seeing it's all true."

"Are those real glasses, or are you trying to be retro for appearance's sake?"

"Forget about my glasses; I can see you perfectly with or without them."

"So, they're fake."

"Do you mind if I sit down with you?"

"That depends, does sitting down *with* me entail you also sitting down *next* to me?"

"That was the hope."

"Only if you get me some popcorn."

"That's not too great a cost for getting to sit down next to you, and with you."

"Kind of redundant, don't you think? Get two baskets, I have a thing about sharing."

Alina downed both shots and gently placed them back down on the bar. It wasn't necessary for her to turn and see when her popcorn would arrive; the belabored steps of flip-flops on a sticky floor audibly smacked.

"What can I get for you ladies?"

"I'll have a Pimm's cup."

"What's in a Pimm's cup?"

"How does a bartender not know what that is? You know, the summer gin drink."

"No, I don't know the summer gin drink. Do you know what else is in it besides gin, or do you want a shot of gin?"

"Two shots of gin, depending on who you ask, three to four parts 7up or Sprite, ginger ale if you're feeling frisky, then a whole shit ton of fruit which I'm guessing you don't have. I think you might have some oranges and mint. Throw those in there and screw the cucumber."

"Mmmmm, I love a girl who knows her drinks."

"And what can I get you? Another shot of Whiskey?"

"I'll take another two. This one seems like a mindless talker."

"You're mean."

"I know."

"So why are you here so early during the day? Are you trying to forget your woes? I can..."

"If you're going to sit anywhere near my vicinity, I ask you please leave the bullshit at the door. If you need to go back there and have a physical process of doing that, like going back to the front door and throwing away those ridiculous glasses, or getting rid of those flip flops, you might as well be barefoot, then please, by all means go back there and do it. If you need to retroactively go back to the door through a mental process, I can give you a minute of silence so you can metaphorically throw away those ridiculous glasses. Either way, just putting it out there, I'll wait."

"Here are your drinks ladies, on the house."

Alina's sidekick smiled politely to the bartender in the hopes she was conveying an authentic sentiment of gratitude; Alina stared at the two filled glasses on the bar.

"I'm Jess by the way. I had this drink when I was in New Orleans; it's supposed to be a NOLA special. We, my friends and I, went down there for spring break. We studied hard and wanted to blow off some steam, so when we all got the grades we needed, our parents bought us this amazing travel package: all-inclusive, five-night stay in the French Quarter. It was to die for. I would definitely go back in a heartbeat, but you know, the real-world beckons. Growing up and all that."

In the exhilaration of reliving her time in New Orleans, Jess unconsciously placed her hand on top of Alina's.

"I have butter all over my fingers from the popcorn. I don't want to soil that pretty hand of yours."

"I don't mind, really; I work with clay and all kinds of dirty materials. I'm an artist. Well, I studied psychology at DePaul, but my true calling is sculpting, painting, creating, and just birthing more creative energy and force into this world."

"When I asked you to drop the bullshit earlier, remember the whole sunglasses, flip-flop, dropping the act ordeal, did you accidentally drop your dick somewhere back there?"

With the Pimm's Cup halfway to her mouth, Jess stood in awe at the insinuation. Her cheeks began to darken with a near-red hue, some color in between cerise and crimson. Alina looked intently at Jess; her pupils dilated with the anticipation of a response. Jess brought the rest of the glass to her mouth and gulped. She looked to the bartender and asked for another. Swirling on the barstool, she whooshed ninety-degrees to her right and looked directly at Alina. Alina, in return, picked up the first shot glass, emptied it, then the other, each time lightly placing the emptied glass back upright on the bar.

Two echoing smacks emanated from underneath the bar counter as Jess' flip flops fell to the floor. Billy Ray Cyrus' *Achy Breaky Heart* blared over the sound system.

"Sorry about the music, ladies. We had a country theme night, cowboy hats and all that shit, and last night's bartender forgot to turn it off. Any music requests?"

"This is fine."

The regulars filed into Friar Tuck like clockwork, refusing to deviate from their habitual body sacrifice to Bacchus and the other drink gods who lived on the stools, whipping their slaves into submission. Conversations began to lull and wilt with the sounds of Billy Ray, and the front door slammed with each new participant: evidence of the cacophony yet to come. Jess drank her second Pimm's cup all while gawking at Alina. Her bare toes gripped the metallic barstool base; each petite aubergine painted toenail glistened with the overlay of silver sparkles. Alina quietly tapped her fingers on the bar top, occasionally striking the shot glasses with her nails.

After taking a mouthful of stale bar air, Jess exhaled for several seconds, controlling the pressure and expulsion rate of her breath. She released her toes from the bar stool, planted her bare feet onto the laminate floor, turned around and walked out of the bar with the emptied glass still in her hand.

Two more echoing smacks echoed from beneath the bar counter.

"Going over to a friend's house for dinner after you're married isn't the most comfortable of affairs. It gets infinitely more complicated if the friend is also married, making it kind of awkward. I don't believe someone completely turns off the part of their brain which was developed and strengthened during single life, during the era of free-love and calculated advances. It's not a date, but a tiny bit of your brain thinks it is, so any itty-bitty whiff of what you once construed as flirting during your single years becomes both circumspect and arousing. A simple, "You look good," while single could be taken as an invitation to begin flirtatious banter. When you're married, and having dinner with another married couple, you're not sure if they think you look good, which let's be honest doesn't really happen after you get married, or they haven't been able to shut off the whiny single voice in the attic of their brain. You smile politely, but you can't stop thinking about the possible deeper meaning.

"I don't give credence to the false impression that once you're married, you don't find anyone else attractive. I also don't prescribe to the notion you aren't supposed to think anyone else is attractive. It's the same chemistry, same hormones, same sex-drive, same body that served us for one-night stands as it does when we are in a committed, monogamous relationship. Whether or not one *should* curb those appetites, vices, transgressions, impulses, whatever the hell the kids are saying nowadays, that's altogether a matter of choice, or in the instance of an open-communication of partners, a consensual agreement.

"Let me put it bluntly; you meet some married friends who are acquaintances of your partner and you've only met them once before. The wife has an amazing ass, and you're an ass person from the day you first felt the hormone monster ravage your mind and body. What are you proving by not looking at, what clearly, is preoccupying the shit out of your mind? It wouldn't matter what board game, or what delicious meal, or topic of conversation, you name it, you're thinking about her ass. Even if you fight the urge, those peripherals you've honed throughout your adolescence and teen years sneak a peek and store a subconscious snapshot. Then you wonder why you're so horny when you get home...

"Unless, of course, you were never an ass person. Maybe you admire how you looked better than anyone else ever could. What if you found yourself so appealing you couldn't even touch yourself? Everyone around looks so pathetic and scraggly to you; it repulses you to even breathe the same air as they do. After a while, you don't see an ass, or a bulge, or two bulges, or curves, or contours, or anything. It's all just a giant blob of skin that can never be pulled taut enough to match how perfect you are. To complicate things further, if your spouse does somehow, in their utter lunacy, find anyone else attractive, you despise them just like the others. You wish they would have an affair so you can make yourself sick thinking about two blobs of imperfection mounting and swooshing around. I tend to also imagine silk sheets because it adds a considerable amount of humor to the potential muddling of corpses. Best visual I can give you is two pigs, weltering in their own squalor. You look like you're an ass man, a regular Bottom. Let me crown you with your rightful headpiece."

One by one they sat, listened for some time, for amusement or in hopes of fulfilling their lusts, but eventually parted, baffled and confused as to whether or not they had been offended. There was never a shortage of suitors eager to pay for Alina's drinks, even though she had refined her preference from well whiskey to Four Roses. None of her aspiring paramours minded the cost as long as she kept them thinking they had somehow obtained her attention.

"Do you think if those devout followers replaced the four roses they carry for the virgin with bottles of Four Roses, they wouldn't care much about commemorating her as much as replenishing her? That might've been a little crude, but she is the most visited site by her zealots. She has to have some goods to keep them coming back time after time. Offensive, I know, but there maybe a little truth in it. You don't think it's odd for grown-ass men to race four roses in remembrance of a virgin? Sounds like a fetish to me.

"According to *Der Rosenkavalier,* it's supposed to be a silver rose, but I don't think those have been around since the time of Glaurung; I'm sure he had at least one hidden away in his mound of stash, or booty if you are also an ass-man, or just an ass like Bottom over there.

"What do you think Octavian was thinking when presenting the silver rose to either Sophie or the Marschallin? Who was actually the virgin? On the one hand, an oldy but a goody who was either a shrew or a sure thing, and on the other you have a sprightly thing who was either silvery-pristine just like good ole' Guadalup, or rosy and red like this whiskey, bourbon, whatever."

"Is that from a show? I'm recent on almost all the new ones, but I don't remember that particular plot line. Name it, I've seen them all. It's kind of my thing. Sounds maybe like a soap opera, if I'm not mistaken?"

"You're definitely mistaken. It's from an opera."

"Isn't that what I said?"

"That's exactly what you said."

"By the way, I meant to ask you earlier, are these your flip flops on the floor?"

"Yes."

"Did you accidentally drop them? I don't want you to forget and leave without them."

"I couldn't forget them if I tried. They're perfectly content where they are, or at least they haven't complained to me. Do you have a special ear, specially evolved to hear the wee whimpering of inanimate objects, yet completely unable to register the most obvious? It's a wicked thing, evolution."

"Please don't tell me you're a flat Earther? Nevermind, I don't even want to know. Don't tell me. I'd rather go on believing you people don't exist."

Billy Ray Cyrus and his lot gave up the stage to the Bee-Gees and Queen; each act had to deal with the persistent scraping of barstools as one distraught admirer after another whisked off to mow greener pastures as far away from Alina's prairie as possible. No longer was she able to take the shots with the quick efficiency she had demonstrated in the initial hours of her bout at Friar Tuck's. Resorting to sipping was deemed a failure by her standards, but somehow it titillated others into yearning for the breadcrumbs of her allure which fell onto the alcohol-soaked floor.

"What are you drinking?"

"The drink that's in front of me."

"What's your name?"

"Goodfellow."

"You don't look like a Goodfellow."

"Neither do you."

"You haven't even given me a chance."

"Then a chance you shall have. I would like a shot of Pappy Van Winkle. Would you be willing, in your eagerness, to procure one for me?"

"Sure. What is it?"

"A very manly drink."

"Can I please have two shots of Pappy Van Winkle. One for me and one for, what was your name again?"

"Billy Ray Cyrus was just on the radio and he insinuated his heart was masculine. Makes sense at cursory glance; man equals man parts, equals man heart, a heroic heart."

"No way, hearts are definitely feminine."

"The Valentine's, Disney rendition of the heart, or the vascular, violent heart of darkness?"

"People are innately good, so no heart of, what did you say, darkness?"

"Do you consider yourself a great man, a hero even?"

"No, I consider myself an ally for every person."

"And therefore a hero cannot represent those disenfranchised, cannot bring light to those hiding?"

"Of course, it's our responsibility to bring the light into the darkness."

"What if the light blinds those we seek to help? What if living so long in the pitch black alters their perspective, their ability to understand and reason in the light? What if their life remained in the dark? What if to bring the light is to doom them, to blind them, to take away who they have become, who they believe they essentially are? What if by bringing the light we cripple them, force them to rely on other blind travelers? If Sisyphus was doomed to an eternity of rolling up a boulder, at what moment in the infinite timeline would a point-of-no-return exist? What if Sisyphus needs to roll the boulder to exist, for his survival to make sense, for him to grasp what is real and what is finite? What if it became his comfort, his dismantling of the chaotic, of the infinite, of the pointless, of the light which doesn't make sense to one who spends their life in the dark? What if it wasn't a damnation for Sisyphus but a grace, a mercy on the part of the gods for him to spend eternity drudging the boulder up, time and time again?"

"I've never thought of it that way."

"Of course you haven't, you idiot. You've become so accustomed to listening to Orpheus' stringless lyre, calling chaotic machinations into existence with your skewed imaginations, that you've forgotten the sound of real music, of beautiful music. You call the silence beautiful because otherwise you admit your folly and allow the gods who have deceived you to host banquets in honor of your own demise. You cower in the corner of your own hearts, unheroic, un-masculine, un-feminine. Your effort of perpetually toiling with the boulder is your own undoing for all eternity. It is better to allow that boulder to crush you, allowing its weight to pulverize everything that remains human within you, though there is little to destroy."

"What the hell are you talking about? Are you insane? I was just trying to make friendly conversation. You are clearly out of your mind. I'm sorry I ever walked over here."

The hair on the back of his neck raised and tugged painfully on his skin. Pappy ended up on the floor due to the shaking of his hand, adding to the perpetual stickiness on the laminate. There was no place far enough from the words, the accusation or the smell of iron in his nose. He walked through the bar, away from the massacre which lay behind him.

Alina pushed the emptied shot glass of Four Roses away from the newly supplied shot of Pappy Van Winkle. There was no need to fill a new shot glass with inferior liquid.

The preceding exchange warded off any other prospective admirer; the tumult of raised voices was off-putting even to the inebriated. No more heroes meant no more drinks for Alina. Without the need for fulfillment or propensity to savor the last drop of whiskey, she gulped down the shot and thumped the empty glass on the counter. The gavel dropped and she finished her day drinking. All eyes zoomed downward as she walked across the bar; the bottoms of her feet stuck to the laminate and popped as she exited. The door to Friar Tuck whacked closed again.

"Do you mind if I bum one off of you?"

"No, not at all."

Ambient Broadway street noise drowned out the delicate click of the lighter, and the offensive glare of the sun scattered the billowing smoke. Alina held the smoke stack in her right hand, staring intently at the feverish glow and the ensuing ash.

"It always smells like the world is burning to a smoker. The scent of fire lingers in their nostrils. The suffocating thickness of smoke is ever-present within their lungs. The world is always burning to a smoker.

"It isn't the pleasant, infantile notion of campfires or the reminisces of sing-alongs around a pit with their closest friends when they breathe in the outside air. There's a realization the world is ablaze, emitting a tar stained perfume. Behind the idyllic swaying of trees and blossoming rosebuds there is a looming flame there to threaten the stage design of the comforted and assuaged."

Alina flicked the newly lit American Spirit into the bustle of oncoming traffic.

"What the hell? Why did you ask for one if you were just going to toss it?"

All the way down Broadway, Alina did not totter, stumble or allude to her pronounced intoxication. All indications pointed to complete and utter sobriety, except for the blaring omission of foot wear. Even the Chicago homeless had shoes.

Travelling barefoot in a place she chose as her home, in a land she felt like herself, she was punished by the *ought* of her heritage and the *should* of her upbringing. Undressing the slavish robes of her ancestors, bestowed on their progeny with a perverted sense of pride and elevated sense of humility, she preferred the stark nudity of fitting into a land with a populace of newly heralded emperors and empresses wearing the finest of translucent clothing.

18

Miriam was genuinely concerned about being a good sibling to Rachel. At least twice a month, more frequently if Rachel had time to spare or willingness to engage, Miriam video chatted with her sister to prevent physical distance between them from turning into a vast divide. Miriam inherited an uncanny ability to divide herself among numerous relationships, giving her counterpart more than adequate attention, love and understanding. When the same consideration and empathy was not reciprocated, the miniscule portion of her character that desired an equal exchange was muted in hopes of maintaining an equilibrium within her relationships. She learned in order to obtain peace, to nurture a genuine atmosphere of placid homeostasis, she could not realistically expect the person on the receiving end of her generosity to return the favor. With Rachel, the tempest and natural perturbation that riles up the calmest of seas, Miriam needed super-human patience.

Communication between the sisters often depended on the temperament of Rachel: her mindset, circumstance, mood, moon phase, Venus positioning, or random selection of odds. Miriam loved her sister beyond human limits of understanding.

Video chatting was scheduled for the first and third Saturday of the month, though rescheduling was a built-in expectation. Attempts to keep the hearth of their sisterly connection, kindled in traumatic loss and strengthened through physical proximity, was genuine for both sisters. A healthy dose of nostalgia fueled their conversations. Reliving their New York days, the food they ate, the men they dated, the drama that never left their minds, were added blankets across a frosty ocean which separated them.

A silent pact existed between the two sisters, initiated when they were children, that it would be the eldest of the two, Rachel, in all her firstborn glory, to have sole rights to experience the *firsts* which life offered. It had never been a priority for Rachel to settle down with one man. She coveted a lifestyle surrounded by glitz and glamor, yet upon hearing of Miriam's rekindling love with Lennox, she deemed it was her birthright to enjoy a domestic life first.

Within a few short weeks of Miriam's reconciliation, Rachel moved to London, and announced her engagement to a real-life Jacob from a far-off land. Maxime Fenton was a mid-level exec for Tesco, having been with the company since its turnaround in the 90s and proudly declaring to anyone who listened how his efforts brought a remarkable change to London. The two, Maxime and Rachel, were almost equal, ounce per ounce, in their self-interest, self-assuredness, and lack of self-realization. After speaking to Maxime over video chat for the first time, Miriam acknowledged that Maxime and Rachel had found their fabled counterpart in the most random and unexpected way.

Miriam ignored the coincidence of Rachel's engagement one week before hers, and took no notice when Maxime and Rachel Fenton's nuptials were hastily scheduled three months before the Adler's. It was the birthright of the first born to fill their purse with *firsts,* and no matter the circumstance, it would be honored either naturally or by force.

It was the same routine—laptop, room, time, and identical rolling office chair—but Miriam couldn't dispose of her growing apprehension. Opening the laptop was woefully difficult because she had violated the natural order of the whispered pact. Rachel hadn't changed since birth. The reaction was decided; the fate was determined. There were no surprises between the two sisters, at least until Miriam opened up the laptop.

"Can you hear me?"

"Can you see me?"

"I can't see you, is your video on mute?"

Like clockwork, the picture disappeared from Miriam's laptop, and moments later a new incoming call.

"You know you do this every time, right? You don't have to exit out, just unmute the video in settings."

"It works just fine when I reboot it. Whatever, it's fixed now. How are you? Any good happen lately? Oh, before I forget, can you please send me your good reminiscences from the last time I visited? I've been waiting forever to add them to our good memories scrapbook. Please."

"I've been meaning to get around to it, I promise. I know how much it means to you."

"To us. It really does mean a lot to both me and Maxime. We want to remember the good time we had."

Rachel caught breath and new life with her sister as a willing audience. Miriam noticed the lack of Rachel ramblings and babblings during the past year's video chats. Often, she wondered whether or not Rachel felt abandoned and alone in London, apart from the little family she had, and married to a man who seemed to be more engaged, married, and sexually attracted to mid-level busy work than to his wife. From the gatherings of shared experience, and from a sisterly intuition, Miriam suspected something was pent up inside her sister. It wasn't like Rachel not to express everything, every modicum, morsel, speck, dust of her opinion or to share her life's woes with any pair of ears. To hear the labyrinthine chatter was a welcomed comfort; at least Rachel was trying to work it out.

Miriam sat in front of the screen as a mere bookmark. A nod or a side smile at the end of key phrases, or an eyebrow raise at the sound of an elevated pitch was enough to keep her sister convinced.

The first time Miriam walked into the Division Street apartment, she fell in love. She was all alone. The landlord was working outside on the balcony, the realtor was taking a call, and Lennox wandered off to inspect the neighborhood. It was decided: the beautiful hardwood floors, the high ceilings, the windows, the space, the rooms, the antithesis of everything she left in New York. When all the men finally came in, there was no further discussion about the issue. They signed the lease that day.

"What is that sound? Is someone at your door?"

"No, we have the windows open and the cross breeze is moving the blinds."

"Can you fix it? It's so loud on my end I can barely hear

myself talk. It's really bad."

"Hang on."

There was no fixing the issue. One downfall of the apartment was the lack of centralized air, encouraging the Adlers to either use a window ac unit, or to rely on the windows to produce a whispering draft. Once opened, the windows remained fixed; it was like finding a unicorn. Nonetheless, Rachel needed to see Miriam doing something about the noise, so per usual, Miriam left the office and wandered around the apartment until the lack of human interaction drove Rachel to forego the convenience of complete and utter silence for the need to hear herself talk.

Chicago humidity made the floors sticky, but the sensation against the soles of Miriam's bare feet compensated for the inconvenience of not having an AC unit. A walk from the second room to the balcony sufficed to refocus Rachel. It had begun to warm up in the city, but had not yet reached the zenith temperatures of summer. View of Division Street from the balcony affirmed others were taking advantage of the resplendent weather, even if only for a few hours. The outside brick was still warm but the wood underfoot had cooled with the unseasonable abatement of the summertime heat. Leaning up against the wooden railing and stepping up onto the tips of her toes, she watched the strollers and grocery bags of the passersby. She loved the city; she loved New York more, but Chicago felt closer to home. It was the city of her adventurous and iron-clad aunt, her mother and father's beginning and end, and a city near enough to the riches and wealth she sought.

Her heels touched the ground again and she turned to

revisit with Rachel; enough time had passed for the problem to not be resolved.

Great effort was required to close the door to the balcony due to the expansion of the wood and the poorly constructed door frame. The slamming sound gave the impression items were being moved around and perhaps, to the willing mind, the shutting of windows.

"I tried closing all the windows in the living room. If that doesn't work, I'm sorry, I'm all out of options."

"That's fine, I can deal with it. So, as I was saying, we visited this small, tiny, I guess you can call it apartment in Paris to spend the night, except we had paid for a luxury-sized suite..."

The cross breeze besieged the blinds, but the unbearable effect dissipated and the one-sided dialogue commenced in full. There was talk in the Adler apartment of converting the second room into a nursery, but the issue of the heat in the winter prevented a firm agreement. There was no central heating unit, so the wall-furnace warmed only the living room with most of the heat escaping through cracks and poorly insulated walls. The residual warmth was warded off by the gaps underneath every door. Space heaters were an option, but the newly publicized fear spreading of the myriad of ways to die by space heaters deterred even the soundest of minds. A crib in their bedroom was the only alternative which seemed to work within the constraints of remaining in the Humboldt Park apartment.

"I don't think it's funny, though."

"Neither do I."

"Then why are you smiling?"

"Because I'm pregnant."

Physicists sit, stand, bend over, bend backwards, upside down, all thinking about the possibility of nothingness; of infinite silence filled to the brim with infinite loudness, and at one point exploding infinitely fast into infinite nothing. Miriam comprehended better than any physicist did. The entirety of the room, of the apartment, of the building, of the street, of the neighborhood, of the city was swallowed up into the space in between Miriam's face and the laptop screen. It hinged on the oval space which contoured Rachel Fenton's face, which did not move or flinch. Then, Ragnarok.

"You selfish bitch. Why didn't you tell me you were trying? Why the fuck didn't you tell your only sister you were starting to try? I can't believe how big of a twat you are."

"No one uses 'twat' in the States."

"Fuck you and your jokes. You couldn't let me have this, could you? You had to take this away from me. You promised you would tell me, you promised we would share everything, you promised me and Mom I would know before anyone else."

"We didn't plan for this to happen so soon, Rachel."

"You've probably been trying all along. You're always trying to grab attention and always trying to show everyone else up. You've been like that your entire life. News flash, you're not special. You're not the center of the universe, you're only living in a tiny apartment in a shitty neighborhood, with a shitty job, and a shit life. Mom would be so disappointed in you."

"No, she wouldn't!"

"We were supposed to do this together. Fuck you."

It wasn't an attempt to reboot the video call when

Rachel's screen went blank. Rachel purposefully disconnected the video chat.

Anne Lehr unbearably loved her daughters, almost to the point of fallibility. Though they were two years apart in age, Anne treated them equally and instilled the possibility of utopia within them. Rachel and Miriam were both exposed to the same activities, lessons, music, toys, and games so Anne could never be accused of favoritism. By doing so, away from the cautious eyes of Anne Lehr, the two daughters competed not for the love and affection of a mother, but for the admiration and praise of a sister. For Rachel, there was a need to prove her birth order, to prove she was the first and best version of their mother. Though Miriam, being the younger, more agile-minded child, was disparagingly more successful at any task or activity the two shared, it was the overbearing attitude and demeanor of Rachel which sought to equal the playing field. In her mind, an older sister ought to be first, ought to be better, ought to be in charge, ought to be a mother.

Anne's daughters could do no wrong in her own eyes. Even in their adult years, Anne patiently absorbed their mistakes, outbursts, envies, jealousies, and even their childishness. Though all Anne's love was inexhaustibly given as inheritance to both daughters, one wisely used it, but the other squandered it into a negative energy, focused on supplanting the memory of their mother with the artificial embrace of a sister-mother. In their remembrance of her, their mother merged into an amalgamation of two personalities: Grace Ann Flint and Anne Lehr, and eventually one behemoth monument of a demi-god.

It was the image of her mother's disappointment

which caused Miriam to slam the laptop closed: an uncharacteristic display of rage and hostility towards the sister she cared deeply for. No sacrifice, no burnt offering, no tithing could have assuaged the abstract consternation of Anne Lehr creeping into Miriam's imagination. The mere visualization of sadness and discontent molded a pile of dormant woe into a durable and reinforced basin of grief.

Without the carefully crafted shelter of presumed acceptance, the gripping fear and paranoia that Miriam had undone all the teachings of her mother began to kindle. Almost instantly, a firestorm set fire to a hay barn of uncertainty, held up by buried guilt and regret. The offering smoke rose no higher than Miriam's nose, enough to nauseate her insides and suffocate her.

There was just enough time for her to reach the bathroom before she expelled the entirety of her stomach. The bathroom sink once again filled with vomit.

The light in the bathroom was off. Miriam couldn't handle the brazen clamor of the exhaust fan. She slouched over the slowly emptying sink. The drain was struggling to facilitate the ridding of the evidence, so Miriam pulled the stopper and allowed the mess to pool underneath her nose. She instinctively whipped her face up and away from the basin. Speckles of toothpaste and other foreign flecks were dried onto the unlit mirror, and even in the darkness, amid a minefield of foreign debris, the form of Miriam's reflection was still visible.

The all too familiar sound of Miriam's phone: I'M SORRY, PLEASE CAN WE VIDEO CHAT AGAIN?

Attempts at a cleanup would be delayed until an armistice. Reconciliation was prioritized over allowing time for Miriam to collect herself. Miriam elected to relay a feigned sense of composure for the sake of Rachel's well-being. She deliberately chose to belabor the process of opening up the laptop for half an hour in hopes that one more second, a sliver of a moment, would freeze the world.

"I reacted poorly, but your news is shocking. I wasn't prepared for it, but I want to know how you're doing."

Rachel's hair was frazzled and her breaths were shallow. There was an indistinct contour in the background of Rachel's apartment which seemed to be a man's shadow. By all indications, either an altercation took place, or she recently concluded a rage-induced frenzy. Both seemed probable.

"I know how important babies are for us, Rachel. I know we had expectations and we anticipated it to be a certain way, but this is life. I won't feel bad for being pregnant, and you were wrong; Mom would be happy there's another life being born. I vividly recall the first time I saw my reflection in a mirror. We were at the farm. Mom was holding me in her arms, and you were holding my hand. I had my red mittens on..."

"The ones sewn into your jacket."

"Mom anticipated I was going to drop them in some parking lot or in a store bathroom. I remember us girls together as though we were posing for a picture in the mirror. Maybe Mom was taking a snapshot. Maybe Mom foresaw what was going to happen. Maybe Mom divined what could happened to us if we weren't careful. Maybe Mom saw this day, I don't know, but I like to believe that somewhere, somehow, that moment will live on forever, just like Mom. I want to tell my baby about Mom, and I want you to be an aunt, and I want us to be together just like in the mirror at the farm. I don't want to do this without you. It never crossed my mind to have a family without you."

"I'm sorry, Miriam."

Their exchange carried on without words. Rachel and Miriam both looked down at their hands folded atop their laps, unable to maintain eye contact for fear the moment would pass. Gusts of wind blew through the Humboldt apartment and shuffling was heard in the background of the London abode. The air gradually cleared, the mist of remembrance and the array of memories fell to the floor. One by one they glided down to the ground, momentarily stalling next to the sisters' hands, and then continued down until they clicked in harmony with the billowing blinds as they bound themselves to the physical existence of both apartments.

Miriam and Rachel grew up on a family farm. Filled with the desire to revive her mother's memory and reconnect with her story, Miriam, during her time in Iowa, made the trek to Southern Illinois to revisit the site of her family's history and stunted progress. The surrounding corn fields, which had once been the splendor and envy of all neighbors, had been sold to larger farms that grew the Midwest cash crops of corn and soy. The man-made lake had shrunk and vanished, and the farmhouse was poorly maintained. She couldn't help but relive all the nostalgia of an ethereal home.

James and Shirley Flint settled in the fecund farming area of Findlay, Illinois, in the hopes of creating a bloodline that would value the land and the idea of family enough to hold onto the property for lifetimes extending beyond their physical existence. They had three children; Grace Ann, Pearl and Dale were all born and raised in Shelby County. According to extant genealogies and family histories, the Flint family lived in Illinois since putting pen to paper. Tracing the origin of the family was rooted more in myth than in factual evidence. It was believed, but never proven, that the Flints of old were actually the Flickensteins of very old. Sometime from somewhere, the Flickensteins came to the United States and settled in Illinois, changing their name to Flint and creating their idea of a family utopia in the Midwest. James and Shirley rarely mentioned the alleged origins of a Jewish identity, but on sentimental holidays, when the inside of the farmhouse was bedecked with multi-colored lights and festive floral arrangements, a faint whisper of guilt and longing, as though innately programmed, persuaded them to share the fable with their children. Thus, the myth of the Flickensteins was born, and reborn.

Grace Ann moved to Chicago after graduating from Northern Illinois University. While coming back to Findlay for a class reunion, she was reintroduced to a former classmate, and a one-time track star, by the name of Liam Lehr. They'd lost contact after high school, but felt a bourgeoning connection after the reuttered hello. Liam acquiesced to forsake his insulated life, and move to Chicago to be with Grace Ann. The holiday whisperings of James and Shirley Flint affected Grace Ann the most. Stories of a mysterious past with dubious origins firmly latched onto her thoughts, and patiently awaited the birth of her children before creating a crisis of identity. It was in a flurry of elation and euphoria that she heard her ancestors call and devoted her mind and soul to reconnecting with her forbearers. She desperately sought to accumulate an inheritance she could offer her two girls. Within the zeal and ardor of that search, she took up the name Anne and bestowed upon her daughters the names Rachel and Miriam.

Pearl Flint moved to Chicago with her sister Grace Ann, taking the initiative as first born to manufacture a destiny for herself, but after two became three with the addition of Liam, Pearl moved out and built a successful career as an executive assistant at a financial firm. She accumulated physical wealth in the form of furniture, high-quality silks, rugs, crystal, and paintings. She never married, and her affluence was redistributed as an inheritance to mostly unknown individuals.

Dale Flint was a brilliant man who floated from one interest to the other, amassing a wealth of knowledge which was unsteadily constricted to one human mind. He provisionally settled his precariousness and joined the Marines, joining an elite intelligence gathering team and keeping the contents of his work concealed, even from his family. He married his high school sweetheart, moved to Raleigh, North Carolina, and had one son. In an infantile stage of information, at a point where the growing understanding of drug interactions and side effects was still relatively nascent, Dale Flint lost control of his bipolar disorder. He took the lives of his family, and his own, far from the safe haven of the Flint farm.

Shirley remained in Shelby County and moved to Shelbyville, Illinois, after James died. They both loved the farm, but James loved Shirley more than the failed prospect of a family community centered around the land. He insisted they sell the property so Shirley could appreciate the rest of her days without the constant reminder of what could have been, and the reality of what had transpired. The farm faded to the back of the Flint children's minds, laying latent for several years until the motivation to see it again rekindled lost hopes.

Miriam closed her eyes and saw, as through a blur, the gravel up the farmhouse driveway; it crunched underfoot but didn't give way. The ice froze the entirety of the pebbles together like a mosaic of uniform rounds. Snow drifts were two feet high on either side. In the fields, random stalks of corn protruded the snow, creating a minimalist, pointillism painting for the birds. The lake was frozen, but no one dared tread on it lest they fall in. Gusts of wind blew the dusted snow, swirling overhead as though mimicking a starry night. Miriam, her eyes closing tighter, stopped halfway up the drive, listened to the whistling and smelled the ice and buried soil. There was one light on in the farmhouse and voices laughing in the fields. She settled herself, inhaled deeply, and looked out across the barren countryside. It was the genuine sound of happiness and feeling of comfort.

Miriam opened her eyes and saw the screen that glided between her and Rachel. Still standing outside the farm in her mind, she expected the gulp of air to shock her as it harrowed down her throat, her bronchial tree to crunch with the same frozen stiffness that she felt as a child.

Cars began to travers Division street, neighbors were walking their dogs, the uprising commotion of the weekend commenced, and the cold, unbearable air became humid and thick in Miriam's lungs. After all the worlds had passed, Miriam readjusted her gaze and noticed Rachel mocking up a smile.

"How far along are you?"

Sentimentality fell by the wayside and Rachel's facial muscles contorted and tensed. There was no simple answer, and no pure truth which would allow the situation between the sisters to remain amicable and sans argument. Miriam's dread had been realized. All strategies failed when Rachel asked further about the pregnancy. Miriam would not hold back the truth no matter how difficult or tumultuous the consequence.

"A little more than a month."

Rachel's face slackened and her eyes narrowed. She anticipated the moment and, since the beginning of the conversation, discreetly fanned the fanatical flame rousing within her innards. Reconciliation and amicability did not suit her. A brute force slowly released from the bellows of her insecurity, and she hissed through clenched teeth.

"You mean you kept this from me for more than a month. You unbelievably selfish bitch. I can't believe you would do this to me when we've been through so much. I tell you everything when it happens, and here you are, bloating up to have a kid, and you conveniently wait one month to tell me. You are the worst sister I could ever have imagined for myself."

For the second time, the screen went blank. Miriam closed the laptop because the conversation was over. She knew her sister well enough.

The longest stretch of time the sisters went without communication was two months. After the Adlers moved to Chicago, Rachel requested a video chat during the week. The lone request made by Rachel was that it would be a conversation only between sisters, implying no spouses would take part. It was an odd demand considering

Saturday video chats always excluded spouses, regardless of circumstance. On that Tuesday, Maxime and Rachel were on-screen, smiling and leaning forward to convey a sense of closeness and familiarity. The mid-level manager and her sister needed money. They were not forthright about their need, but Miriam didn't expect a PowerPoint presentation outlining their financial situation. Miriam assured them she would discuss it with Lennox and get back to them with a response within two days. Miriam politely denied their request. Rachel yelled, 'You're a selfish bitch!" and ended all communication.

Miriam tilted back into the chair, and as she did, the wood creaked and the joints further weakened. A nauseating waft of smoke snuck in through the window facing the hallway. Miriam closed off the only hope of a cross-breeze and latched the window closed.

No amount of nuisance could diminish the delight Miriam felt in the Division Street apartment, not even a sister who couldn't understand her. It didn't faze Miriam that there was still puke in the bathroom sink or that the smell of smoke stimulated her gag reflex. Finally arriving at a place that epitomized comfort kept Miriam optimistic. She wanted to be on the balcony, so she ignored the alerting ring tone on her phone and walked across the tacky apartment floor.

19

Lennox received an address and a time. Alastor tendered no explanation as to the why, how, or even an insight into the thought process he utilized to elect moving into the city. His brother had asked a favor, and Lennox was more than willing to comply with the request. It was an exchange honed throughout their fraternal relationship, through countless arguments in their youth, and ample misunderstandings. Seeds of discontent were only sown in circumstances when either of the two brothers tried to explicate the seeming irrational and mercurial nature of the other's decision-making. Years of interaction between the two unlocked an intelligibility that reeked of maddening senselessness to outsiders. The yearning to know, to explain, to define, to compartmentalize, to employ instruments of the sane and responsible, all rusted away in neglect.

Punctuality was expected of the Adler children: a byproduct of a father water-boarded in the discipline of a military life, who in an attempt to raise proper children, drilled the habit into the minds of the four rapscallions.

"I brought coffee. It's Dark Matter."

"Had I known that to be the case, I would've stolen IV bags from work to have our fix while we expend ourselves into exhaustive oblivion."

"A simple 'thank you' would've sufficed for even the most greedy and self-serving of us all."

"Then I wouldn't be me, and we know that's why you're here. Why not give the people what they want?"

"I want to be in bed, not moving all your shit."

"Well, give to Caesar what is Caesar's."

"He ended up with a knife in his back."

"I'll make sure you're always the first one up the steps, and I'll keep a keen and brotherly eye out for shiny daggers."

Lennox handed the coffee to Alastor and the two rested before moving the truckload of personal items into the outside world.

"Did you pack all the stuff by yourself?"

"No, the cats helped."

"That was very saintly of them."

"They take after their uncle."

"That was a shitty attempt at flattery."

"Awfully presumptuous of you to assume I was talking about you. Graham has been an incredible presence in their lives, though as always, work and family take him far from their growing needs."

"We're still talking about your cats, right?"

"No, we're talking about Andrew Lloyd Weber's adaptation of T.S. Eliot's story."

"That's what I thought. Either that or you were making fun of Graham's parenting of his own children."

The rhythmic blinking of the hazard lights on the back of the rental truck soothed Lennox into a trance. Both brothers leaned up against the rear fender of the truck with a sullen awareness of the heaps and stacks that silently stalked them from behind the closed door. Still recovering from the end-of-week festivities and Bacchus worship, the city dwellers were yet tucked into their abodes awaiting the sultry crooning of the afternoon hours.

Two bus rides were the only feasible options for Lennox to arrive at Alastor's new Lakeview residence. It was fortuitous for Lennox that the hiccupping prophets and wandering riffraff didn't use the city's transportation system until the city-dwellers awoke from their mattress warbling. Lennox had a knack for running into the most unpleasant and seedy individuals when he took the bus, regardless of the destination.

"Did you run into your friend from the bus?"

"No, otherwise I'm fairly certain I would be in prison right now."

A stalwart steward of sanity mistook Lennox's errant glance as an affront and proceeded to expose himself in defiance and gesture circles around his ear and pointed back at Lennox.

"You know you've seen it all when a crazy person calls you crazy. He must've known something. He must've seen deeper than anyone ever has."

"Yes Alastor, he peered deeply into my very being and concluded his dick absolutely had to bear witness to *my* insanity."

"Should I even ask?"

"No. Let it be."

"Was it..."

"Damn it, Alastor, I said let it be."

"I was just going to ask if it was crooked like his smile!"

"There isn't enough coffee in all of the world right now."

"This is as good a time as any to make you aware that my apartment number is 308. Meaning, I have the great fortune of living on the third floor of this astonishing building. Upside, there is carpet. That might lessen the wear on our knee ligaments. Silver lining."

"Days like this I almost wish the Mayans were right."

"That won't make the process any less painful. Leave the Mayans in peace and embrace the certainty. I have a lot of books; I mean, a lot. You might look into the bed of the truck and be tempted to think it's not so bad, but it is. It's worse. There are deceptive little critters hiding in boxes. Remember, lift with your back."

As though a starter gun fired directly into Lennox's ear, he leaped off from the fender and stood in front of Alastor in an act of defiance and annoyance. Alastor, still seated, lifted the latch and flung the door open as far as he could. There was no need for him to look back at the monster that stared into the fear-stricken eyes of his brother. He was familiar with the towering heap because he had pieced it together, centimeter by centimeter.

"Holy shit you have a lot of stuff. How did you not tell me you were a hoarder?"

"Then you wouldn't have showed up."

"Why didn't you also ask Graham to help, or Dad, or anyone else? It's not too late to find someone crazy enough to aid us. There is still hope."

"There is no hope. You should've let that illusion go a long time ago. It's just me and you: bonding time."

"More like bondage time."

"Like…"

"Like indentured servitude."

There was no easiest place to start. All the components of the truck were haphazardly dispersed with no cohesion or logic to their stacking or arrangement.

"You work in a damn lab, don't you?"

"Yeah, and?"

"It looks like a four-year-old decided to pack for you. I see, what I can only assume, are heavy-ass boxes all the way in the back, light pillows and furniture in the front, boxes unsoundly stacked atop cushions, and is that an old typewriter?"

"Yeah, I think it weighs thirty kilograms. Easily thirty kilograms. You're looking at this all wrong, Len."

"Al…"

"Sorry. Lennox. Just think how much more agitated and aggravated you would've been if I invited you to pack the truck with me. You would've lost your mind watching me use all the wrong logic and ignoring decency and common sense. This way, you only have to unload the insanity. Half glass full."

There had never been more of a motivation for Lennox to control time to his whim, to wrestle it to the ground, than when he climbed up and down three flights of stairs to Alastor's Lakeview apartment. Lungs, legs, forearms, knees burned in agony; muscles seized up and every step a new cramp surfaced. He wished time to speed up during intermittent bouts of placidity and to deaccelerate when rest minutes sprinted past.

"*Yonder comes a man with a sack on his back, honey…*"

"Oh dear god, I need to stop for a minute. How is it possible you have breath left to even half mutter a song? I hate this so much. I hate you so much right now. I left my wife for this."

"No, Lennox, *I* left my wife for this. Yours is still at home."

"Do you remember the alley behind the 83rd street house before we moved to the suburbs and how we used to look for discarded treasure in the neighbor's trash cans?"

"I think the term is 'dumpster diving'?"

"I don't give a shit if it's called 'muff diving,' I will continue to call it 'searching for treasure'. I don't think we ever found anything we kept. We held out that one time, sometime, someone would discard a treasure. Looking back, our neighborhood was comprised entirely of immigrants. There was no way anyone was throwing something useful away. And now, as I sit here, expelling bits of my lungs onto this cat-piss smelling carpet, I wonder if somehow you managed to collect all the treasure and box it up for us to carry into your apartment. Except, now I know better; I know this isn't treasure, it's just shit I have to carry with you."

"I ain't heavy, I'm just your brother."

"You're no spring chicken."

"Are you referencing my weight? You calling me fat?"

"Just observing both our inabilities to cope with physical exertion. My excuse is age, what's yours?"

"General disinterest and a broad sense of I don't give a rat's ass."

"A true, authentic modern man."

"*The man fell down and he broke that sack, honey...*"

Lennox's saving grace throughout the moving process was the numbness from having woken up too early. The incessant humming of the same tune and the paralysis of his forearms allotted him scarce moments of patience and a limited willingness to endure. As the afternoon dragged on, the stairs bent back in incline, the boxes gained weight, and the coffee was sweated out with a large human's worth of water. They had no change of clothes and no plan to stop for meals. The Adler way was to bulldoze through a task, finishing any started undertaking and completing it as quickly as possible. Automatically reaching for another box, without any concern for their well-being, the brothers drudged up and down the three flights of stairs almost a hundred times. Little was said and even fewer glances were exchanged.

"Watch out, Lennox."

"Thank you. Are you new to the building?"

"I am; he's just here for moral support and general annoyance. Hi, I'm Alastor."

"Hi, I'm Jess. I live in apartment 208."

"I live in 308. I guess this means I live right above you."

"You'll have to excuse my brother, he's a little slow in picking up cues like if you live in an apartment that ends in 8, and he lives in an apartment that ends in 8, chances are you're either living above or below one another."

"Don't mind him, he's morbidly out of shape and is probably going to have a heart attack at any moment. He's old, as you can probably tell by looking at him. Don't mind the beard. I know, it's off-putting, and honestly, kind of scary. He's not homeless, just lazy."

"So, you two are brothers then? You seem very close."

"Not by choice. We're part of a cruel deistic joke."

"We're not very fond of the cosmic laughter."

"Okay. Well, let me know if you want to grab a drink

sometime. There's this cool neighborhood bar a few blocks away. It's called Friar Tuck and there are always interesting people there."

"I'll keep that in mind, Jess from apartment 208."

"That sounds like a sitcom title."

"Lennox, don't be rude; let the lady pass. Sorry he takes up so much of the stairwell. It's something we're working to help him overcome."

"Bye, brothers."

An interruption in the mechanical flow of the process permitted their brains to commence sending pain signals pinging throughout their entire bodies. Their motivation to complete their task dwindled while they stood on the landing of the first floor.

"If I sit down, I'm not getting up again."

"Speaking of getting up."

"Seriously? She looks like trouble."

"She's Jess from apartment 208."

"And you're the dumbass from 308. I don't see your point."

"Fine, you win. Let's get this over with. You know, I've never been fortunate enough to trust my instincts. 'Trust your gut' was advice I ignored, and more so, used as a compass to execute the exact opposite. In chess, my instinct was to always sacrifice my minor pieces with no compensation in site. In love, my urge was to immediately open myself up to the possibility I found a unicorn. In life, my intuition was always wrong. I gradually learned my lesson over the course of my mid-20s; identify my tendencies then do the exact opposite. It isn't a flawless process, but it's way better than the fallout from trusting my gut. When my compulsion was to tip the delivery driver $10 for an $8 tab when they were an hour late and made me go downstairs to get the food, I simply did the opposite; I tipped the driver zero dollars and told him to take it up with management.

"If I ever joined the military, I would be the first person to die. In a pressure situation, I would have the unfortunate displeasure of relying on my instincts and take a bullet right in the noggin. No amount of conditioning or muscle memory would save me from standing during a gunfight. I strongly considered applying to be a Marine, or a Navy Seal in hopes I would forget my inner promptings and formulate a second sight: the mind and body conditioning of a soldier. The epiphany came to me when I was twenty-six, considerably overripe for the age requirement of starting a military career.

"If the United States ever institutes the draft again, my gut tells me I'd be the first drafted and the first dead."

"If we get through this move, and in the end we are both alive, I'll consider it a win. If you're lucky, I might pity you a bit, but I can't promise anything."

No other interruptions were permitted to slow down progress. Neither Lennox nor Alastor halted their mindless lifting and toiling, no matter how attractive the passersby. Hunger, aches and pains were ignored in the expectation it would all end soon. As one brother dropped off a load of boxes on the carpeted floor of the Lakeview apartment, the next would already be on his way up the flights of stairs: two passing shadows hiding from the outside light.

"I got a tattoo earlier this week."

"No shit! Where? Of what? How drunk were you? Come one, you can tell me. Were you ass up in an alley, or gangway, whatever they call it in Chicago? Did some hoodlum take advantage of your bare ass and draw two handle bars on the small of your back? Although, more like a large of your back; you're no Georgia peach."

"It's five letters from Linear A on my chest."

"What does it say?"

"No one knows, still un-deciphered."

"What if one day they find out it means mushu pork, or 'call Jimbo for a good time,' or better yet, what if it translates to 'flying squirrel hidden dung beetle'? I feel the last option is by far the most authentic, or maybe the mushu pork."

"Well then, I'll always wear a shirt."

"Make sure it's not a white shirt, that shit is see-through. Did they need to shave your hairy chest to ink you?"

"I'm Eastern European, what the hell do you expect, a naked mole rat?"

"Well, you could've done them the courtesy of, oh I don't know, shaving beforehand and sparing them the agony of hedging a forest."

"You're pulled from the same genetic pond, dumbass."

"Yeah, but unlike you, I pay homage to our ancestors."

"Again, Eastern European."

"Further back than that, I mean before we had limbs. I bet we were as naked and hairless as any living thing can get. Somewhere down the road, gene splicing thought it would be funny for some of us to look more like Wooly Mammoths than humans."

"Dear god, I think that was the last one."

"I think you're right. I can't breathe in here though; I'm overheating. Now that we've arrived, let's get the hell out of here."

Exhaustion and fatigue wore the two brothers down. Not yet knowing the ventilation situation in the new apartment, they ventured outside into the courtyard and collapsed on the grass. Inertia and gravity carried them down the steps, like gamboling children rolling and thrashing down a grassy hill, until they arrived at their destination without remembering the journey. Their legs and arms gave out and they sprawled out as far as their limbs could reach. The summer heat mingled above them, invisibly reacting with the elements, and heat lightning intermittently skittered across the darkened sky.

"Do you ever see lightning and think of Storm?"

"The 90's cartoon or later movie Storm?"

"Either?"

"No, but wouldn't it be incredible if Halle Berry were up there giving us a show?"

"I think it's safe to say Halle Berry had a profound impact on our adolescent minds."

"And our adolescent anatomy."

"Truer words have ne'er been spoken."

"Do you still talk to McKenzie?"

"Holy shit, it's been a while since I heard that name. We didn't even date that long. No, I stopped seeing her a while back. Where the hell did that come from?"

"She wrote me an email confessing how worried she was about you. While reading it, I feel like I should've been holding a microphone and trying to make a love connection with two people who weren't in the same room."

"Not even in the same head space. She wanted more than I could give, than I wanted to give. I built her up too much in my head. Either that or I was just too damn backed up."

"Too many berries and twigs?"

"Something like that."

"She made it seem like you just disappeared on her."

"Did Mom tell you Katelyn was at the funeral?"

"What?"

"Yeah, she popped in to experience all she had been missing, or thought she had been missing."

"Katelyn told Mom that?"

"Yeah. It could have been such a great reunion for all us Adler kids. Better luck at the next funeral."

Most of the units overlooking the grassy courtyard had their curtains drawn; however, several units defied their privilege to privacy and opened both windows and drapes. A few onlookers came to the window to identify the source of the chatter emanating from the grassy mound, but the cover of dark hid the Adler brothers away from scrutinizing eyes.

"I was on choir tour one year and there was this frat guy who was obsessed with sex. We were on a bus on the way back to campus. It was spring break so all the other students were still flashing cameras or whatever they do. I couldn't help but notice how intently he was staring out the window because, honestly, the man was only obsessed with sex. I asked him what he was looking at and he responded he was trying to calculate how many people were having sex on campus. The man was trying to Rain Man the statistical probability of, one, how many people were actually on campus who didn't go on spring break, and two, how many of those people were having sex. He threw out some number as though he were counting pretzel sticks scattered on the floor, and he made a believer out of me."

"Are you wondering how many of my neighbors are having sex?"

"No, I'm wondering what he's doing now."

"Car salesman, or is that too obvious?"

"What does selling cars have to do with what I just said?"

"Consider it a rhetorical question then."

"What the hell prompted you to move? I didn't know you were even slightly contemplating it."

"I needed a change of scenery. There was too much slime on those walls at all hours of the day."

"Like Slimer shat all over your walls?"

"Except I didn't have a ghost trap to confine and discard it."

"I still can't get over the fact that Katelyn was at the funeral and didn't tell me. It screams of Katelyn, but for some reason it seems she went a little further than she usually does. I was in their house, for crying out loud. She tried so hard to seem disinterested in going."

"We come from a long, rich line of half-truths and lies of omission. Why not just expect everyone you know to not tell you everything? That way you always know they're never telling you everything."

"That's quite a mouthful."

"Speaking of which, I was in a cab the other day. Some friends from college were in town and they invited me out to the bars."

"In town? What town, this town?"

"No, I mean River City where everyone is really gearing up for a new boy's brass band with big trombones and evil pool tables."

"So then, Elmore City?"

"Chicago, you ass-hat. I don't know how it happened, but I was in the cab with another random person. I don't know how or where I met her, or even why the hell she seemed to be taking care of me, but the tequila and tacos were not sitting well. I could have sworn the cabbie purposefully braked every two-hundred meters just to get me sick."

"Meters, really?"

"As you know, Lennox, the mind of a scientist never turns off. I felt the rumblings progressively get stronger, but it wasn't until I projectile vomited all over the plastic barrier that I realized how relieved I was to puke it all out. The cabbie pulled over and shrieked he was charging me an extra fifty bucks to clean it all. I thought that was fair."

"What did the mystery woman do?"

"I don't actually remember. She didn't end up in my apartment, at least I don't think so. She could still be hiding in the closet. Damn it, I just freaked myself out."

Summertime in the Midwest housed the cricketing annoyance of a cicada infestation, yet Chicago was an unfit mating ground for the insects. City life killed them off without any regard for their survival. Trees were lined with a dense layer of insecticide, potent enough to send the squirrels into early hibernation accompanied by internal bleeding and permanent genetic defects in their encoding.

Nightlife in the new neighborhood was lively, and the streets were polluted with the sound of clicking heels and slurred words; humans as pests replaced the buzzing and clicks of the natural nuisances. Bourgeoning city life, with all its amenities and indemnities, offered little room for silence and less allotment for repose. Alastor welcomed the constant motion of the Lakeview landscape over the static disturbance of what haunted him. In the distance of the blackened city sky, the faint rumbling of an anxious heaven connected with the reverberation in the brothers' chests.

"If Dad saw us lying here, watching the sky, he would think we were wasting away our lives."

"Would he though, or would he be proud we're watching and hopefully learning? Dad always tried to teach us by watching him. He would say, 'You don't have to do anything. Just watch and learn. All you have to do is watch.' I would ask him while watching if I can try it myself. I would study him changing the car breaks, and asked if I could unscrew the nuts on the hubcap or try to empty the brake line of fluid. He would tell me to just stand there and watch. I would look on as he fixed the heater in the basement. I asked if I could unscrew something or hold the broken pieces. He handed me the flashlight and told me to watch. He must have thought he was making it simple for me, or maybe he believed I would learn. So, I watched. I watched him fix the roof, cut down trees, build a chicken coup, change engine parts on the car, remodel the bathroom, replace lightbulbs, put down hardwood floor in the living room, change the oil on all the cars, build his retirement funds, till the garden in the spring. Then it came time for me to buy my first car. I paid attention as the dealer ripped me off. It came time for me to buy my own house. I monitored as the market took all of my money. It came time for me to fix the leaky roof. I surveilled the repair guy charging me three times as much because I made a hole the size of Nantucket where the small leak used to be. The time came for me to get married. She divorced me two years later. The time came for me to build a career. I worked as a peon and got peed on, and eventually I just stayed locked up in my apartment all day. All that watching and I learned nothing.

"Now, I watch smut on my phone, my siblings having kids, classmates succeeding in their jobs, beggars on the corner of North and Western with their Styrofoam cups, my rent go up every year, voting booths in November, and drooping faces taking the bus into the Loop. I watch every day go by. Too bad I haven't learned a damn thing. "

"It's always in the best interest of the children to tear down their parents."

"If I had a chance to do it differently had I been Dad, I probably would, but I don't want the chance. I don't want kids. I don't want progeny. I don't want to deal with me, with my genetic inheritance, with my mannerisms on a different person. It would be like watching a puppet come to life and mimic you. Too many people in the world anyway."

"I think I remember the first time I saw myself in a mirror. I was two. I must've fallen because I was sitting on the rug we used to have in the living room of our old house. You know we weren't allowed to sit on that rug; Dad always said the floor was too cold and we would get sick. I must have wandered off without supervision. I stared at myself in the mirror for an eternity. It was the first time I remember seeing my reflection. I felt awkward looking at the things around me, so I stared at myself. My shirt was plaid, orange and white, the buttons were metallic and the sleeves were a little too long for me. My brown corduroy pants were worn at the knees and my white socks were tucked into them. I don't know why I was more comfortable taking note of what I was wearing and not of the sofa I knew was behind me, or the gold lampstand I'd knocked over so many times before, or any other discernible objects. I remember a vague sensation of not being in the right clothes.

"Aren't children supposed to relate their first experience of *self* with a parent, sibling, or with someone else, anyone else? Isn't it normal for babies to see their reflection in the comforting arms of a mother or father, surrounded by things that welcome a sense of identity, individuality, or uniqueness? Aren't we supposed to see ourselves connected with others, to a concept of shared humanity, or togetherness, or family? Aren't those the pivotal moments we formulate in our ever-expanding minds?

"Yet, there I was, alone, sitting, staring at the inconsequentiality of my worn clothes, uncomfortably moving my head in the hopes that the top button would come undone so I could breathe easier."

"My ass hurts from laying here too long. I've been sitting on a twig for the past hour, at least I hope it's a twig. You want to go upstairs and check out my tiny balcony that stares at my neighbor's brick wall? It's going to start storming. May as well stay ahead of it."

"I'm hoping your tiny balcony is a literal balcony and not some euphemism."

"The night is young."

"Creep."

Getting up was a process made increasingly difficult by the lack of feeling throughout their appendages. Having carried dozens of boxes and countless pieces of furniture rendered their muscles obsolete, and no amount of groans or exasperated whelps would have made it easier.

The weight of their exhaustion bore witness as two indents in the soft grass plot between the two apartment buildings: two molds of rotund contour.

"Oh god, the sheer agony of it all."

"You can just call me Alastor."

"This is how Odysseus must've felt after he escaped from Calypso's island. I feel like I'm being torn apart. I need to start working out."

"Look, we've left our marks on this world. Our big, fat-ass dents on this pliable and muddy world."

"Do you really feel that way about Dad?"

"I don't know and I don't think I want to know. I'm okay not understanding the schadenfreude of having children. It's definitely easier to criticize from afar."

"I saw Dad cry once. Mom and Dad flew down to the armpit of America and surprised me when I was in grad school. It was my final recital and they sat in the middle of the auditorium. I find it humorous performers believe dimming the lights will make all the gawking faces disappear.

"It was during *The Lament of Ian the Proud*. I looked out and saw him crying. I nearly lost it. Almost like fast forwarding and rewinding through the woes of his own family, the hardships of his children, the inevitability we all contemplate at least once, I witnessed what it could be like for Mom and Dad. I didn't much care for it. All the times we had to make phone calls because the assholes on the other side would take advantage of him because he had an accent. He didn't seem to care as long as it was resolved.

It didn't matter if there were people who laughed, or people who didn't understand him, or even family who hated him. He never cried through all of it, at least not in front of us. Then, in that auditorium, he lost it."

"I don't ever want to feel like that."

"I don't know if I'm able to feel like that."

The two brothers were deliberately slowing their pace from the courtyard to their destination. It was the dread of climbing three flights of stairs that convinced them to take smaller steps. With a harmonious consonance, and subliminal unity, each muscle communicated with the other the limits of their strength and consented to lengthen the duration of the journey by tenfold.

"Is this the longest you've left the pious duo unattended?"

"My cats will be fine. They have plenty of crevices to explore without me."

"Look at you, all grown up."

"Bright side, they'll know the layout better than I do by the time we get back up there."

"When do you reckon humans first decided to run from storms? At what point do you think we, as a species, drew a correlation between barometric disturbances and danger? When did natural occurrences become natural disasters?"

"Is this your way of telling me you don't want to climb up the stairs? If we get caught in the rain, there is a good chance we'll drown."

"At this rate, we won't be able to outrun the storm even if we wanted to."

"Damn it, Lennox, why didn't you bring this up when we were comfortably laying on the supple ground?"

Sensing the futility of their efforts to outrun the eminent Chicago storm, the two brothers turned around with great effort and retreated to their indentations in the softened ground.

"I had a dream I was treading water in this murky lake. I looked to my left and there were all our loved ones, everyone we grew up, but they were in a channel leading to an unknown destination. I desperately tried to swim to them, but a withered tree crashed down right in front of me and blocked my path. I never felt so alone in all my life. The water was so murky. It struck me with a fear of the unknown and the unseen. I couldn't see the bottom of whatever I was floating in and it terrified me. I made my way to the shore. As soon as I got out of the water, I was carrying a child and holding hands with someone I knew I loved. I grieved so much that I couldn't see my loved ones, but the path before me was dry and paved."

"You know, for admitting to not being a Joseph, you sure do have a lot of dreams. Every time we talk, you had another dream. Do you ever just sleep? I mean, a restful sleep where you're at peace and you don't see some other world, dimension, or future event? Does the augur in you ever rest?"

The gradual patter of raindrops on their skin did not stimulate a response. A beating exhaustion overtook their bodies and numbed their stimulus receptors from alerting them of the oncoming deluge.

"It seems our molded cavities have awaited our return."

It was with an utter lack of grace and caution that the two brothers plopped down onto the courtyard lawn. Their pain receptors were frayed beyond recognition, a byproduct of ignoring the warning signs of physical fatigue.

"I've been thinking, Lennox, maybe a small god, a pocket-sized god, is better than none at all. Maybe a miniaturized, misrepresentation of a higher power is favorable to the depravity of our humanity. Do you ever think carrying around a small piece of a god with us takes focus away from the cavernous dark? Maybe a life spent with the bulge of a god within our chest pocket is better than allowing the inner misery of our true selves to drip out, and seep into the very soil we trod. Deflecting the trapping of our innate selves by putting an idol between us and our fellow man seems like a good idea to me. It might be our only hope of surviving this thing."

"I don't remember this twig digging into my back ten minutes ago."

"Now you know how Miriam feels every morning."

"This isn't morning wood."

"You're right, it's evening wood."

"Does that mean I've aroused the ground?"

"You must be doing something right."

"Alastor, do you think there is a place...a place big enough to fit all the people I have ever met into one place? A place where I can take all the people I've ever said hello to, all the people I've ever loved, all the people I've glanced at in passing on the street, all the people I've hated, all the people I've hit, all the people I've thought about, all the people who were ever around me, in my proximity, all the people I've imagined, that aren't here anymore. If our galaxy collides with another larger galaxy and all the streets are torn asunder and every molecule is ripped apart and scattered among the infinite expansiveness, do you think there is a place we can all go?"

"Lennox, exactly how many people have you hit in your lifetime that you need a separate category for them?"

"When the universe gets tired and decides to contract or expand into infinity, do you think there is a place after, above, around, or outside of this place that can accommodate all those people? Do you think there's a place we can't destroy, that we choose not to destroy? Do you think there's a place we can go back to? Is there a Canaan for us to return, but not just a place for my people, or their people, or our people, but a Canaan for everyone? I really hope there is, because I want to go there. I want to be there with everyone, being happy and peaceful in infinite nothingness and everythingness. I really want there to be a place like that, Alastor. I really want to go home."

"Will Halle Berry be there?"

"Obviously."

"It's a deal breaker for me if she's not there."

"She'll be there."

"I mean, I'd rather wander aimlessly in space."

"You mean to tell me that your decision-making process will still be controlled by your pocket-rocket even after this life?"

"It will help launch me into another world."

"That's disappointing."

"Why do you think I've only had three-and-a-half blowjobs."

"Ah, the mysteries of this existence."

The city sky above the brothers twinkled with slight changes in hue as each streak of lightning ran across the speckled rink. Backgrounds of deep blue and woeful magenta surrendered to instances of profound green as the brightened bolts selected the palette above their heads.

"Hey, Lennox."

"I'm still right here, Alastor. I haven't gone anywhere."

"Do you know a good joke?"

"No."

"Neither do I."

Lennox pulled out the red lighter from inside his sweatshirt. He engaged the striker wheel three times with no success. Sparks flew from the top of the red lighter without giving way to a flame. He looked up at the descending droplets and welcomed the rhythmic tapping on his face. Alastor quietly extended his hand towards Lennox, supplying a new red lighter for his brother to use. Within the silence that gently grew between the two brothers, enveloping them and nudging the outside world further outward, Lennox flicked Alastor's lighter on and set the silence ablaze. As the brothers of thunder sacrificed their pure oxygen and bodies, the rolling smoke drew higher, wobbling through the open spaces, expanding through the staleness of the city air, and reaching skyward, ascending unimpeded and unrelenting.

ABOUT ATMOSPHERE PRESS

Atmosphere Press is an independent, full-service publisher for excellent books in all genres and for all audiences. Learn more about what we do at atmospherepress.com.

We encourage you to check out some of Atmosphere's latest releases, which are available at Amazon.com and via order from your local bookstore:

An Expectation of Plenty, a novel by Thomas Bazar
Sink or Swim, Brooklyn, a novel by Ron Kemper
Lost and Found, a novel by Kevin Gardner
Skinny Vanilla Crisis, a novel by Colleen Alles
The Mommy Clique, a novel by Barbara Altamirano
Eaten Alive, a novel by Tim Galati
The Sacrifice Zone, a novel by Roger S. Gottlieb
Olive, a novel by Barbara Braendlein
Itsuki, a novel by Zach MacDonald
A Surprising Measure of Subliminal Sadness, short stories by Sue Powers
Saint Lazarus Day, short stories by R. Conrad Speer
The Lower Canyons, a novel by John Manuel
Shiftless, a novel by Anthony C. Murphy
Connie Undone, a novel by Kristine Brown
A Cage Called Freedom, a novel by Paul P.S. Berg
The Escapist, a novel by Karahn Washington
Buildings Without Murders, a novel by Dan Gutstein

ABOUT THE AUTHOR

James Stoia was born and forged in the Marquette Park neighborhood of Chicago, Illinois. He completed both his undergraduate and graduate coursework in Opera Performance before shifting to a literary career. He plays piano, mandolin, euph-  onium, composes, sings, plays chess, and attempts triathlons. His perspective and style borrow from his experiences in stage performance, academic research, and his fondness for cinema. He lives in Illinois and *This Side of Babylon* is his debut novel.

CPSIA information can be obtained
at www.ICGtesting.com
Printed in the USA
LVHW050727291020
669934LV00003B/95